"If you'll permit me to say so, sir, I think your choice of words is a little inexact. The recon platoon's not like a violin. They're just a bunch of bad eggs, and this Bannon is as bad as any of them. You know yourself that he beat up an officer a few weeks back, and if that officer hadn't subsequently been killed in battle, Bannon could have gotten a firing squad. I don't trust Bannon or any of the other hoodlums in the recon platoon, and I've never thought that much of Butsko either. He's worse than all the rest of them put together."

"That's why he can handle them." Colonel Stockton's briar was out, and he placed it next to his ashtray. "You seem to forget, Major, that the recon platoon has done some pretty incredible things out here."

"That's true, they've been nothing but trouble otherwise."

"We have to pay a price for everything, and I guess that's the price we have to pay for the recon platoon."

Also in THE RAT BASTARDS series from Jove

Meat Grinder Hill

by
John Mackie

A JOVE BOOK

Excepting basic historical events, places, and personages, this series of books is fictional, and anything that appears otherwise is coincidental and unintentional.

The principal characters are imaginary, although they might remind veterans of specific men whom they knew. The Twenty-third Infantry Regiment, in which the characters serve, is used fictitiously—it doesn't represent the real historical Twenty-third Infantry, which has distinguished itself in so many battles from the Civil War to Vietnam—but it could have been any American line regiment that fought and bled during World War II.

These novels are dedicated to the men who were there. May their deeds and gallantry never be forgotten.

MEAT GRINDER HILL

A Jove Book/published by arrangement with
the author

PRINTING HISTORY
Jove edition/January 1984

ISBN: 0-515-07260-5

Jove books are published by The Berkley Publishing Group,
200 Madison Avenue, New York, N.Y. 10016. The words
"A JOVE BOOK" and the "J" with sunburst are trademarks
belonging to Jove Publications, Inc.
PRINTED IN THE UNITED STATES OF AMERICA

ONE . . .

"I believe that's your Headquarters Company over there," the jeep driver said.

Private Homer Gladley, a big farm boy from Nebraska, looked into the jungle to the right of the dirt road and saw men wearing helmets and no shirts moving among the branches and leaves. The sound of gunfire could be heard in the distance. The sky was clear and the sun shone with burning intensity on Guadalcanal.

"Well, thanks for the lift," Gladley said.

The jeep driver said nothing; he didn't even look at Gladley. The jeep driver hadn't given him the ride as a favor but had been ordered to do so. He looked grumpily through the windshield and waited for Gladley to depart.

Gladley swung his long, thick legs to the ground and stood up. He was six feet two inches tall, with mountainous shoulders and an expression of innocence, or maybe stupidity, on his face. He reached into the back of the jeep and pulled out his full field pack and M 1 rifle. The jeep driver revved his engine, turning around in the middle of the narrow dirt road. Gladley waved his rifle in the air as a good-bye gesture, but the jeep driver hunched over his wheel and paid no attention, roaring back toward Henderson Field.

The rebuff didn't bother Gladley; he just smiled happily as he lifted his pack and ran his arms through the shoulder straps.

He picked up his rifle and carried it in his big right hand as he trudged toward the jungle, anxious to see his old buddies again. Nearly six weeks earlier he'd been wounded near Tassafaronga Point and had been evacuated to the Army hospital in New Caledonia. The doctors had taken the bullets out of his stomach and sewed him up, and now he was returning to duty again.

"You know where the recon platoon is?" Homer Gladley asked some soldiers cleaning the parts of a stripped-down .30 caliber machine gun.

"Thataway," said one of the soldiers, pointing with the trigger assembly of the machine gun.

Homer Gladley turned in that direction and stepped out, thinking about Butsko and Bannon and all the other guys in the recon platoon. They'd landed on Guadalcanal in October and had been through a lot together. He'd missed them while he was in the hospital.

Homer Gladley made his way through the jungle. Wherever he looked, there were shell craters and trees knocked down by explosions. Evidently a big battle had taken place here recently. He could smell gunpowder and the stench of putrefying human bodies, which lay in bits on the ground and in the bushes, indistinguishable from the ordinary muck and slime of the island. Soldiers everywhere were cleaning weapons and sharpening bayonets. It looked to Homer Gladley as if the Twenty-third Infantry Regiment was moving out soon.

Homer Gladley looked at a soldier with dark craggy features and a cigarette dangling from the corner of his mouth, pulling a patch of cotton through the barrel of his M 1, and recognized him as Pfc. Sam Longtree, the full-blooded Apache from Arizona.

"Hey, Longtree!" Homer shouted, waving his M 1 in the air. "How're you doing?"

Longtree glanced up and saw Gladley approaching. "What the hell are you doing here? We thought you'd be back in the States by now!"

"They just returned me to duty," Gladley said, reaching down and shaking Longtree's hand. "What the hell's going on?"

"The same old shit. How're you feeling?"

"Real good. The doctor said I'm fit for the front lines again."

"I bet you weren't too happy to hear that."

"There ain't nothing I can do about it, so there ain't no use complaining. I guess I'd better report in to Butsko. Where's he at."

"He got shot up about two weeks ago. He must be in that hospital that you just came from."

"No shit? If I knew he was there, I woulda gone looking for him."

"A lot of the guys are there: Frankie La Barbara, Craig Delane, Simpson, Larraby. Madonia is dead, and so's Atwell." Longtree took off his helmet and wiped his forehead with the back of his sleeve. "We've been through some bad shit. You're lucky you missed it."

"Looks like everybody's getting fixed to move out."

"The Japs have been pulling back and we're going after them."

"Who's in charge around here?"

"Bannon."

"Bannon? He was just a corporal when I left."

"Well, he's a buck sergeant now, and they turned the platoon over to him."

"How's he doing?"

"He's okay, but there's only one Butsko."

"Where's Bannon at?"

"Over there someplace."

"I'd better report in to him. See you later, Chief."

Gladley straightened up, adjusted his pack, and walked toward the section of the jungle where Longtree said Bannon was located. He looked around and saw a destroyed Japanese tank lying on its side, the turret stained with dried blood. Empty C ration cans were scattered about, and Gladley caught a whiff of a latrine that couldn't be far away. He checked every foxhole, saying hello to his old buddies and seeing many new faces—men who'd come to replace the ones who'd been killed.

Finally he saw Bannon, a tall, lanky Texan, sitting cross-legged in a hole, looking at a map and moving his finger across it.

"Hiya, Bannon," Gladley said, dropping into the foxhole. "Guess who's back?"

Bannon looked up, keeping his finger on the map. "I thought you were dead!"

"That's what everybody says." Gladley sat on his haunches. "I heard Butsko got shot and you're the new platoon sergeant."

Bannon nodded.

"I never thought the Japs'd stop Butsko."

"Well, they did."

"I hear you've taken his place."

"Yeah, and you might as well take your place back in the First Squad. Longtree's the new squad leader."

"I was just talking to him. He didn't say he was the squad leader."

"Yeah, well, he's always been kinda strange."

"Is the Reverend still around?"

"He's still in the First Squad. Listen, I'm busy right now. Report to Longtree and get yourself squared away. We're moving out pretty soon."

"Where we going?"

"The Japs are up in those hills out there and we've got to clean 'em out."

Bannon returned his concentration to his map, and Gladley stared at him for a few seconds. Bannon used to be a friendly, happy-go-lucky guy, but now he was all business. *His rank must be going to his head,* Gladley thought as he stood up. He climbed out of the foxhole and walked back to Longtree and the First Squad.

At the Army hospital in New Caledonia, Master Sergeant John Butsko made his way through the ward, passing soldiers lying on their cots, sleeping or reading magazines. Butsko's chest ached constantly from his wounds, and he was still weak from loss of blood and the operation, but he could feel his strength returning steadily and figured he'd be back at the front in another month.

He pushed open the screened door and saw the green lawn inclining toward more barracklike buildings like the one he'd just left. He could smell salt water from the bay, and a squadron of American fighter planes roared across the clear blue sky. Butsko wore white pajama bottoms and a white T-shirt puffed out in front by the bandages on his chest and stomach. He was deeply tanned and had scars, some of them fresh, on his cheeks, chin, and forehead.

A group of GIs sat around on chairs, shooting the shit, but Butsko didn't like small talk. He took a chair and carried it toward a coconut palm tree, sitting down in the shade, leaning back, and feeling weird to be in such a quiet, peaceful place, so far from the fighting on Guadalcanal.

Butsko wasn't adjusting well to the hospital. It was too tranquil for a sensibility accustomed to the constant dangers of the front lines. He thought there was something false about his hospital existence, because the real world was the green hell of Guadalcanal, the machine-gun fire and artillery barrages, the Jap banzai bayonet attacks at night and your men getting cut down before your eyes. Butsko felt like a fuck-off here, away from the action. He thought he was evading his responsibilities, although common sense told him he had been wounded badly and was in no condition to fight or lead men. Butsko was afraid he'd be soft and dull by the time he returned, not able to lead his platoon anymore, and too slow to stay alive.

He thought of Bannon, Longtree, Jones, and all the others. They were probably glad he was gone and hoped he'd never come back, because he was hard on them. Well, he had to be hard on his men: He didn't know how to be any other way, and he didn't think any other way would be effective anyway. When your life was on the line, you had to stay tough all the time. Lie back for a moment and you'd be food for the rats and flies that infested Guadalcanal.

Butsko took out a Camel and lit it up with his trusty old Zippo. He glanced at his watch and saw that chow would be served in two more hours. All he did was go to chow, watch movies, and get examined by doctors. He was bored to death.

"Sergeant Butsko, you know you shouldn't be smoking!"

Butsko shielded his eyes from the sun and looked up at Nurse Crawford, blond and full-bosomed, the prettiest nurse he'd seen so far on New Caledonia. She wore a white dress and cap and stood with her hands on her hips, looking at him sternly. "The doctor said you shouldn't smoke until your wounds are completely healed."

"They're almost healed," Butsko said.

"I think you should put that cigarette out right now, Sergeant Butsko, and that's an order!"

Butsko wasn't accustomed to taking orders from a woman, but she was a lieutenant and he was a master sergeant. He took one last deep drag and stubbed the cigarette out against the bottom of his hospital slippers. "You're a hard woman, Nurse Crawford."

"It's for your own good, Sergeant Butsko. And I'd better not see you smoking anymore until Dr. Henderson gives you permission."

"Yes, ma'am."

Her face softened. "How do you feel otherwise, Sergeant Butsko."

"Good enough to smoke."

"When Dr. Henderson examines you today, why don't you ask him about it?"

"I'll do that, ma'am."

Nurse Crawford looked at the group of men sitting not far away, talking and laughing. Butsko examined her profile, the small upturned nose, the finely sculpted chin. She was like the girl next door trying to be a tough Army nurse.

She turned to him. "Why do you always stay by yourself, Sergeant? Why don't you mix with the other men?"

Butsko met her gaze. "What you wanna know for?"

She wrinkled her brow, momentarily surprised by his question. "Just curious. We don't think it's healthy for recovering soldiers to spend too much time alone, brooding."

"What makes you think I'm brooding?"

"Then what are you thinking about?"

"I'm just biding my time, that's all."

"Until what?"

"Until I go back to the front."

"Do you want to go back?"

"As opposed to what?"

"Staying here?"

"I'd rather go back."

She smiled. "Most of the men would rather stay here."

"I ain't them."

Nurse Crawford wanted to stay and talk to Butsko, but she

didn't think he wanted to talk with her, and on top of that she had her rounds to make. "I've got to be going," she said. "Hope you feel better, Sergeant."

She turned and walked away and Butsko watched her caboose swing from side to side under her white skirt. *What a cute little piece of ass she is,* he thought. *I wonder if anybody's plunking her.*

Nurse Crawford walked across the green lawn, her arms crossed beneath her breasts, thinking about Sergeant Butsko. He was such a strange man, so unlike the others who sat around complaining or telling each other lies all day long. They all made advances to her, but not Butsko. He acted as if he didn't like her very much, but she didn't take it seriously; he didn't seem to like anybody else much either. She'd seen his records and knew he was married, but he never got mail from anybody and never wrote letters. He was an old professional soldier busted up and down the ranks many times, and he'd been on the Bataan Death March, escaping from a Japanese prison camp in northern Luzon. There was something intriguing about him, and she could sense his strength and his rough-and-ready sense of dignity. She thought him the most interesting man in her ward.

She approached one of the barrack buildings and turned the corner, nearly bumping into a tall dark-haired soldier with tanned features.

"Well, hello there!" the soldier said, his eyes widening. "Where have you been all my life?"

Nurse Crawford smiled and tried to get around him, but he sidestepped in her way. "Boy, you're a real doll!" he said. "What's your name, sweetheart?"

"Get out of my way, soldier. I've got work to do."

"Hey, let's get together sometime?"

"I said get out of my way, soldier, and I'm not going to tell you again."

The soldier stepped backward and made a serious face. "Hey-hey, you're pulling rank on me, huh? Listen, I got this terrific pain and I wonder if you'd help me out with it?"

She knew he was putting her on, but she had to ask, "Where's the pain?"

He winked. "You know where."

His impertinence infuriated her. "What's your name, soldier?"

He winked again. "You can call me Frankie."

"I mean your last name!"

"La Barbara."

"Your rank?"

"Pfc."

"I'm an officer in the United States Army, Pfc. La Barbara, and if you don't get out of my way, I'll bring you up on charges!"

Frankie realized she meant business. This one was no pushover, like some of the other nurses he'd run into at the hospital. "Sorry, sir," he said, stepping out of the way. "I was just trying to be friendly."

"You're not from this ward. What are you doing over here."

"I heard my old platoon sergeant is in this section, sir. Sergeant John Butsko. Know him?"

Nurse Crawford pointed toward the lawn. "He's seated back there."

Frankie saluted. "Yes, sir. Thank you, sir. Nice talking to you, sir. Hope to see you again sometime, sir."

Still saluting, Frankie walked by her, and she knew he was mocking her. He was a wise guy with a New York accent. She didn't like his type and never did. She watched him walk across the lawn toward Sergeant Butsko, and suddenly he stopped, turned, and blew her a kiss.

He'd known that she was watching him. Irritated, she turned and walked away. *It's so easy to hate men,* she thought. *Most of them are disgusting.*

"Hey, big Sarge!" Frankie said, bouncing up and down and rubbing his hands together as he approached Butsko. "How're ya doin'?"

Butsko looked up; his face was like a block of stone. "Well, well, well," he said, "look who's here."

Frankie sat down at Butsko's feet. "I heard you were here and thought I'd come over to say hello. How're you feeling?"

"Not bad. How're you feeling?"

"They say I'm just about all better. They're gonna send me

back to the front any day now. Hope they take their time. I'm trying to figure out who to pay off so's I can stick around here for a while."

Butsko shrugged. He didn't like Frankie but didn't dislike him either. Frankie had been in his platoon and Butsko felt a certain closeness to him for that reason only.

Frankie sensed that Butsko wasn't overjoyed to see him, but that didn't stop him. He was overjoyed to see Butsko. Like most of the men in the recon platoon, Frankie worshipped Butsko.

"You fucking any of these nurses yet, Sarge?"

"Are you?"

"You're goddamn right I am. Some of them are real easy, and the others play a little hard to get, but they all give in sooner or later. The ugliest ones are the easiest. I guess they never got so much attention in their lives. I just ran into a real fabulous blonde who told me where you were. You know who she is?"

"She kinda tall?"

"Yeah, around five seven, I'd say."

"That's Nurse Crawford. She's the head nurse of this section."

"She can give me some head anytime."

Butsko scowled. "She's a tough broad. She don't look it but she is."

"I think she needs a good stiff cock, and I'm just the man to give it to her."

"Good luck," Butsko said.

"You try to fuck her yet, Sarge?"

Butsko gave Frankie an angry look that made Frankie turn away.

"It's real nice here," Frankie said, anxious to change the subject. "It's hard to believe there's a war going on back at Guadalcanal, huh?"

"It ain't hard for me to believe."

"I wonder what the guys in the old platoon are doing right now."

"Probably up to their asses in shit someplace."

"Probably. I wish I didn't have to go back there."

"Maybe they'll send you someplace else."

"I wish I could stay here. If I could type, I could get one of them office jobs. That'd be fine with me. Three hots and a cot and whole lots of pussy."

Butsko didn't reply. It was tiresome to make conversation about nothing.

"You hurt bad?" Frankie asked.

"Not that bad."

"You don't think they'll send you back to the States."

"No."

"I bet you could stay here if you wanted to."

"I don't want to."

"Why not?"

"I don't like it here."

"There's cunt all over the place, and nobody's shooting at you, and you don't like it here?"

Butsko looked around and didn't see Nurse Crawford anyplace. He took out another Camel and lit it up.

"I know where there's a good crap game tonight," Frankie said. "You interested?"

"Take a walk, willya, Frankie."

Frankie couldn't believe his ears. "Whatja say, Sarge?"

"I said take a fucking walk."

"Whatsa matter, Sarge? I do something wrong?"

"I got no time for your bullshit, Frankie. Take a fucking walk."

"Sure thing, Sarge. Anything you say."

Stung, Frankie got up and walked away, his hands in his pockets and his head inclined toward the ground. He thought of himself as a dashing, interesting guy and couldn't understand why Butsko wanted him to take a walk. *Well, Butsko's always been a psycho case,* Frankie thought. *He's been shot up too many times. I wonder where that pretty nurse went. Maybe if I play my cards right, I can get into her pants.*

TWO . . .

Bannon approached the desk of Sergeant Major Ramsay. "I'm Sergeant Bannon from the recon platoon. I understand the colonel wants to see me."

"He's busy right now. Have a seat."

Bannon sat on a folding chair inside the big walled tent, laying his carbine across his lap. His face had darkened to the color of mahogany, due to the Guadalcanal sun, and his uniform was dusty and frayed. He'd shaved before coming to Regimental Headquarters, but his straw-colored hair covered the tops of his ears and grew low on his neck. He was twenty-five years old and had been a ranch hand and foreman in Texas before the war.

He felt ill at ease at Headquarters, having the enlisted man's normal fear and hatred of officers. He knew that Butsko had often been called by Colonel Stockton for conferences and figured he'd have to go too someday.

"Mind if I light one up, Sarge?"

"Go ahead."

Bannon took out a Chesterfield and lit it, inhaling deeply but not too deeply, because he had a bayonet wound in his side that still bothered him. He'd gotten it in the big battle after the regiment had crossed the Matanikau River ten days earlier, and he'd lost a lot of blood, but the medics said nothing vital had been damaged, and in fact one of them had taken the stitches out yesterday. If you could walk, the bastards would send you right back to the front.

Officers entered and left Colonel Stockton's office in a steady stream, and Bannon recognized the colonel's battalion commanders and staff personnel, the big, heavy brass in the regiment. Bannon puffed his cigarette and flicked the ashes into a nearby butt can with an inch of water in the bottom. The day was heating up and his uniform stuck to his body. *I must smell like hell,* he thought.

"You can go in now, Bannon," Sergeant Major Ramsay said. "Put out your cigarette first."

Bannon dropped his cigarette into the butt can, stood, slung his carbine, and carried his helmet under his left arm as he approached the tent flap that led to Colonel Stockton's office. He pushed the flap aside and saw Colonel Stockton sitting behind his desk, while Major Cobb, the regimental operations officer, sat on a chair in front of the desk. Bannon marched to the desk and saluted smartly.

"Sergeant Charles Bannon reporting, sir!"

"Have a seat Bannon."

"Yes, sir."

Bannon sat stiffly on one of the chairs. Colonel Stockton was a lean, silver-haired West Pointer from Maine; Major Cobb was shorter, heavyset, bald, and wearing glasses.

"Well, how's my recon platoon doing?" Colonel Stockton asked.

"Just fine, sir," Bannon replied, although the recon platoon was just as fucked up as ever.

"How're you getting along without Butsko?"

"Not so bad, but we all miss him, sir."

"I know you've got a rough bunch of boys in that platoon, Bannon. You handling them all right?"

"Yes, sir."

"No problems?"

"None I can't handle, sir."

"Good. Glad to hear it." Colonel Stockton lifted his briar out of his West Point ashtray and filled it with fine old Virginia burley. "You may smoke if you like, Bannon."

"Thank you, sir."

Bannon took out another Chesterfield and lit it up, aware

that Major Cobb was scrutinizing him. *What are these two fucking officers setting me up for?* Bannon wondered, puffing his cigarette.

"You know, Bannon," Colonel Stockton said, "that the recon platoon is very important in this regiment."

"Oh, yes, sir. I know that."

"You know because you've been in the recon platoon since the beginning, and the recon platoon's been in a lot of tight spots. I guess it's no secret that I organized the recon platoon myself and I make the decision on every man who gets assigned to it. I've put the toughest men in the regiment into the recon platoon, men who couldn't get along anywhere else, men who've been in and out of the stockade. You were in the stockade recently yourself, so you know what I'm talking about."

"Yes, sir."

"Well, Butsko was the kind of NCO who could keep men like that in line, but now that he's gone, I haven't really known what to do with the recon platoon." Colonel Stockton lit his pipe, and his head disappeared in a cloud of blue smoke. "I've been under pressure to put an officer in charge of the platoon, but quite frankly I'm short of officers as it is, and I couldn't think of anybody suitable anyway. The same is true of top-rankings NCOs. Therefore I've decided to leave you in charge of the recon platoon if you think you can handle it."

Bannon shrugged. "I think I can handle it, sir."

"Maybe you'd better think that over a little, Bannon. The recon platoon hasn't done much since we crossed the Matanikau, but we're moving out tomorrow and your men will be our advance screen into no-man's land. There can't be any slip-ups or funny business, because there are too many lives on the line. There'll be a lot of pressure on you, let's make no bones about that. If you're not sure, I can put somebody else in charge."

"I don't know, sir," Bannon said. "It's up to you."

"I know it's up to me. I just asked you how sure you are that you can handle the recon platoon in combat."

"I've already led some of them during the times Butsko wasn't around. I guess I could do it about as well as most people, but you understand, sir, that I don't have the experience of somebody like Sergeant Butsko."

"Neither does anybody else around here."

The room was silent for a few moments. Bannon puffed his cigarette as both officers looked at him, evidently waiting for him to say something.

"Well," Bannon drawled, "if you don't have anybody around like Butsko, I guess I could handle the recon platoon about as well as anybody. On top of that, I already know all the men—what their strengths and weaknesses are. Somebody new would have to learn all that."

Colonel Stockton looked at Major Cobb, then turned to Bannon again. "That's good enough for me. You'll continue to lead the recon platoon until Butsko gets back or unless circumstances change."

Bannon knew what Colonel Stockton meant by that. If Bannon fucked up, someone else would be put in charge of the recon platoon.

"From now on you'll report directly to Major Cobb here," Colonel Stockton said.

"Yes, sir."

"The regiment will move out in the morning, as I said, but I'll want the recon platoon to get into position tonight. Come behind the desk here and I'll show you where I want you to go."

Bannon rose and sauntered behind the desk, looking down at the map. He recognized all the geographical configurations immediately, because ever since Butsko had been wounded, Bannon had been spending half his life looking at maps.

"The Japs have pulled back to these hills and mountains," Colonel Stockton said, pointing at them, "and it's there that they evidently intend to make their last stand on Guadalcanal. The only problem is that we don't know exactly where they are. Our Air Corps spotters can't find them, so the recon platoon will have to do it. The regiment will be traveling through this area here tomorrow, and I want the recon platoon to go first and be the screen. Do you understand?"

"Yes, sir."

"After chow tonight, move your men into position. Stay in close touch with Major Cobb on your radio. At daybreak tomorrow, move your men out and, again, stay in touch with Major Cobb. Report anything unusual. Don't let the regiment walk into a hornets' nest of trouble. We'll be depending on you."

"Yes, sir."

"Anything you want to say?"

"Yes, sir: We need a medic. We ain't had a medic since we crossed the Matanikau."

"I'll get you a medic. Do you have any questions about the operation?"

"No, sir."

"Are you sure?"

"Yes, sir."

"All right, Sergeant. You're dismissed. Good luck, and don't forget to stay in touch."

Bannon moved in front of Colonel Stockton's desk, saluted, and marched out of the office. Colonel Stockton looked at Major Cobb, who shook his head.

"What's the matter?" Colonel Stockton said.

"I still think you should put an officer in charge of the recon platoon."

"Who?"

"I don't know who. Anybody would be better than nobody."

"I don't agree. The recon platoon is like a violin: Start monkeying with it and it'll go out of tune."

"If you'll permit me to say so, sir, I think your choice of words is a little inexact. The recon platoon's not like a violin. They're just a bunch of bad eggs, and this Bannon is as bad as any of them. You know yourself that he beat up an officer a few weeks back, and if that officer hadn't subsequently been killed in battle, Bannon could have gotten a firing squad. I don't trust Bannon or any of the other hoodlums in the recon platoon, and I've never thought that much of Butsko either. He's worse than all the rest of them put together."

"That's why he can handle them." Colonel Stockton's briar was out, and he placed it next to his ashtray. "You seem to forget, Major, that the recon platoon has done some pretty incredible things out here."

"That's true, they've been nothing but trouble otherwise."

"We have to pay a price for everything, and I guess that's the price we have to pay for the recon platoon."

"I still think you ought to break them up and ship them to

other units and then form a new recon platoon."

"Out of what?"

"Out of the best men in the regiment."

Colonel Stockton leaned forward. "Major Cobb, I think the recon platoon already contains the best men in the regiment. War isn't a parade, you know. I'd hate to have the recon platoon in a parade, and if I was on an Army post with them back in the States, I'd probably have to put the whole bunch of them in the stockade. But out here, on Guadalcanal, I need fighters, and if there's anything the recon platoon is good at, it's fighting."

"Yes, but sometimes they forget who they're supposed to be fighting."

"It'll be up to you to keep that clear in their minds. It shouldn't be that much trouble. Bannon seems to be a sensible man, doesn't he?"

"He'd better be," Major Cobb said, "because I will not tolerate any insubordination."

"No, or course not. This is still the Army, after all."

"Just as long as Bannon and the others understand that, everything'll be all right," Major Cobb said.

Deep in the jungle, twenty miles from Colonel Stockton's tent, was the headquarters encampment of the Japanese Seventeenth Army on Guadalcanal. In one of the tents sat Colonel Tsuji, stern and slender, studying his maps and planning the last-ditch defense of Guadalcanal. The order had already gone out, under General Hyakutake's signature, that they would fight to the last man. Tsuji had planned most of the disastrous (for the Japanese Army) battles on Guadalcanal and now was organizing a series of impregnable defensive positions to hold off the Americans until General Imperial Headquarters in Tokyo decided what to do.

The afternoon was hot, and sweat dripped down Tsuji's face. He had plenty of water to drink, but food was in short supply, and a hundred soldiers were dying of starvation each day. The Imperial Navy had been unable to resupply the Imperial Army, due to the aggressive patrolling of the US Navy. Reports had been received of cannibalism in the field. Even General Hyakutake was losing weight on his diet of rice, boiled grass, and small quantities of rationed canned meat and fish. General Hyakutake had ordered that all troops be placed in one of three classifications:

(1) able to fight and walk
(2) able to fight but not walk
(3) unable to fight or walk.

The situation had become more desperate than anything Colonel Tsuji could have imagined, but the men were dug into strong defensive positions and prepared to fight to the death. They were well camouflaged, and the Americans wouldn't see them until it was too late. Tsuji was making certain that the Americans would pay a heavy price for Guadalcanal.

"Sir!" said Sergeant Kaburagi, outside the tent. "A message has just arrived for you from Imperial Headquarters in Tokyo!"

Tsuji sat erect in his chair. "Bring it here at once!"

Sergeant Kaburagi entered the tent and held out the message, which Colonel Tsuji snatched from his hand.

YOUR APPLICATION FOR TRANSFER TO SEVENTEENTH ARMY NOT APPROVED. RETURN HERE TO REPORT ON BATTLE SITUATION.

Tsuji sank into his chair. "You may leave, Sergeant Kaburagi."

"Yes, sir."

Sergeant Kaburagi saluted, turned, and marched out of the tent. Colonel Tsuji stared at the message, trying to digest it. He'd previously requested a formal transfer to the Seventeenth Army on Guadalcanal, because technically he'd only been on temporary duty with General Hyakutake, supervising operations in the field for Imperial Headquarters in Tokyo. He'd wanted to make sure he'd stay on Guadalcanal and defeat the Americans or die an honorable death instead of leaving the battlefield on which he'd made so many erroneous decisions.

But now he had to return to Tokyo. Orders were orders. How ignominious it would be to leave the battle now that it was approaching its final hour. But at least he could tell the generals and admirals of their complicity in the defeats, because they'd never taken Guadalcanal seriously enough and never supplied enough men, ammunition, food, air cover, or anything else.

If I have to leave, Tsuji thought, *the sooner the better. Perhaps I can convince the generals and admirals to give us what we need to win on Guadalcanal, so that all those who died will not have died in vain.* Standing, he put on a fresh shirt and positioned his cap squarely on his head. He strapped on his samurai sword and stormed out of his tent, walking swiftly across the clearing, which was covered with camouflage netting so that American planes wouldn't spot them. He tried not to look at the emaciated soldiers listlessly cleaning their weapons or digging ditches. Some chewed leaves, green scum covering their lips. *What a disaster,* Tsuji thought. *Who would ever have guessed it would come to this?*

He entered General Hyakutake's command tent, nodded to the staff officers at their desks, their eyes dull with hunger and defeat, and entered the office of General Hyakutake, who was lying on his cot, taking a nap. General Hyakutake opened his eyes and reached for his sword at the approach of Tsuji.

"Oh, it's you," General Hyakutake said, sitting up. "What's wrong now?"

Tsuji handed him the message. "I just received this from Imperial Headquarters."

General Hyakutake read the message. "They want you back in Tokyo," he said. "How unfortunate for you."

"It is indeed unfortunate sir, but at least they'll find out the true situation here."

"It won't matter. I've told them in a hundred communiqués and they've done nothing. I only hope they'll let us die here with honor instead of making us run away like dogs with our tails between our legs."

"I will convey that sentiment to them, sir," Colonel Tsuji said, looking down at his boots. "It's the least I can do for the Seventeenth Army. It's my fault that we've failed here, because I consistently underestimated the enemy's fighting power and always insisted on my own operations plans, which proved to be wrong. I deserve a sentence of ten thousand deaths for my failures here on Guadalcanal."

"Come, come, Tsuji," General Hyakutake said. "All of us

are to blame, especially the generals and admirals in Tokyo, who never gave us what we needed. But the battle isn't lost yet. We can still fight. Thanks to you, we have a string of insurmountable defenses laid out against the Americans. They shall not pass."

Tsuji knew his general was engaging in wishful thinking, because no defense was insurmountable. The Americans would break through sooner or later—probably sooner, because half-starved Japanese soldiers could not hold out indefinitely against the American juggernaut.

"Yes, sir," Tsuji said.

"You might as well get busy right away on your travel arrangements. No use staying around if you don't have to. The sooner you get to Tokyo, the sooner you can plead our cause."

Colonel Tsuji took a step backward and saluted. "Yes, sir. I'll go to the radio shack and arrange for transportation right now."

"Carry on, Colonel Tsuji."

Tsuji marched out of the tent and stomped across the clearing to the radio shack, the jungle buzzing with insects as the full heat and humidity of the day descended on the island.

It wasn't nearly so hot in Nouméa on New Caledonia, and Frankie La Barbara sat on the steps of one of the barracks buildings that faced the nurses' quarters, waiting for Lieutenant Crawford to come out. He'd been sitting there for a couple of hours, smoking cigarettes and glancing at his watch. He'd decided she was the prettiest nurse on the island and he wanted to get her goodies before he was shipped back to the front.

Frankie La Barbara was a handsome young man and he knew it. Women had always told him that he resembled the actor Victor Mature, and back in New York City he'd had a whole bunch of girl friends in addition to his wife, Francesca, who loved him dearly and put up with all his bullshit. Frankie knew that women were attracted to him just as he was attracted to them. He'd had so many women in his young life that he had a lot of confidence. He'd found out long ago that women like to fuck just as much as men do, and pretty women like it even more.

Where is she? he thought, puffing a Chesterfield. He'd been trying to find her all day, checking her ward, the mess hall, and now sitting in front of the nurses' quarters. Frankie was getting discouraged. He thought of Nurse Gleason in his own ward. *Maybe I ought to go and get a blowjob from her. Then I can come back and wait for Nurse Crawford.*

Frankie stubbed out his cigarette on the ground and field-stripped it, scattering the shreds of tobacco into the air and balling up the paper. He tossed the paper to the side and stood, then spotted two nurses leave the building across the street; one of them was Betty Crawford. The nurses walked to the street, continued talking for a few minutes, and then split up. The other nurse was headed in Frankie's direction and Nurse Crawford was going the other way.

Frankie stood up and walked swiftly across the lawn. He passed the other nurse on the street, a gawky old-maid type, and caught up with Nurse Crawford.

"Hi, there," Frankie said, flashing his best smile. "Remember me?"

Betty Crawford was startled by the sound of his voice, looked at him, and remembered him instantly. "Oh, yes, you're the friend of Sargeant Butsko."

The sun gleamed on Frankie's pearly-white teeth. "Well, I wouldn't exactly call us friends. He was my platoon sergeant. Ugly son of a bitch, isn't he?"

"He's certainly seen a lot of war."

Frankie looked around furtively. "Say, I know you're an officer and I'm an ordinary soldier, but how'd you like to take a ride around the island with me tonight?"

Nurse Crawford smiled at the earnest expression on Frank ie's face. She was no dumb broad and it was not hard for her to perceive that he was the basic good-looking Don Juan type who didn't have a shred of decency in his body.

"No, thank you," she said politely. "I'm going to the movies tonight."

"Aw, you can see the movies anytime. But a ride around the island with old Frankie? You can't get that anytime." He winked.

She almost laughed, but knew that Don Juan types take themselves seriously, so she kept a straight face. "I'm very flattered, but I'm engaged to be married, and I think I'd rather go to the movies."

"Where's the guy you're engaged to?"

"He's in the Army—in North Africa."

"Hey, that's a long ways off." Frankie winked and flashed his smile again. "I'm married, you know. My wife's in New York. But you and me are here together, and who's gonna know?"

"There's no point in talking about it," she said. "You just don't understand."

"I understand that people get lonely sometimes. Don't you get lonely sometimes?"

"What did you say your name was?"

"Just call me Frankie. What's your first name?"

"None of your business." She looked sternly at him. "Now listen to me, Frankie. I'm sure you're a good soldier, but I'm not interested in talking with you any further, so why don't you go your way and I'll go mine."

Frankie turned down the corners of his mouth. "Hey, baby, I'm a good thing. You don't want to throw away a good thing."

"If you don't start walking away from me right now, I'm going to call for an MP."

"Shit, you wouldn't dare."

"No?"

"No."

She opened her mouth to scream and Frankie took a quick step backward, holding up his hand. "Okay, I guess you would dare. Sorry to bother you, sweetheart. See you around like a doughnut."

Frankie walked away quickly, taking a cigarette from his pack, not looking back. What a cunt she had turned out to be. Well, the *no*'s don't count. Only the *yes*'s count. His Uncle Tony from Brooklyn had told him that once and he always found it to be true. He headed back to his own ward and Nurse Gleason, who was a little on the chubby side but usually said yes.

THREE . . .

Bannon returned to the recon platoon, where Pfc. Shaw had organized a lively crap game around a filthy Army blanket, everybody playing for payday stakes.

"All right, let's break it up!" Bannon shouted. "We're moving out *now*!"

"Aw, Sarge!" complained Corporal Gomez, an ex-pachuco from Los Angeles, who held the dice. "I was just starting to win back what I lost!"

"I said we're moving out! *Let's go!*"

"But, Sarge . . . !"

Bannon charged forward and snatched the dice out of his hands. *"I said saddle up and move out!"*

Everything became quiet. Bannon was aware that all eyes were on him, and he could feel the hate. It was odd, because he'd been one of the boys until only three weeks earlier, but now he'd become The Enemy to all his former friends.

Bannon put the dice in his shirt pocket. "You'll get these back when we get to were we're going."

"Where we going?" Private Billie Jones asked.

"You'll find out when you get there."

Bannon turned his back to them and headed for his foxhole. He was tense because he thought one of them might jump him from behind, but he didn't look back; it was a trick he'd seen Butsko use many times. The only difference was that all the men were scared shitless of Butsko, but he knew that none of them were that scared of him. He'd had to punch a few of them out during the past few weeks, but it hadn't been enough. *If I was built like a tank like Butsko and scarred from head to foot, then I bet they'd be afraid of me.*

He returned to his foxhole and saw his runner, Pfc. Alfred DelFranco from River Rouge, Michigan, inside it, praying his rosary. DelFranco was a spidery little man with a wispy mustache who was very serious and conscientious, which was why Bannon had made him his runner, although Bannon thought the platoon definitely didn't need another religious fanatic. The Reverend Billie Jones had been almost more than Bannon could tolerate, but DelFranco was the quiet type of religious fanatic who prayed silently and never delivered impromptu sermons, so there had been no problems with him so far.

"We're moving out," Bannon told him. "Get your shit squared away."

"Hup, Sarge."

Bannon gathered together his equipment and stuffed it into his pack. DelFranco struck their pup tent and unbuttoned the halves, bringing Bannon his half, which Bannon rolled up with his blanket, tying it to the top and sides of his pack so that it resembled a horseshoe. From the corner of his eye he could see DelFranco scurrying about, gathering together his equipment, all concentration and no wasted effort. Like most of the men in the recon platoon, DelFranco was there because of a fight. Someone in his former company had made a disparaging remark about the pope, and DelFranco had let him have it. Now he was the smallest man in the recon platoon. He had no friends and appeared not to want any: another eight ball in a platoon of eight balls.

After Bannon's pack was ready, he roamed through the platoon area, shouting orders, telling the men to get a move on. He wanted to reach his new position before chow that night and then get his men to bed early so he could make an early start in the morning. They grumbled and snarled, just the way he grumbled and snarled when Butsko gave him orders, but now he was in Butsko's position and knew what he'd gone through. Maintaining discipline among thirty-two maniacs wasn't easy.

Finally all the men were ready. Bannon lined them up in a column of twos and moved them off. He led the column with DelFranco at his side, and behind him was the First Squad with Corporal Sam Longtree at its head.

The recon platoon passed other units in the regiment, and some of the old soldiers looked up as they passed, because they knew of the exploits of the recon platoon and recognized some of its members.

The march was slow, because the jungle was thick and the trail twisted like a demented snake. Several times Bannon had to stop and check his compass or ask directions. Around 1600 hours the platoon landed in Fox Company, the approximate point from which they were to jump off in the morning. Bannon asked around, found out where the company command post was, and marched the platoon there, telling them to take a break while he went into the tent and talked with the company commander.

Bannon entered the tent and saw the company's first sergeant, a grizzled old war dog with a big red whiskey nose, sitting at a portable field desk.

"Hi, there," Bannon said. "I wonder if I could talk with your CO for a moment."

"Who the fuck are you?" the old master sergeant asked in a raspy voice.

"I'm Sergeant Bannon from the recon platoon."

"What the fuck you want?"

"That's what I got to talk with your CO about. I don't feel like explaining everything twice."

"You're not getting in there until you tell me what you want."

"Kiss my ass," Bannon said, moving toward the tent flap and pushing it aside. He stepped into the office of the company commander and saw him, a young captain, seated behind the desk. Two lieutenants were seated in front of the desk. Everyone looked up in surprise at Bannon, who threw a snappy salute.

"Hate to bother you, gentlemen," Bannon said, "but I'm Sergeant Bannon from the recon platoon and I thought I ought to tell you that we're going to be in the area for the night."

The old first sergeant barged into the office and grabbed Bannon's arm. "Now just a minute!" he roared.

Bannon pulled away from him. "Get your fucking hands off me."

The officer behind the desk stood up. "Now hold on—the both of you!"

"Sir," said the first sergeant, "this man barged into your office without my permission."

"I don't have time to play games with you," Bannon said.

The captain behind the desk looked back and forth at each of them and tried to size up the situation. He knew that his first sergeant was a drunken old fool and that the recon platoon was Colonel Stockton's baby.

"I'll handle this, Sergeant Page," he said.

"Yes, sir," the old first sergeant said gruffly. He turned and left the office.

The captain looked at Bannon. "You shouldn't have walked in here without my first sergeant's permission."

"Sorry, sir, but I didn't have time for a song and dance with him. My platoon has to move out ahead of the regiment in the morning, and I wanted to get my men settled in as soon as I can. If you have any questions about what I'm doing here, you can call Major Cobb at Regiment."

The captain was a graduate of West Point, wise in the ways of Army protocol. "I don't think that'll be necessary. You can bivouac anywhere around here that you want. I'll pass the word along so that you don't have any problems. Do you need any rations or anything like that?"

"No, sir."

The captain smiled. "By the way, I'm Captain Leach. This is Lieutenant Bova and that's Lieutenant Martin."

"Hiya," Bannon said.

The officers nodded and grinned. All of them knew how Colonel Stockton felt about his recon platoon.

"Well," Bannon said. "I guess I'd better get rolling along. Got a lot to do. Nice talking to you, gentlemen."

He threw another of his smart salutes and left the office, passing the desk of First Sergeant Page, who gave him a dirty look.

"Fuck you," Bannon said out the corner of his mouth.

Sergeant Page jumped to his feet. *"What'd you say?"*

But Bannon was already out of the tent.

Sergeant Page was so angry, his hands were trembling and his face was turning purple with rage. He bared his teeth, snarled, took out a cigarette, and lit it up.

"You okay, Sarge?" asked the company clerk, Pfc. Andy Sawyer from Raleigh, North Carolina, who was seated behind the desk on the other side of the tent.

"Watch the phones for a few minutes. I gotta go take care of something."

"Hup, Sarge."

Sergeant Page put on his helmet and charged out of the tent like an angry bull moose. His enormous beer belly hung over his belt and his helmet was low over his eyes as he made his way to the weapons platoon, where he found Sergeant Fowler putting one of his mortar squads through an aiming-and-firing exercise.

"Fowler, come here a minute."

Sergeant Fowler had been a drinking buddy of Sergeant Page's when the Twenty-third Infantry Regiment was in Australia, and they also used to visit whorehouses together. Fowler was thirty-five and husky, with coarse features and malevolent eyes. "Yeah, whataya want?" he said, slapping the dirt off his hands as he approached Sergeant Page.

Sergeant Page led him away from the mortar squad. "Guess what?" he said.

"What?" asked Fowler.

"We got the fucking recon platoon with us for the night."

"Oh, that must be the guys I saw around here a few minutes ago."

"That's them."

"They're supposed to be a bunch of real tough rat bastards."

Sergeant Page scowled and spat at the trunk of a coconut palm tree. "They look like a bunch of wise guys and fags to me. I don't think they're so tough. Why don't you take some of the boys over there in a little while and we'll see how tough they really are."

Sergeant Fowler showed the palms of his hands. "Hey, I don't want any trouble, Les. The captain wouldn't go for any rough stuff."

"Fuck the captain. I'm the one who runs this company, and everybody knows it. He just signs what I put in front of him.

Listen, that recon platoon is in trouble all the time, because they're a bunch of fuck-ups. If anything happens, we can just blame it on them."

"They're supposed to be the colonel's fair-haired boys, ain't they?"

"Yeah, he bails them out whenever they fuck up."

Sergeant Fowler wiped his nose with the back of his hand. "When I was a kid at school, I always hated the teacher's pet."

"Well the recon platoon is the same fucking thing."

"That's what I was thinking." Sergeant Fowler looked around. "Where are they?"

Sergeant Page pointed. "Somewhere back there."

"How many of them?"

"I don't know. If they're a platoon, there're probably around forty, but if they're understrength, like we are, there're probably around thirty."

"We got that many badasses in this company, at least. I'll round some of them up. Things have been too quiet around here lately anyway."

"Kick their asses," Sergeant Page said. "Stomp their fucking heads. Their platoon sergeant's name is Bannon. You might want to get a piece of him for yourself."

"I always wanted to kick the shit out of the teacher's pet," Fowler said.

"Well, here's your chance. Let me know when you're ready to go, because I'd like to see the fun."

The sun was sinking on the horizon, and Pfc. Tommy Shaw, the former professional heavyweight boxer, was spreading out his blanket in preparation for the evening's crap game. Corporal Gomez had retrieved the dice from Bannon and was rubbing the tiny cubes in his hands, warming them up and praying for the blessings of Lady Luck. The other soldiers crowded around, anxious to bet money they hadn't even been paid yet on a toss of the dice. Pfc. DelFranco walked by on his way to the latrine.

"Hey, DelFranco!" Gomez called out. "Gonna join the game?"

"No, thanks."

Gomez laughed. He'd known DelFranco wouldn't join. DelFranco spent all his time with his Bible. DelFranco didn't believe in gambling, but the Reverend Billie Jones did. The Reverend Billie Jones was a gambling fool, but then he'd turn around and start giving you a sermon on morals and shit. Gomez couldn't figure Billie Jones out.

DelFranco continued on his way to the latrine. He knew the others thought he was odd, and he was totally miserable in the Army, but he was trying to do his duty. Sometimes he thought he should have become a priest when he had the chance, but he hadn't done it because he didn't think he was smart enough or moral enough. He had too many lewd thoughts and believed he was too selfish to be a priest. But he was working on it. You always had to work on it to make yourself worthy of the Kingdom of God.

A group of soldiers whom he didn't know came walking toward him, and they looked like a big, rowdy bunch.

"Hey, this looks like one of them here!" said Sergeant Fowler, who was leading the pack through the jungle.

"He's just a little guy," Private Engle replied. "He looks like a pansy to me."

"Hey, are you a pansy?" Sergeant Fowler asked DelFranco.

DelFranco knew trouble when he saw it. He just kept on walking.

"Hey, I'm talking to you, sissy-boy!"

DelFranco kept on walking.

Fowler rushed toward him and grabbed the front of his shirt. "I just asked you a question, punk!"

DelFranco looked up at Sergeant Fowler, his heart beating like a tom-tom. "I am under no obligation to answer your questions," he said in a voice that was so steady, it surprised him more than it surprised Fowler.

Fowler stared at him in disbelief, then laughed and pushed him out of the way. "Get lost, fag."

DelFranco wanted to tell him to drop dead, but a good Christian was supposed to turn the other cheek, so he just smoothed his shirt and continued on his way to the latrine.

Meanwhile, back at the blanket, Corporal Gomez was getting the crap game under way. He was shaking the dice in his fist three inches from his ear and talking to them. "Come on, *Mamacita, Chiquita, Pupusita*—come on, seven—come on, eleven—*talk to me!*"

He threw the dice; his eyes bulged as the cubes bounced over the blanket, rolling to a stop and coming up snake eyes.

"You son of a bitch bastard!" Gomez said. "You dirty fucking cunt! You *maricón* whore!"

Next to him Private Shilansky, the former bank robber from the Boston area, picked up the dice. He was among the tallest men in the platoon and had a very violent nature, with numerous courts-martial to prove it. He shook the dice high in the air. "Come, seven—come, eleven—and I'll be in heaven."

He let the dice fly, and they came up with a five and a three.

"Eight's your point," said Shaw.

"I can read, asshole," Shilansky said, picking up the dice again. As he was about to shake them again, he heard footsteps. Looking up, he saw Sergeant Fowler and the others approaching in the twilight.

"Well, what we got here?" asked Fowler. "Looks like a little crap game!" He spread his legs and crossed his arms.

"You're welcome to join, boys," Shilansky said, blowing on the dice. "Just lay your money down."

"We don't play dice with scumbags and punks."

Suddenly everything became very quiet. Shilansky looked at Shaw. Shaw looked at Longtree. Longtree looked at Gomez, who already was reaching for the switchblade he'd brought with him all the way from the back alleys of Los Angeles. The recon platoon stood up.

Shilansky smiled. "I don't think I heard you right, friend. What was that again?"

"I ain't your fucking friend, and I said we don't play dice with scumbags, punks, and creeps who spend all their time kissing the colonel's ass."

Shilansky looked at Shaw. Shaw looked at Longtree. Longtree looked at Gomez, whose hand was in his pocket, his thumb on the button of his switch. The rest of the recon platoon crowded around. The group in front of them outnumbered them by around ten men, but they'd faced worse odds than that since they came to Guadalcanal and had come out okay.

"Well," said Shilansky, "I guess it's gonna be one of them days."

"Looks that way," Longtree agreed.

The Reverend Billie Jones looked at the sky. "Lord, we try to stay out of trouble, but what can we do when trouble come looking for us?"

At that point Bannon arrived to join in the crap game. "What's going on here?"

"Who the fuck are you?" asked Sergeant Fowler, rocking back and forth on the balls of his feet.

Bannon glanced around and perceived in an instant that something heavy was about to go down. "Who wants to know?" Bannon asked.

Sergeant Fowler noticed the three stripes on Bannon's arm and figured he must be the recon platoon sergeant, the one Sergeant Page had told him about. "Are you Bannon?"

"What's it to you?"

"I've been wanting to meet the recon platoon sergeant, because I heard he's Colonel Stockton's asshole buddy."

Bannon wanted to take Sergeant Fowler's head off, but he knew, from a court-martial point of view, that he shouldn't be the one to throw the first punch. "I think you'd better turn around and get out of here while you're still in one piece, fuckface."

"What you call me?"

"Fuckface."

"You know, I'll bet you're that Bannon feller, Colonel Stockton's asshole buddy."

"Are you looking for a fight by any chance, Sergeant?"

"Who, me?"

"Yeah, you."

"What makes you think that?"

"Because you're someplace where you shouldn't be. If you come here to fight Bannon, here I stand."

The atmosphere crackled with electricity. The men in the recon platoon knew Bannon was trying to egg the other man on, to make him throw the first punch. Most of the men in the recon platoon had been through courts-martial and knew that score.

Sergeant Fowler uncrossed his arms and lowered his hands to his sides, making fists. "So you're Bannon, huh?"

"Did you come to talk or did you come to fight, shithead."

"I come to rearrange your face."

Sergeant Fowler raised his fists and charged, and the men he'd brought with him charged behind him. He threw an overhead right at Bannon's face, but Bannon got under it and dug an uppercut into Fowler's solar plexus. Fowler wheezed and Bannon punched him in the mouth. Then he went downstairs and hit him in the belly. Fowler swung wildly and Bannon threw a left hook that broke Sergeant Fowler's nose, blood spurting in all directions. Fowler swung wild again and Bannon threw a right hook that landed squarely on Fowler's jaw. Fowler was stunned and reached out to hang on to something, but Bannon smashed him in the mouth again and Fowler went down for the count.

Shaw, the ex-heavyweight pro, was happy to have the opportunity to do some sparring, but his happiness soon turned to boredom. The first guy who came at him was wide open and Shaw knocked him out with a stiff left jab. The next guy telegraphed every punch and Shaw put him down with a left-right combination. The third guy was more tentative, pawing at Shaw with his left while trying to set him up with a right. Shaw let himself get set up, watched the right come, dodged to the side, and buried his fist almost to the wrist in the other soldier's fat stomach. The soldier fell down and Shaw thought, *Oh, shit, isn't there anybody around here who can fight?*

He looked around and saw a big guy who looked stupid, pounding on Private Kroll, one of the smaller men in the recon platoon. "Hey, scumbucket!" Shaw shouted at the big soldier.

The soldier looked at Shaw. Shaw winked and beckoned to him. The soldier turned from Kroll and moved toward Shaw like a big lumbering elephant. Shaw got up on the balls of his feet and started dancing, hoping this guy would give him a workout. The soldier stopped in puzzlement, grinned, and charged, trying to grab Shaw around the waist in a bear hug. Shaw danced backward, throwing a left, a right, and then another left at the soldier's head, connecting each time, but the soldier kept coming. Shaw dodged to the side, but the soldier followed him and lunged suddenly, wrapping his big arms around Shaw's waist. The big soldier squeezed and Shaw could feel sharp pressure on his spine.

There was nothing for him to do except insert one finger in

the soldier's left nostril, another finger in the right corner of the soldier's mouth, and pull. The soldier's face ripped apart in a bloody red jagged line, and he screamed, letting Shaw go. Shaw put all of his two hundred and ten pounds into a left punch that landed squarely on the soldier's mouth, breaking teeth and staggering him. Another punch, exactly the same, sent the big soldier sprawling into the mud.

Gomez ran through the crowd, waving his switchblade in the air, but everyone got out of his way; nobody wanted any part of that cold razor-sharp weapon. A path opened wide in front of Gomez, and at its end stood a Mexican like himself, holding a switchblade pointed straight up in the air.

Gomez stopped. Both men stared at each other. Then they began their deadly dance, circling round each other, waving the blades of their knives back and forth in the air. Gomez could see that his opponent was skilled with a knife, maybe as skilled as he, and he felt that intoxicating rush that accompanied mortal combat. Gomez feinted with his knife and the other man darted backward. He feinted again and the man moved to the side. The man feinted but Gomez didn't budge; he was anxious to get it on. The other man lunged suddenly, and Gomez tried to grab his wrist with his left hand, but he missed and his fingers closed around the blade of the other man's knife. The knife cut Gomez's hand to the bone, but Gomez didn't make a sound as he held on tightly and rammed his switchblade into the man's belly. The man staggered, his eyes rolling up into his head, and collapsed at Gomez's feet. Gomez held his hand in front of his face and looked at the deep gash as soldiers grunted and shouted all around him, throwing punches, kicking, rolling around on the ground, trying to strangle each other.

Homer Gladley, the biggest man in the recon platoon, wasn't a particularly skillful fighter, but he had tremendous power. He waded through the men from Fox Company, swinging wildly, and no one had the strength to block his punches; he sent a succession of men crumbling to the ground, and once they landed they didn't get up again.

Corporal Sam Longtree, built tall and lanky, like Bannon, relied on speed and fighting skill, always throwing more punches than his opponents and landing more, darting about as if his legs had springs in them; he was especially good at slipping punches.

Longtree loved to fight and, as an Apache, had been taught since he was a child that fighting was a man's main function in life. A soldier from Fox Company threw a punch at him, and Longtree bent low, letting the punch fly over his head. Longtree grabbed the soldier by his belt and his shirt, lifted him into the air, and threw him to the ground, the impact of landing knocking the soldier senseless. Longtree jumped on the soldier's face, flattening out his nose, then leaped away and found himself facing another soldier from Fox Company.

The soldier swung, but Longtree swung first, whacking the soldier's head back. The soldier's punch went wild and Longtree punched him twice in the stomach, doubling him over. An uppercut sent the soldier flying through the air.

Another soldier jumped on Longtree's back, wrapping his arms around Longtree's neck. Longtree shot his elbow backward, burying it in the soldier's ribs. The soldier grunted and loosened his hold on Longtree's neck, and Longtree dropped to his knees, slipping out of the soldier's grasp. He turned around, tackled the soldier, and pushed him to the ground, then straddled him and punched his face until the soldier was unconscious.

The recon platoon ripped through the men of Fox Company as if they were made of paper. The battle didn't take long, but it lasted long enough for Captain Leach to hear the commotion and stick his head out of the tent. He couldn't see much through the thick foliage, but he knew something improper was going on. Pulling his head back into the tent, he looked at Sergeant Page's empty chair.

"Where's Sergeant Page?" he asked Pfc. Sawyer.

"I dunno, sir."

Captain Leach put on his helmet and walked in long strides toward the sound of the tumult. When he was halfway there he spotted Sergeant Page walking quickly toward the CP tent, an expression of horror on his face.

"What's going on over there, Sergeant?"

Sergeant Page hadn't noticed Captain Leach because Sergeant Page was stunned by the way the fight had turned out.

The recon platoon was kicking the shit out of Sergeant Fowler and his men. "Huh?"

"I said what's going on over there?"

"Over where?"

Captain Leach pointed. "Over there."

Sergeant Page looked in that direction. "There?"

"Yes, where you're coming from."

"Um . . . I . . ."

"I think you'd better come with me, Sergeant."

They made their way through the jungle, but by the time they got to the scene of the fight, it was all over. The ground was strewn with men from Fox Company, while the men from the recon platoon were jubilant, slapping each other on their backs, lighting up cigarettes, discussing the fun they'd had. The new recon platoon medic, Private Joel Blum, was trying to stop the bleeding of the Mexican who'd been knifed by Gomez. About ten men from Fox Company had fled when they realized the battle was going against them, and they could be heard in the distance, crashing through the jungle.

Captain Leach blinked and his jaw dropped open at the sight of the devastation.

"What's going on here?"

"Sir," said Sergeant Page, "it looks as if the recon platoon has attacked some of our men."

"What were our men doing over here in the recon platoon area?"

"I . . . ah . . ."

Captain Leach saw Bannon laughing and smoking with Longtree and Shilansky. *"Bannon!"*

Bannon's head snapped around. *"Yes, sir!"*

"Get over here!"

Bannon threw away his cigarette and put on a straight face, running toward Captain Leach, saluting. "Yes, sir!"

"What the hell's going on?"

"Well, sir," Bannon explained, "a little while ago, just as my men were getting ready to sack out, some of your men came over and picked a fight with us. We didn't throw the first punch, sir. One of your men did. He's over there someplace." Bannon pointed with his thumb behind him to the spot where

Sergeant Fowler lay, his face like hamburger.

"That's a lie!" Sergeant Page exploded. "My men would never start trouble like this!"

Captain Leach looked at Sergeant Page. "Then what were they doing over here?"

"Over here?" Sergeant Page wrinkled his forehead. "Maybe they came over to welcome the recon platoon to our company area."

Somehow that didn't ring true to Captain Leach. Then he remembered Sergeant Page rushing from the scene of the fight. "What were you doing over here, Page?"

"Who, me?" Sergeant Page took a step backward, pointed to his chest, and shook his head. "I wasn't over here, sir."

"I saw you coming from this direction. What were you doing over here?"

"Um . . . just taking a walk, sir."

"And you didn't hear the fight?"

"No, sir."

Captain Leach knew that Sergeant Page had to be lying, because anyone in the area would have heard the sound of fighting. Moreover, he'd caught Sergeant Page lying numerous times in the past, so he knew Sergeant Page wasn't a particularly truthful person. He recalled the argument Sergeant Page had had with Bannon in the CP tent earlier that day. Captain Leach put two and two together. Sergeant Page had probably connived to have some men from Fox Company beat up the recon platoon, but the recon platoon had turned the tables. "Sergeant Page," he said. "Get the company medics over here right away. And then I want to speak with you in my tent."

"Yes, sir."

Sergeant Page, an unhappy look on his face, walked away, his big belly bouncing up and down over his belt. Some of the men from Fox Company were getting up and staggering back to their company area. Others were still out cold. The man whom Corporal Gomez had knifed had lost a lot of blood, and Private Blum was struggling to keep him alive.

Bannon shrugged. "I'm awfully sorry about this, sir, but your people came over here; we didn't go over there."

"Yes, I can see that." Lieutenant Leach felt as if he should apologize to Bannon, but one doesn't apologize to one's inferiors. "If any of your men need medical attention, just ask our medics for help. They'll be here soon."

"We got our own medic, sir."

"I doubt whether anything like this will happen again, but if it does, I hope you'll come directly to me before it gets out of hand."

"Yes, sir."

"That is all. Carry on."

"Yes, sir."

Bannon saluted and Captain Leach walked away. Bannon turned around and smiled, joining the men from the recon platoon who gathered around him, bruised, their knuckles bleeding.

"What he say?" asked Shaw.

"What could he say?" replied Bannon. "He knows what happened. Evidently that fat fuck of a first sergeant set the whole thing up. Anyway, let's get cleaned up and hit the sack. We gotta get up early tomorrow."

The men dispersed and headed for their pup tents. Shaw looked back at the men from Fox Company who were still lying unconscious on the ground. *Gee,* he thought, *I bet Frankie La Barbara would've liked to have been here for this.*

The 1939 Chevrolet staff car, painted khaki, came to a stop in a desolate part of the jungle on new Caledonia. Frankie La Barbara pulled up the emergency brake and turned off the ignition, then faced chubby brunette Lieutenant Wanda Gleason from Toledo, Ohio. "Let's take our clothes off," he said.

"Frankie, we just got here!"

"I know we just got here. Let's take our clothes off."

"What's the hurry?"

"I wanna go back to see the movie."

Wanda groaned. "Frankie, you're awful."

He reached over and unbuttoned the top button of her khaki blouse. "Lemme see your tits, baby."

She slapped his hand away. "Frankie!"

"What's the matter?"

"Slow down."

"What for?"

"You're going too fast."

"Hey, c'mon. It ain't like this is the first time we're gonna do it."

She looked at him with annoyance. "You were so romantic at first, but you're not romantic at all anymore."

Frankie realized he wouldn't get anything unless he played it her way, so he decided to cool it. "Okay, okay." He decided he'd have a cigarette and chat for a while, then go to work on her slowly. If he missed the movie, there'd be other movies.

"Want one?" he asked, holding out his pack to her.

"Thank you."

He lit them both with his Zippo. "Nice night, isn't it?"

She looked at him and wrinkled her brow. "You know, Frankie, you're really a terrible person."

"What makes you say that?"

"You don't care about me at all."

"That's not true! Would I be here with you if I didn't care about you?"

"Yes, because you'll do anything to get laid."

"Well, what else is there to do?"

"Sometimes it's nice just to be with somebody else. You don't have to have sex."

"Who don't have to have sex?" Frankie asked.

"People don't."

"Bullshit, and let me tell you, there are a lot of nurses on this island who'd give their left tits to be with me right now, but I'm with you because I like you best."

"That's a lie and you know it."

"It is not a lie!"

"Yes, it is, but I'll believe it because I want to." She looked out the window at the palm trees and, beyond them, at the half-moon in the sky. She knew Frankie was just using her, but he was so sexy that she didn't care. She'd never had so many boyfriends in her life since becoming an Army nurse and was realistic enough to understand that that was because the GIs had such limited choice among women. A man like Frankie La Barbara never would look at her twice back in Toledo.

"I feel bad," Frankie said. "You think I'm a heel. Maybe I should drive you back to the base."

"Since we're here, we might as well stay here."

Frankie went limp behind the wheel and looked unhappy.

She knew he was trying to get her sympathy, and it was working. He was handsome enough to be a movie star, exept there always was something nasty and evil on his face, and that's the part that really turned her on.

She bent toward him and kissed his cheek. "God, you're really something."

He didn't move a muscle. "No, you don't have to do that. It's okay. We can just talk."

"You bastard," she said, nuzzling his neck. "You know you've got me where you want me."

He stubbed out his cigarette in the ashtray and grabbed her, squeezing her soft, full body, pressing his lips against hers and sticking his tongue in. She let him push her down in the front seat, and he kissed her cheeks and chin, becoming intoxicated by her sweet fragrance and brushing his lips against hers again, licking them with her tongue.

"Am I going too fast?" he asked, tantalizing her.

"No," she whispered.

"There's not a helluva lot of room in this car. Let's get the blanket and go into the woods."

"Don't move. Just stay where you are for a few moments."

Frankie counted to three, then slapped her ass. "Okay, let's go."

He got out of the car, took the blanket from the backseat, then went around to her side and opened the door.

She stepped out and looked at the moonlight on the palm trees. He took her hand and led her into the woods, stopping at the first clearing and laying out the blanket. Then he stood and looked at her.

"Frankie," she said, "you really do kind of like me, don't you? I mean, you're not just doing this for the sex, are you?"

"I don't like you baby," Frankie said. "I *love* you."

"You don't mean that."

"No?"

He moved toward her and squeezed her against him, covering her face with kisses. His hands roved up and down her back and grabbed her meaty haunches, while he thrilled to the touch of her gigantic breasts against his shirt. Feeling dizzy, her knees gave way, and Frankie lowered her gently to the ground. She lay with her eyes closed, and he unbuttoned the front of her blouse, uncovering her brassiere, which stuck out like two torpedoes. Frankie bent down and bit one of the peaks.

"You got the best tits in the world," he told her.

She shivered as he chewed on the end of her boob and worked his hands underneath to unsnap the strap. She raised herself an inch to help him and the strap came loose. Frankie pushed her bra up, baring her huge breasts, and buried his face in them, lapping and slobbering, kissing and sucking the nipples. Wanda squirmed and felt juicy. She ran her fingers through Frankie's thick black hair and saw the moon through half-closed eyes. Her nipples extended and became hard under the pressure of his tongue. His left hand steadied one breast while his right pulled up her skirt, his fingers seeking that soft spot between her legs, sneaking in underneath the legband of her underpants, and burrowing into the hot, moist flesh.

She arched her back and moaned, Frankie, nearly suffocated by tits, figured she was about ready. He sank his middle finger into her whirlpool and she moaned, moving her head from side to side on the blanket. It was greasy and hot in there, the magic spot he craved. He wiggled his finger around and raised his face until it was level with hers.

"You're hot stuff, baby," he said through a throat constricted with raw animal lust. He pulled his finger out a bit and twiddled her gumdrop.

She spread her legs and closed her eyes, and he knew the time had come to get her clothes off before she changed her mind. In lightning movements he pulled down her skirt and underpants, showing her thick, firm legs and the wispy brown curls where they formed a juncture. Then he took off her blouse and brassiere while she kicked off her shoes. Frankie jumped up like a rabbit, tore off his shirt, and leaped out of his pants, but his shoes were still on and they'd stay on because he didn't want to waste any time taking them off.

He looked down at her; she was like a big healthy nymph of the forest, all pink and smooth, soft as marshmallow and heaven to touch. He lowered himself on top of her, laying his prong on her belly, and she wrapped her arms around him, hugging him tightly to her and pursing her lips.

He kissed her, and her lips tasted like wild raspberries. Women's saliva always tasted like ambrosia to him once he got them aroused. He slurped inside her mouth with his tongue, and she slurped back, saliva dripping down their chins, both getting a little crazy. Frankie grabbed his flaming, throbbing dork, wiggled his hips, and touched it to the delicate petallike lips between her legs.

She made a soft high-pitched animal noise as he worked it up and down against those wonderful gooey lips, and she raised her ass off the ground to bring him more deeply into her. He pulled his equipment away.

"I think maybe we're going too fast," he said.

"You bastard."

"Maybe we should talk a while."

"Don't do this to me."

"Sometimes I get the feeling you only want me for sex."

She looked into his eyes. "Frankie, if you continue to tease me like this, I'll kill you."

"Well, I guess I wouldn't want you to do that," he said with a grin as he slid it in all the way.

The tingles and tickles and twitches were so good she had to bite her lip to keep from screaming out loud. Frankie rested for a few moments, letting it soak, and then kissed her, pushing his tongue deep in her mouth, almost against her throat, while his cock pulsated inside her softest, most tender place. Then he pulled out, paused, and shoved it in again. She squirmed and whimpered; he could tell that she liked it.

"Pretty good, huh?" he asked in a whisper.

She nodded.

He plunged in again, working her slowly at first so he could build up to a crescendo at the end. She wagged her hips from side to side and raised her knees in the air as he invaded her premises first from the left and then from the right, charging from the top and withdrawing from the bottom. Their lips clashed passionately, and she scratched her fingernails across his back.

Oh, boy, Frankie thought wildly, pumping away, *if only the guys could see me now.*

Betty Crawford returned to her ward to check the orderlies and see how her sickest patients were doing before she went to the movies. First she went to the nurses' station to see if there were any messages for her, and then she strolled through the ward to make sure that everything had been done that needed to be done, because her orderlies were regular GIs and they had a tendency to goldbrick.

She stepped outside to look at the lawn and saw a bulky figure sitting in the distance, a faint red glow coming from the vicinity of one of his hands. She'd figured he'd be there, because that's where he spent most of his time, just staring off into the distance and thinking about something; she often wondered what.

She felt uncomfortable and wrinkled her brow, because she knew in her heart that she'd returned to the ward basically to see him; she was off duty after all, and she'd never checked up on things so much before he became a patient of hers. She didn't know what to think of him; he was so strange, so obviously embittered.

She walked toward him, her feet moving almost by themselves. *If I were silly like some of the other girls around here, I might think I had a crush on him, but it's only a matter of one person finding another person interesting*. She had to tell herself this because she was engaged to marry a young lieutenant on General George Patton's staff in North Africa, a man she'd met at UCLA when they were students.

She approached him from the left, and he turned around and looked at her.

"Hi, Sergeant Butsko," she said cheerily, "How're you feeling tonight?"

He groaned. "I guess you just caught me smoking again."

She waved her hand. "Oh, that's all right. You're mending well. I guess it's okay if you smoke now. I can't seem to stop you anyway."

Butsko puffed his cigarette and grinned. "You're a good nurse. You're not a pain in the ass like some of the others."

"Aren't you going to the movie?"

"No."

"Why not?"

"Because I don't feel like it."

"James Cagney and Joan Blondell are in it."

"So what?"

She held her hands behind her back. "Don't you ever get tired of just sitting here?"

"Yeah, but there's nothing else to do."

"You could go to the movies."

"Movies are stupid."

"They're a distraction at least."

"I don't need any distractions. I don't have anything that I wanna run away from."

"Don't you want to forget the war?" she asked softly. "Don't you get tired of it?"

"Yeah, I'm tired of it. I'm so tired of it, you wouldn't believe it."

"Then come to the movies with me?" Suddenly she realized what she said and was glad it was dark, so he wouldn't see her blushing.

He looked up at her, his face immobile. "I don't wanna see the movie. Maybe later I'll take a walk."

She almost said, *Can I go with you?* but bit her tongue. "Do you feel well enough?"

"Yeah, I been feeling pretty good lately."

"Well, I wish you'd go to the movie. I think it'd do you good."

Butsko shrugged. Betty wanted to stay and talk with him, but he might think it odd. "Well, I'll be seeing you," she said.

"Right."

"Have a nice walk."

"Yeah."

She turned and walked off across the lawn, putting her hands in the pockets of her khaki trousers, feeling perplexed. She was afraid he might suspect that she liked him and take it the wrong way. *I basically treat him like everybody else, more or less,* she told herself. *I'm friendly with all my patients.*

But she had to admit to herself that she'd never invited one of them to go to the movies before, and she didn't particularly like James Cagney or Joan Blondell either, but she was going out of boredom, like everybody else on the base. Everybody else except Sergeant Butsko.

There's something about him that I like, she thought as she passed between two barracks. *I really wonder what it is.*

FOUR . . .

The recon platoon moved out early in the morning, an hour before dawn. They passed easily through the American forward positions and entered no-man's-land, with Longtree on the point and the rest of the platoon following. Bannon and his runner, DelFranco, were about halfway back.

The molten tropical sun was just below the horizon, making the eastern sky red and casting a hellish glow onto the jungle. The platoon moved forward stealthily, aware that Japanese suicide patrols could be all around them, sighting in for the kill.

On the point Longtree was glad to be getting away from the regiment for a while, because he couldn't stand the chickenshit. He heard a sound in the bushes ahead and froze, holding up his hand. The rest of the platoon stopped behind him. He got down on his stomach, and so did everyone to the rear. It could be a wild pig or a bird or a land crab, or it could be the Jap who would send Longtree to the Happy Hunting Ground. Longtree inched forward as silently as a snake. He heard the sound again; it was coming from the underbrush to the right of the road. He crawled off the trail and into the foliage, then was swallowed up by the treeline.

It was like being in a strange green world tinged with red. Birds chirped and monkeys chattered high in the trees. But the sound he'd heard had been on the ground. He hoped it wasn't a lost wandering crocodile, because there were a lot of them on Guadalcanal too.

He heard the sound again and crawled toward it, making no sound himself. The noise became more distinct as he moved forward; then he peeked around a tree and saw them: two land crabs fucking next to a boulder. Longtree didn't know whether to be angry or amused. He decided to get the hell out of there. Standing up, he turned to walk back to the trail, when he heard the snick of metal. He'd never heard land crabs, whether fucking or not, make a sound like that.

He dropped to the ground again just as a bullet cracked over his head and slammed into a tree behind him.

"Japs in here!" he screamed.

Back on the trail Bannon didn't know if it was one Jap or a hundred Japs, but there was only one way to find out. "Into the woods!" he hollered, waving his arm. "Keep your heads down!"

The recon platoon was like a well-oiled machine as it fanned out and entered the woods. Meanwhile, Longtree strained his eyes trying to see where the shot had come from. Maybe it was an American patrol returning.

"Who goes there!" Longtree said.

A fusillade of rifle fire erupted from the woods in front of Longtree, all the bullets flying over his head. The Japs were firing at the rest of the recon platoon entering the woods, but the GIs were keeping their heads low, and at the first sound of the fusillade they were down on their stomachs.

"Can anybody see them?" Bannon asked.

"They're someplace in front of me!" Longtree said.

"First and Second squads, form a skirmish line on Longtree's left! Third and Fourth squads, form a skirmish line on Longtree's right!"

"Where the fuck is Longtree?" Corporal Gomez asked, his left hand covered with a thick bandage.

"Over here!" said Longtree.

The squads moved into position, making a lot of noise. Longtree heard rustling in front of him and could perceive that the Japs were moving out. It sounded like there were five or six of them. They probably figured they were outnumbered and it was best to get the hell out of there.

"They're moving out!"

"Keep your heads down!" Bannon shouted. Bannon crawled to where Longtree was. "Where were the Japs?" Bannon asked Longtree.

Longtree pointed. "Over there. There were maybe five or six of them. I think they ran away."

"Maybe some left and some didn't. It might be a trap. We'll have to check. *Everybody forward, but watch your asses!"*

In a long wave the recon platoon crawled across the moist, stinking floor of the jungle, through piles of rat shit and little stagnant pools full of mosquito larvae. Adult mosquitoes buzzed around their heads and bit their bare arms. Lizards scampered out of their way. Finally, Longtree and Bannon came to footprints in the muck.

"This must be where they were," Longtree said, examining the footprints. "Looks like they went that way."

"It still might be a trap. You'd better go up there and check it out."

Longtree nodded and crawled forward, his rifle cradled in his arms. Bannon motioned for DelFranco to join him with the walkie-talkie and the bazooka. DelFranco wiggled forward, lugging his equipment.

"How're you doing?" Bannon asked, because DelFranco had never been out on patrol with the recon platoon before.

"Okay."

"Stay close in case I need that radio."

"Yo."

Meanwhile, Longtree crawled more deeply into the jungle, and for all he knew a hundred Japs could be waiting for him to come. *Why does it always have to be me who goes forward to check everything out?* he thought. But he knew the answer. He was the best scout in the recon platoon—maybe the best in the entire regiment. None of the others really understood how to track an enemy. None of them had the ears or the eyes he had. He wouldn't feel safe if somebody else was on the point. He crawled deeper into the jungle, following impressions in the mud, torn leaves, scratches on the bark of trees.

Bannon sat with his back against a tree, smoking a cigarette and waiting for Longtree to come back. DelFranco lay on the ground nearby with his head on his pack and his eyes closed. With his pointy nose, mustache, and receding chin, Bannon thought DelFranco looked something like a rodent.

Bannon wished Butsko was there. It was weird being in command of so many men. You were afraid to make a mistake for fear of getting some of them killed. And out here in no-man's-land on patrol, there was no one higher up to whom you could pass the buck. You were on your own and had to make all the decisions.

Longtree returned about fifteen minutes after he went out. "The tracks just keep going," he said.

"They're probably on their way back to wherever they came from. I'd better report them to Major Cobb. DelFranco, gimme the walkie-talkie."

DelFranco handed the portable radio over and Bannon held it to his face. "This is Red Dog calling Hot Dog Three. This is Red Dog calling Hot Dog Three. Do you read me? Do you read me? Over."

A few seconds later the reply came from Lieutenant Hutchinson at the regiment's operations section. "This is Hot Dog Three. This is Hot Dog Three. I read you loud and clear. I read you loud and clear. Over."

"Is the major there?" Bannon asked.

"Just a moment."

Bannon waited, then heard the deep, calm voice of Major Cobb. "What is it, Bannon?"

"We've just run into an enemy patrol of approximately squad strength. Nobody was hurt and the Japs ran away. Should we go after them?"

"No, your mission is to screen the regiment. Keep moving ahead as ordered."

"But the Japs'll probably go right back to their base. We can follow them back and find out where it is."

Major Cobb thought for a few moments. "Okay, you can follow them, provided you don't deviate too much from the general direction of the regimental advance. You're our eyes up there, understand?"

"Yes, sir. Has the regiment moved out yet?"

"We're moving out now. Anything else?"

"No, sir."

"Stay in touch. Over and out."

Bannon handed the radio back to DelFranco. "All right, everybody, assemble around me!"

The GIs got up from their resting spots and gathered around. Bannon told them they were going after the Jap patrol, with his old First Squad on the point and Longtree leading. The men adjusted their packs, and the squad moved out. The sun was a big red basketball on the horizon as the recon platoon set out through the jungle in a column of twos.

The sun rose in the sky and the day became hotter. The soldiers' uniforms were plastered to their bodies by perspiration, which also trickled into their eyes and burned. The jungle was thick, smelly, and dark. Longtree moved among the branches and leaves as if he'd lived there all his life, but the rest of the men were scratched and bruised. They sank to their knees in muck and were eaten alive by swarms of insects. Bannon kept checking his map and compass to make sure he was moving in the same general direction as the regimental advance.

It took two hours to get through the jungle, and then they came to a field of kunai grass. The grass was as tall as they were and so thick you couldn't see somebody hiding a few feet away. Longtree went in first, still following the trail left by the Japanese patrol, but soon encountered a number of other trails crisscrossing through the field; many patrols had come through there. He was able to discern the freshest and follow it, the rest of the platoon behind him.

Bannon also realized that many patrols had come through the field and figured a concentration of Japs must be someplace up ahead. It took an hour to get through the kunai grass. On the other side were palm trees and more jungle.

"Take a break!" Bannon said as soon as they were in the jungle. "DelFranco, gimme the radio!"

Bannon sat heavily on the ground and DelFranco handed him the walkie-talkie. Bannon called Major Cobb again and told him of the heavy patrol activity in the kunai grass.

"Where are you?" Major Cobb asked.

Bannon looked down at his map. "Grid Four Twenty-five."

"You're moving into the hills and mountains now. That's probably where the Japs are holed up. Watch your step and report immediately any contact with the enemy."

"Yes, sir."

"Over and out."

Bannon handed the radio back to DelFranco, then looked at his maps. The Japanese patrol was evidently heading toward the foothills to the southwest of Mount Austin, which also was the direction in which the regiment was going. Bannon took out a cigarette and lit it up, looking around at his men, feeling a sense of satisfaction because everything was going okay so far. Even old Butsko couldn't have done any better, he thought.

Butsko lay on the examining table as Nurse Betty Crawford removed the bandages from his chest and Dr. Henderson looked on.

"This might hurt a little," Betty said.

"Don't worry about it," Butsko replied.

Betty peeled the last layer of gauze away, revealing the ugly stitched-up red gash on Butsko's chest two inches above his nipple. It looked to Betty as if it were healing normally. She noticed all the other scars on his torso. The poor man looked as if he'd been through a meat grinder.

"I'll examine him now," said Dr. Henderson, wearing a tan uniform with the collar unbuttoned. He bent over Butsko, probing and searching around the wound, testing the stitches, looking for infections. Standing to the side, Betty Crawford looked down at Butsko's naked upper body and felt a weird tickle deep inside her.

"How does the wound look, Doctor?" she asked.

"He's healing nicely. You've got a healthy constitution, Sergeant."

Butsko grunted. The doctor turned to Betty. "The stitches can come out on Monday. Bandage him up again, will you?"

"Yes, sir."

Butsko looked up at the doctor. "When will I go back to my outfit?"

"Another three or four weeks or so, I'd say."

Dr. Henderson looked at his watch. "I have to be at a

meeting. Nurse Crawford, I'll be back on the ward this afternoon around one."

"Yes, sir."

Dr. Henderson left the tiny room.

"Just relax, Sergeant Butsko, and I'll have you bandaged up in a minute."

"Mind if I smoke?"

"Go ahead."

"They're in the pocket of my robe over there."

She plucked the pack of cigarettes out of his robe and handed it to him, watching him light up.

"Lie still, now."

He smoked his cigarette, holding it away from her as she cleaned the wound and taped on a new bandage, her fingers touching his hairy chest, while he appeared unconcerned, as if his mind were far off someplace. She glanced down at his flat stomach and then the white pajama bottoms. He flinched as she pressed down the tape.

"Sorry," she said.

"S'okay."

He was so bulky and muscular that he reminded her of a horse—not an elegant Arabian stallion or a racehorse, but one of those big incredibly powerful workhorses she used to see on the farms in California.

"Ouch!" he said.

"Sorry."

She pressed down another strip of tape.

"You can put your shirt on now."

Butsko got up from the table, the cigarette dangling from the corner of his mouth. "Is there any way I can get out of this hospital sooner than the doctor said?"

"I don't think so. Everybody has to go through the same procedures. What's your hurry."

"I'm getting bored around here."

"If you kept busy, you wouldn't be so bored."

"Busy doing what?"

"The other men play checkers, read books, go to the movies, play cards . . ."

"I hate all that crap."

"What do you like?" she asked.

"Nothing around here."

She could not conceal the hurt in her expression. "*Nothing* around here?"

Butsko shuffled his feet awkwardly. "I didn't mean you, Nurse Crawford. You're an awfully nice nurse and a real sweet kid too. I'm talking about this hospital here. I don't like hospitals."

"When you leave here, you'll only go back to the front. Are you in a hurry to get into the war again?"

"I don't know. I just want to get the hell out of here."

"I'll do whatever I can, Sergeant Butsko."

"I'd appreciate it, Nurse Crawford. And thanks for bandaging me up. You got the hands of an angel."

"Thank you, Sergeant Butsko."

"See you around." Butsko winked, opened the door, and left the room.

Nurse Crawford stood in the silence for a few moments, then stripped the sheet from the examining table, feeling the warmth of his body in her hands.

FIVE . . .

At noon the recon platoon was approaching the grassy open slopes of Hill Thirty-one. Longtree was still in the lead, following the trail of the Japanese patrol. The sun was straight overhead and the GIs gasped for breath. Their uniforms were soaked with sweat and their brains roasted inside their heads. Bannon wanted to get the men into the treeline ahead before breaking for chow.

The men climbed the lower slopes of the hill, bending forward under the weight of their packs, their knees aching, each one wishing he was someplace else.

They entered the treeline, and the shade made everything cooler. The forest was thick, with wide green leaves everywhere. Bannon decided to continue until 1300 hours and then break for lunch. The men were tired and hungry, but the more ground they covered now, the less they'd have to go in the latter part of the afternoon, when the temperature rose.

They continued up Hill Thirty-one with Longtree in the lead. Longtree peered ahead through the wall of leaves and branches, trying to see what was ahead, but he couldn't see more than ten or twenty feet. The Japanese patrol had gone straight up that way; it was easy to follow their trail. He stepped over a rotting fallen tree and was suddenly struck by the awareness that something was wrong. Pausing, he crouched and looked around. He couldn't see anything, but his old Apache sixth ense told him that danger was ahead. He could almost smell it in the air. He raised his hand, and the recon platoon stopped behind him.

Longtree dropped to one knee behind the log. Behind him, the men of the recon platoon dropped onto their stomachs. Bannon held his rifle in his right hand and ran crouched over toward Longtree.

"What's the problem?" Bannon asked, dropping down beside Longtree.

"Something's up there."

"Where?"

"I don't know exactly."

"Then what makes you think there's something there?"

"I smell Japs."

Bannon sniffed the air. "I don't smell nothing. Maybe you've been on point too long, Chief. I'll send Shaw up here."

"Naw, I'm okay," Longtree said. "I can keep going."

"I think you need a rest."

"I'm not tired. I'm just telling you there are Japs up there." Longtree pointed up the hill.

"How do you know?"

"I know."

Bannon spat at the floor of the jungle and tried to think of what to do. He couldn't tell Major Cobb that he was stopping because he thought there were Japs up ahead. He'd need proof. He looked at Longtree and wondered if he was imagining things or if Japs really were up there. Bannon recalled that Butsko had always trusted Longtree's judgment one hundred percent.

"If there are Japs up there," Bannon said, "we'll have to find out where they are and tell regiment."

He made a circular motion above his head with his hand, the signal for his men to gather around him. They slouched up the hill, keeping their heads low, and gathered around him.

"The Chief thinks there's Japs up ahead," Bannon said, "so form a skirmish line and let's go find them. I want the First and Second squads on my left and the Third and Fourth squads on my right. Let's go, move it out!"

The squads formed up to the left and right of him, a straight skirmish line with six feet between men. Longtree went back to the First Squad, which he normally led, and Bannon and

DelFranco positioned themselves behind the skirmish line so Bannon could see what everybody was doing.

Bannon waved his arm forward, and the skirmish line advanced up Hill Thirty-one. The men kept their heads low and moved slowly, being especially cautious, holding their rifles in both hands, ready to fire. It was like swimming through a sea of green leaves, and Bannon realized it would be an ideal area to set up a defensive position. Nutsy Gafooley from the Second Squad tripped over a rock and fell on his face. Billy Klump from the Fourth Squad found the going so tough he had to take out his machete and hack his way through the green tangle. The soldiers grunted and farted as they pushed their way up the hill, looking for Japs.

Suddenly a machine gun opened fire somewhere in front of them, and three men from the Second Squad were mowed down. The rest of the platoon hit the dirt as soon as the first bullets started to fly.

"Medic!" screamed Bannon.

"Yo!" replied Private Joel Blum.

"Get the fuck over there!"

"Yo!"

"Anybody see where that machine gun is?"

Nobody said anything.

"Longtree, take the First Squad and find out where that machine gun is!"

Longtree motioned with his hand and the members of the First Squad moved out on their bellies. Private Blum made his way toward the three men who'd been shot down. The first one had stopped a bullet with his face and was almost unrecognizable. The second had a bullet in his gut. The third had been hit in the leg. Blum went to work on the one who'd been shot in the stomach.

Meanwhile, Longtree and the First Squad crawled up the hill. They'd only gone fifteen yards when two machine guns opened fire on them, stopping them cold. The jungle was so thick that they couldn't see where the machine guns were; individual rifles were firing also.

"We can't move!" Longtree called back.

"Gimme the radio!" Bannon said.

DelFranco passed it to him and Bannon called Major Cobb.

"Sir," he said, "we've run into two Japanese machine guns on Hill Thirty-one but we can't see where they are."

"Have you sent somebody up to find out?"

"Yes, but they didn't get very far."

"Try to take it on the flank. We'll have to know if it's just an isolated nest or part of something bigger."

"Yes, sir."

"Over and out."

Bannon tried to work out a plan. He figured the machine-gun nest was probably straight ahead, so he'd send one squad way out to the left and another squad way out to the right. That ought to determine if the machine-gun nest was isolated or not.

"Everybody assemble around me!"

The men crawled back on their stomachs and crowded around him. Nearby, Blum worked frantically on the wounded man.

"Longtree, swing the First Squad about one hundred yards to the left and probe for that nest. Stravopoulis, take the Fourth Squad to the right about a hundred yards and do the same thing. Don't take any chances. Get going."

The two squads separated themselves from the platoon and swung out on the flanks to probe for the machine-gun nest. Bannon took out a cigarette and lit it up.

"How's those men?" Bannon asked Blum.

"One dead, one not too bad, and the other needs a doctor quick."

Bannon debated in his mind whether two men should be assigned to carry the wounded man back. He decided to do it. "Pinkston! Duffy! Carry that man back!"

Pinkston and Duffy tied their shirts together into a makeshift stretcher while Bannon looked ahead in the direction of the machine-gun nest. The First Squad and the Fourth Squad were already out of sight. There was nothing to do now except wait.

Sergeant Stravopoulis led the Fourth Squad to the right and then, after two hundred yards, turned them up the slope of Hill Thirty-one. They'd only gone another hundred yards before they came under intense machine-gun fire directly in front of them. They couldn't see exactly where it was coming from, but it was one gun supported by small-arms fire. Stravopoulis, black-haired with a thick growth of beard, called Bannon on the walkie-talkie.

"We just ran into another nest," Stravopoulis said. "We can't move forward."

"Can you see where it's coming from?"

"Nope, but it's someplace in front of us."

"Stay where you are. If things get hot, get back here on the double."

Longtree led the First Squad up the left side of the hill, and after a short distance machine guns and rifles stopped him cold. He called Bannon to report his situation, and Bannon gave him the same orders: Stay put unless there was trouble. Then Bannon radioed Major Cobb and told him what had happened.

Major Cobb was with the Regimental Headquarters Company in a grove of coconut trees about three miles away. Troops streamed past on their way forward, and a company of engineers nearby was clearing a road for jeeps and trucks. Major Cobb spread a map out on the ground and found Hill Thirty-one.

"Stay where you are," he told Bannon. "Don't take any chances. I'll send a couple of companies up there to wipe out those machine-gun nests and then you'll continue with your mission. Any questions?"

"When'll they get here?"

"A few hours."

"I hope that's before dark."

"It'll be before dark. Anything else?"

"No, sir."

"Over and out."

The jungle was a mass of GIs and equipment moving toward the parts of the island held by the Japanese. Major Cobb found Colonel Stockton sitting in his jeep, talking on the radio to one of his forward units. Colonel Stockton wore his steel pot, puffed his pipe, and wore strapped to his waist a samurai sword that Sergeant Butsko had given him. He looked every inch the frontline combat officer, eager for battle and smart as a fox. He finished his radio transmission, and Major Cobb told him about the machine-gun nests the recon platoon had found.

"I'm sending two companies to clear them out," Major Cobb said. "Which ones would you suggest, sir?"

Colonel Stockton looked at his map. Hill Thirty-one was in the sector in front of the Second Battalion, commanded by Lieutenant Colonel Joe Smith, a cigar-smoking pugnacious old combat veteran. "It's in Colonel Smith's sector," Colonel Stockton said. "Apprise him of the situation and let him handle it."

"Yes, sir."

Colonel Stockton turned to accept a message handed him by Lieutenant Harper, and Major Cobb returned to his operations section to call Colonel Smith and tell him to clear up the mess on Hill Thirty-one.

SIX . . .

Bannon didn't know it, but he'd stumbled on the strongest Japanese defensive position on Guadalcanal, the Gifu Line. Manned by five hundred fanatical soldiers from General Hyakutake's Seventeenth Army, it consisted of forty-five interconnected pillboxes deployed in a horseshoe-shaped line between hills Thirty-one and Twenty-seven. Most of the soldiers were from the Gifu Prefecture on the island of Honshu, hence the name they'd given to their fortifications.

The pillboxes were mutually supporting, dug deeply into the ground, built up with logs, and revetted inside and out with dirt. Each rose only three feet above ground level and was well camouflaged. The ceilings were three logs thick and covered with boulders and dirt, and the walls were two logs thick.

Each pillbox contained one or two machine guns and several riflemen. Every approach to the Gifu was covered by interlocking fields of fire, and the line was invisible from the air. Its only flaw was that it could not be reinforced or resupplied. Every Japanese soldier in the Gifu knew that he was in a suicidal situation, because any fortification, no matter how strong, could be overwhelmed if the enemy chose to devote sufficient men and material to the task. Another serious shortcoming was that the Gifu had no artillery.

The Gifu was commanded by Major Yoshinari Uchikoshi, who made his headquarters in one of the larger bunkers. He was a sinewy man with an abrupt military manner. He sported a Fu Manchu mustache and his head was shaved smooth. Like most of his men, he was a fanatic, willing and anxious to die for his Emperor.

It was sweltering hot inside his bunker on that afternoon in December, and he fanned himself with an old communiqué while reading a new one that had just arrived from General Hyakutake. It was an "Address of Instruction" to be read to all commands on Guadalcanal. It said:

The Americans have thrown all their vaunted skill and equipment against the Seventeenth Army, and yet we are still here, full of courage, full of love for our Emperor, and determined to carry on until we win a great victory. I am aware of the suffering and deprivations of all of you, but I want you to know that we, your commanders, share the same suffering and deprivations and that we stand shoulder to shoulder with you in the fighting that lies before us. But the picture is not all grim. The Americans are a weak, cowardly people, and they are rapidly losing their fighting spirit. Your courage and determination has been too much for them. I urge you to be patient, to fight like demons, and to remember the great rewards for brave soldiers in the world to come. The Americans have only their firepower and material substance to sustain them in this fight, whereas we have our Emperor, our ancestors, and our fine Japanese spirit. In addition to that, we have air, ground, and naval reinforcements coming soon. So hold on. Have faith. Obey your officers and remember your training. A great victory will be ours if we just hold on a little while longer. Hail to the Emperor!

The communiqué was signed by General Hyakutake, and Major Uchikoshi wondered how he was going to read it to all his troops. He was a conscientious officer and decided the only proper thing to do would be to go from pillbox to pillbox and read it personally to each group of men. He glanced at his watch to see what time it was, when he heard a burst of machine-gun fire in the distance.

He jumped nearly two feet off his chair, because the machine guns in the Gifu Line had never fired before.

"Sir!" said his radio operator, Private Takemoto. "Bunker Twenty-five has spotted an American patrol!"

Major Uchikoshi snatched the earphones and microphone off Private Takemoto's head. "Who's speaking?" he commanded.

"Sergeant Watanabe, sir!"

"How many Americans?"

"From twenty to thirty, sir! They're retreating now!"

"They'll be back. Keep your eyes open!"

"Yes, sir!"

Major Uchikoshi lit a cigarette and paced the floor. The inevitable had finally happened: The Americans had stumbled upon the Gifu Line. But they didn't know what they were up against, and a lot of them would die before they did. Perhaps by then the reinforcements General Hyakutake had promised would arrive.

During the next half hour there were two more contacts with American patrols. Then everything became quiet again on the Gifu Line, as the patrols withdrew. Major Uchikoshi paced back and forth and deduced that the American patrols hadn't left the area but were still out there, waiting for reinforcements to arrive.

Maybe it would be a good idea to send some of his own men out to wipe out the American patrols before the reinforcements arrived. Then the Americans would have to probe for the Gifu Line from scratch again.

"Lieutenant Hatakeyma!"

"Yes, sir!"

"Come here!"

"Yes, sir!"

Lieutenant Hatakeyma, only twenty years old, the son of a judge in Tokyo, sprang up from his mat of interwoven palm leaves and marched toward Major Uchikoshi.

"Lieutenant Hatakeyma, take a company of men, locate that American patrol out there, and wipe them out!"

"Yes, sir!"

Lieutenant Hatakeyma spun around and ran from the command bunker into the deep concealed trench leading to the next bunker to gather the men together. Major Uchikoshi continued pacing the floor and wondered how long the Gifu Line could hold out once the Americans arrived in force.

It was late in the afternoon and the shadows were growing long. Bannon had learned from Butsko that whenever you stopped you dug in, and now the men in his platoon were hacking the ground with their entrenching tools, having a difficult time because of the thick network of roots beneath the surface.

On his flanks the First and Fourth squads were also digging in. Listening posts had been set up in advance of the positions, in case the Japs tried something cute.

In the Fourth Squad, the listening post was manned by Private Marion Gafooley, better known as Nutsy Gafooley, who had been a hobo before being drafted, and now sat alone in the middle of dense underbrush, his rifle lying on his lap, remembering those big freight trains roaring through the night from one hobo jungle to another, going *clackety-clackety-clackety* as he rode the rails in his mind. What a wonderful life of freedom it had been. He remembered the mulligan stew beside the railroad tracks. The Depression had caused a lot of young women to take up the hobo life, too, so a hobo could even get laid once in a while, but now all that was over for him, and he thought sadly of how low he'd fallen in the world.

He heard the snap of a twig breaking in front of him, and it sounded as if a man's foot had come down on the twig. Peering through the bush in the direction of the sound, he saw nothing at first, but then the foliage moved and he watched a Japanese soldier emerge, carrying a long Arisaka rifle with bayonet affixed to the end. Nutsy Gafooley raised his M 1 to his shoulder, aimed at the soldier, and squeezed his trigger. *Blam*—the M 1 fired, the sound echoing across the woods. The soldier fell back behind a wall of gunsmoke, and Nutsy Gafooley was on his feet, running wildly toward the Fourth Squad.

"Japs!" he screamed as he charged into the area where the GIs were digging.

Everybody dived into their half-dug holes.

Sergeant Stravopoulis grabbed his walkie-talkie and called Bannon.

"Japs are coming!" he said excitedly.

"How many?"

"Don't know."

"We'll be right there!" Bannon looked around at the men of the Second and Third squads. "Stravopoulis is being attacked! Everybody over there on the double!"

The men dropped their entrenching tools and grabbed their rifles, running through the jungle toward the Fourth Squad. Bannon called Longtree.

"The Fourth Squad is being attacked. We're going to help out. You'd better come, too, because we don't know how many they are."

"We'll be right there."

Bannon grabbed his rifle and jumped up, following the Third and Second squads with DelFranco close behind him. A volley of shots erupted from the vicinity of the Fourth Squad.

Lieutenant Hatakeyma swung his samurai sword through the air. *"Banzai!"* he hollered. *"Attack!"*

The Japanese soldiers swarmed through the jungle, heading for the Fourth Squad, who lay in their shallow holes, firing at the indistinct forms hidden by foliage. Their fusillades cut down several of the Japs, but the rest kept coming and erupted out of the jungle, holding their bayonets low, intending to stab the GIs lying on their bellies. The GIs sprang up and got ready as the Japs tore into them. Bayonets clashed against rifle stocks as the Japs overran the Fourth Squad. Private Clemow was felled by one mighty blow from Lieutenant Hatakeyma's samurai sword, and Lieutenant Hatakeyma then hacked off the arm of Pfc. Gary Petty. He turned again and found himself in front of Nutsy Gafooley, tall and skinny, who'd been in countless rough-and-tumble fights in his life.

Lieutenant Hatakeyma swung downward, and Nutsy Gafooley raised his rifle, catching the blow on the stock of his rifle, but Lieutenant Hatakeyma's sword was made of the finest steel, and it rang like a bell in a Buddhist temple. Nutsy Gafooley stepped back and danced from side to side, making himself a difficult target while Lieutenant Hatakeyma raised his sword for another blow. Nutsy lunged forward, pushing his rifle and bayonet toward Lieutenant Hatakeyma's heart, and Lieutenant Hatakeyma swung his sword to the side, blocking the thrust.

Nutsy Gafooley's forward motion brought him to within inches of Lieutenant Hatakeyma, and the aristocratic young officer gazed into the bloodshot eyes of the former hobo, who knew every dirty trick in the book. Nutsy Gafooley raised his knee and hit Lieutenant Hatakeyma in the balls. Lieutenant Hatakeyma's eyes bulged out and he fought the temptation to fall down and give up. He stepped back to get some sword-swinging room, his groin hurting so much that he was half paralyzed, and Nutsy Gafooley lunged with his rifle and bayonet again. This time Lieutenant Hatakeyma could not block the rifle and bayonet streaking toward him, and the bayonet sliced into his stomach to the hilt. Lieutenant Hatakeyma sank to the ground and Nutsy Gafooley pulled out his bayonet.

A rifle butt hit Nutsy Gafooley on the helmet, and he fell down in a daze. He saw a bayonet rocketing toward him and rolled to the side, but he was stopped by the dead body of Corporal Roger Gorham. The bayonet came toward him again and Nutsy thought, *It's all over,* but then a shot rang out and the Japanese soldier above him collapsed beside Corporal Gorham.

The shot had been a wild one fired from the hip by Pfc. Danny Sheehan as the Second and Third squads hit the Japs from the side. The Japs had outnumbered the Fourth Squad, but now everything was even, and the Second and Third squads tore into the Japs.

Sergeant Mitsui saw Lieutenant Hatakeyma fall and realized the raiding party was in danger. "Retreat!" he yelled. "Retreat!"

Corporal Gomez hit Sergeant Mitsui over the head with his rifle butt, and Sergeant Mitsui's skull cracked apart. Blood poured from his ears, nose, and mouth as he dropped to the ground.

The other Japs also had difficulty getting away, because the Second and Third squads had attacked in a line that would cut them off. The Japs fought valiantly for their lives, but they'd bit off more than they could chew. Then Longtree and the First

Squad arrived, and it was all over in a matter of minutes. The ground was strewn with the bodies of the Jap raiding party and Bannon's Fourth Squad, which had nearly been wiped out in the initial stage of the battle.

Bannon's bayonet was covered with blood, but he didn't have a scratch on him. He wasn't even breathing hard and had only been able to kill one Jap. But he didn't have time to gloat over the victory. He had to figure out what to do next, because more Japs might arrive at any moment. He decided to retreat down the hill and dig in.

"Let's go!" he said. "We'll pull back and set up a defensive perimeter. Take the wounded but leave the dead. We don't have much time."

The wounded were hoisted onto the shoulders of the GIs nearest them. The recon platoon retreated down the hill, leaving behind a scene of horrible carnage.

The GIs disappeared into the jungle, and one of the Japanese soldiers stirred. He was Private Yuto Kobayashi, bleeding from a slash on the left side of his face. His left eye had been cut open like a seedless grape, and he had a fractured skull, but he was alive. His first thought was that he must commit hara-kiri, because the raid had failed, but then he told himself he must return to Major Uchikoshi and report what had happened. He pulled himself to his feet, but his legs gave out and he fell to the ground, so he gritted his teeth and crawled toward the Gifu Line, looking ahead through his one good eye at the strange new perspective of the jungle.

It took him a half hour before he drew close to the nearest bunker, and the Japanese soldiers inside, not recognizing him, opened fire with their two machine guns and five rifles.

"It's me—Private Kobayashi!" he wailed. "Don't shoot!"

The soldiers came out to get him, dragging him back to the bunker.

"What happened?" one of them asked.

"It was terrible. Take me to Major Uchikoshi."

"You need a doctor."

"After I see Major Uchikoshi."

They carried him across the network of bunkers and trenches to the command bunker occupied by Major Uchikoshi, who was conferring with his staff officers about the intrusion of American patrols into the area. Major Uchikoshi looked up as Private Kobayashi was carried in.

"What happened?" Major Uchikoshi asked.

"We were wiped out," Private Kobayashi replied.

"What!"

"We were wiped out. At first everything went well, and we were destroying the American patrol, but then many more Americans arrived."

"It was a trap!" Major Uchikoshi said, gnashing his teeth. He cursed himself for letting his men walk into a trap.

"I request permission to commit hara-kiri sir," Private Kobayashi said weakly.

"You will do no such thing! You will report to the medical sergeant for treatment and then you will return to your post!"

"Yes, sir!"

Private Kobayashi tried to salute but fainted from loss of blood. The soldiers carried him away. Major Uchikoshi looked at his staff officers.

"Our vacation is over," he said. "The Americans are here."

SEVEN . . .

The sun sank toward the horizon as the recon platoon was digging in. It was Christmas Eve, and they all thought about how strange it was to be on a far-off tropical island, fighting a war, far from their families.

"Just don't seem like Christmas," Homer Gladley said, shaking his head. "Last year at this time I was home, eating chicken. All the presents were under the tree and we was waiting for Santa Claus to fill up the stockings on the fireplace. My girl friend was there; everybody was there. I wonder if I'll ever see them again."

Nearby, the Reverend Billie Jones was resting, for they were taking turns digging the hole. "The Lord will provide," he said.

"I think he's forgot about us, Billie."

"He never forgets us. We forget Him but he don't forget us."

"Yeah, well he ain't done much for us lately."

Twenty yards away, DelFranco was digging a hole for him and Bannon, who was looking at his maps, marking the spots where he thought Japanese machine-gun nests were situated. He knew of three nests and wondered how many more there might be. It was going to be hell getting those Japs out of there.

DelFranco was listening to the conversation between Homer Gladley and Billie Jones, because religion fascinated him. He also thought that Billie Jones was an idiot, with no realistic perception of God. Jones talked as though God was a benevolent old man with a white beard who lived on a cloud and did favors for people whenever he felt like it. Jones didn't understand that God was more powerful and subtle than that. Jones was too simpleminded. He had a fairy-tale view of God.

Bannon heard sounds in the jungle behind him, and his first reaction was that Japs were sneaking up on the recon platoon from the rear.

"Hit it!"

Everybody grabbed their rifles and dived into their shallow holes. The jungle became silent.

"What's going on?" Shaw asked.

"I heard something," Bannon said.

"Me too," said Longtree.

A voice came out of the jungle. *"Who's there?"*

"The recon platoon!" Bannon replied.

"Christmas!" shouted the voice in the jungle.

"Tree!" replied Bannon.

That was the challenge and countersign for the day, and a squad of American soldiers came out of the jungle, a sergeant leading them.

"Which one's Bannon?" asked the sergeant.

"I am."

"Colonel Smith wants to talk to you."

"Okay." Bannon stood and slung his rifle. "Where's the rest of the battalion?"

"A few hundred yards behind us."

"Saddle up, everybody!" Bannon told the recon platoon. "We're moving out!"

"Hey," said the sergeant, "the colonel wants to talk to you, not your whole platoon."

"Well, I'm not leaving them here. There's a lot of Japs in the vicinity."

The sergeant shrugged. The men from the recon platoon attached their entrenching tools to their packs and hoisted their packs onto their backs. Then they followed the squad from the Second Platoon back down the slope of Hill Thirty-one.

Lieutenant Colonel Smith sat in a pine grove, looking at his map and trying to keep track of his companies as new positions were radioed in. *A battalion commander is nothing more than a coordinator of warm bodies,* he thought as he made marks on his map. The unlit butt of a cigar stuck out the corner of his mouth, and his lips were stained with brown tobacco juice. The faint odor of a saloon clung to him, because he never went anywhere without a flask full of the jungle juice brewed for him by his mess sergeant.

"Here comes Sergeant Shirley," said one of his aides.

Colonel Smith looked up and saw Sergeant Shirley and the recon platoon coming toward him. Colonel Smith stood, hiked up his cartridge belt, and waited for them to approach. Colonel Smith had dealt with the recon platoon before and thought they were a reliable bunch. If they were good enough for Colonel Stockton, they were good enough for him.

Sergeant Shirley saluted. "Here's the recon platoon, sir."

Colonel Smith's eyes narrowed and Bannon stepped forward and saluted. "Sergeant Bannon reporting, sir."

"What the hell's going on up here, Bannon?"

"Japs in machine-gun nests, sir."

"Where are they?"

Bannon took out his map and showed him the marks he'd made. "Here, here, and here."

"Hmmm." Colonel Smith looked up at the sky and saw the sun setting on the horizon. "Well, it's too late to see what's going on up there today. We'll hit them first thing in the morning. Bannon, have your men bivouac somewhere close to my headquarters here. You'll be attached to my battalion until we get through that mess up there."

"Yes, sir."

"That's all."

"Yes, sir."

Bannon led his men away, and Colonel Smith looked at his map. "Major Curry," he said to his operations officer, "have the battalion move up to the base of Hill Thirty-one and dig in for the night."

"Yes, sir."

"Captain Watford?"

"Yes, sir."

"I want my headquarters tent set up right here."

"Yes, sir."

"Everybody else dig in for the night. There'll be a meeting in my tent at two thousand hours. Any questions?"

Nobody said anything.

"You're all dismissed."

Everybody walked away. Colonel Smith sat on the ground again and took out his Zippo, lighting the cigar stub in his mouth. He hoped his tent would be set up quickly so he could go inside and have a swallow of jungle juice where nobody could see him.

It was evening on New Caledonia, and Christmas Eve parties were being held in all the wards. Christmas trees made of local shrubbery were erected, and red and green bunting were draped along the walls.

In Betty Crawford's ward, a Victrola was blaring the Andrews Sisters' recording of "Boogie Woogie Bugle Boy." A few of the men danced and the others watched and clapped their hands in time to the music. The men were given peppermint sticks, candy, and cigarettes by Red Cross workers, some of them reasonably attractive women whom soldiers were trying to lure outside where they could steal kisses and cheap feels.

Betty Crawford tried to smile and appear festive, but inside she was annoyed because Butsko wasn't there. *Where the hell is he?* she wondered. She thought he might be out with some other nurse and realized she was feeling jealous.

She remembered him lying bare-chested on the examining table that afternoon and how strange he'd made her feel. *What's the matter with me? Am I going nuts?* She tried to think of the man she was engaged to marry, but he was in North Africa and it was difficult to conjure him up.

She was afraid Butsko knew how she felt, but if he did, he didn't show it. He treated her just like any other nurse who jabbed needles into his arm. He was cool and respectful toward her, and somehow that was irritating. *I think I've been on this island too long,* she thought. *I'd better pull myself together.*

Butsko walked to the docks of the port of Nouméa and sat on a wharf, smoking a cigarette. He didn't like the Christmas party with all the phony Red Cross women talking their bullshit and the guys acting like idiots. He looked across the bay, which was pitch dark at night so Japanese planes couldn't spot it, and thought of his men back on Guadalcanal. He wondered how they were doing and if any had been killed since he'd been gone. None had been shipped to New Caledonia since he'd been there. As far as he knew, it was just him, Frankie La Barbara, and Craig Delane, the rich guy from New York. Frankie would be sent back to the front any day now, but Delane had been hurt very badly. They might even ship him back to the States.

Butsko wanted to get back to Guadalcanal. He hated the war, the constant anxiety and fatigue, but he felt it was where he belonged. He didn't seem to fit into the world without a gun in his hand and a bandolier hanging from his neck. *Just a few more weeks,* he thought. *That's not so long.*

On Christmas morning three rifle companies from the Second Battalion advanced up Hill Thirty-one with the recon platoon leading the way. The recon platoon was supposed to show the others the spots where they'd come under machine-gun fire, and as soon as they reached those spots, they came under heavy machine-gun fire again. Mortar support was requested, and soon mortar rounds were flying through the air, blowing up the jungle but doing no damage to the heavily fortified bunkers.

The mortar barrage went on for an hour, while the rifle companies lay in the jungle, waiting for the order to charge. Bannon smoked a cigarette and peered through the leaves at the smoke and flames as trees crashed to the ground and huge quantities of real estate were blown into the air.

Finally it was decided that the target area was demolished and any Japs who'd been there had either retreated or were dead. Colonel Smith transmitted the order that all three companies should attack as soon as the mortar barrage stopped. The order was relayed to every platoon and squad, and the men waited tensely for the mortar barrage to end. Finally the last volley was fired. The jungle was still for a few moments and then resounded with the shouts of officers and sergeants.

"Charge!"

The men jumped to their feet and ran up the hill. Bannon pumped his legs and shouted an old Texas cattle call. Longtree let out an Apache was whoop and Shaw screamed bloody blue murder. The three rifle companies surged up the hill in a mighty green wave, and the Japanese machine guns opened fire again with vicious intensity. The jungle became filled with zinging hot lead, and in the first minute innumerable GIs were cut down. The rest hit the dirt, because any farther advance was clearly impossible. The company commanders sized up the situation, or at least they thought they did, and ordered their men to continue the attack on their bellies. The men inched up the hill into the hail of lead, taking more casualties. Medics moved about from man to man, and the Japanese sharpshooters fired at their Red Cross armbands.

Colonel Smith was a hundred yards behind the front line and could see what had happened. Moreover, all the companies were reporting that they couldn't move any farther. Colonel Smith told them to stay put and then ordered another mortar barrage. It lasted a half hour and then the troops were ordered to attack again. Once more they rose to their feet and charged, and once more they were ripped apart by machine-gun fire. Now Colonel Smith realized for the first time that he was up against something serious, but before he relayed any quick evaluations to Colonel Stockton, he wanted to make sure. He ordered all companies to stay where they were and requested that the recon platoon be sent back to him.

The recon platoon disengaged and crawled back down the hill on their stomachs until they were a healthy distance from the machine-gun nests, then stood and double-timed back to Colonel Smith. The morning wasn't even over yet and Bannon already had two dead and three wounded.

Colonel Smith sat amid thick foliage, surrounded by his staff, as Bannon and the recon platoon approached.

"I want you men to go out on a patrol for me," Colonel Smith said. "We need a clearer picture of what's up there, and the only way to do that is to probe for their flanks. Bannon, you take the recon platoon and try to find their left flank. I'll have a platoon from Headquarters Company look for their right flank. Any questions?"

"No, sir."

Colonel Smith drew a line with his finger on the map, and Bannon caught a whiff of alcohol fumes. *Is he drunk?* Bannon wondered.

"Go this way," Colonel Smith said. "If you encounter more fire, keep moving to your left until you find where their shoulder is. Any questions now?"

"No, sir."

"Get going, and good luck."

Colonel Smith ordered the mortar barrage to cease, so that the recon platoon wouldn't get shelled by mistake. Then his own Headquarters Company recon unit showed up and he told them their mission. Up the hill, the machine guns continued firing at the companies that were pinned down.

"The Japs are having their fun now," Colonel Smith told Major Curry, "but their hours are numbered up there."

The recon platoon made its way south through the jungle on a line parallel to the skirmish line of Second Battalion soldiers farther up the hill. They were in a column of twos with Longtree on the point, Shilansky ten yards out on the left flank, and Shaw ten yards out on the right flank. The jungle was thick, but drier than in the valley. In the distance the relentless tattoo of Japanese machine-gun fire could be heard.

The men in the recon platoon said nothing; they'd been on many crummy patrols before, so this was nothing new. They plodded through the jungle until Bannon thought they'd gone far enough out on the left flank and then he moved them up the hill again.

None of them knew what to expect. They could run into more machine-gun fire or they could circle around the Japanese position. Bannon had to make sure they didn't circle around too far and get cut off.

They advanced up the hill in a skirmish line, with Bannon in the middle a few yards behind the others. The tension built as they rose higher and higher up the hill. After twenty minutes Bannon figured he was almost level with the battalion skirmish line, and he expected Japanese machine guns to open up on him at any moment.

He wasn't disappointed. The jungle exploded in front of him and a Japanese machine-gun bullet put a hole in a leaf two inches from his right shoulder. The men of the recon platoon dropped down as bullets whizzed over their heads.

"Pull back!"

They crawled back down the hill as bullets slammed into trees and kicked up dirt all around them. Private O'Conner was hit in the leg and Pfc. Baum dragged him along with the help of Gomez. They continued crawling until they had fifty yards of jungle between them and where they were before, and then Bannon told them to stop.

Blum went to work on O'Conner's leg, while O'Conner writhed in pain, clenching his teeth together in an effort to keep from screaming. Blum gave him a shot of morphine to calm him down and then sprinkled sulfa powder on the wound to disinfect it and start the clotting. The bullet had hit an artery, and blood pumped into the air like a geyser. Blum tied on a tourniquet to cut off the flow of blood.

Bannon would have to send two men to help O'Conner back to the battalion aid station, which would reduce his strength even more. He knew now that he shouldn't have sent the entire platoon up the hill together, because that presented too many targets. He'd send just a few the next time, and the rest of the platoon could stay in support a short distance back. He tried to figure who to send back with O'Conner; it would have to be the two most useless men, but he had no useless men in the platoon.

"DelFranco, Miller, take O'Conner back down the hill!"

DelFranco spun around. "But I'm your runner!"

Bannon could see the look of hurt on DelFranco's face. DelFranco knew Bannon picked him because DelFranco was not as good a soldier as the other men in the platoon. What would Butsko do? Butsko would stick with his decision and get tough.

"I told you what you're gonna do—now do it!"

"But, Sarge . . ."

"Do it!"

DelFranco buckled under. He looked at Miller, who also was on the puny side. *I'm not a priest and Bannon doesn't believe I'm much of a soldier,* DelFranco thought. *What the hell am I?* He laid his walkie-talkie, bazooka, and bazooka ammunition on the ground, then he and Miller got under O'Conner's shoulders and lifted him up.

"We won't be here long," Bannon told DelFranco and Miller, "so stay down at the battalion aid station until we get back."

DelFranco and Miller carried O'Conner down the hill, and O'Conner was humming a crazy tune, because the morphine had finally gotten to his head.

"Gafooley, you're my new runner. Pick up this equipment."

"Hup, Sarge."

Bannon told the rest of them that thereafter Shaw, Shilansky, and Longtree would probe for the Japanese machine-gun nests, with the rest of the platoon hanging back.

"You three watch your step," Bannon told them. "I don't want any more fucking casualties today. Now let's move out, and everybody stay awake."

The platoon headed south again for a few hundred yards, then turned west. They had gone completely around Hill Thirty-one this time and were in a wooded valley, heading for another hill that was designated Hill Thirty on Bannon's map. At the base of the hill he sent Longtree, Shaw, and Shilansky forward.

After a half hour of rough going uphill through the jungle, Longtree, Shaw, and Shilansky came under machine-gun fire. They crawled back to where Bannon and the rest of the recon platoon were.

"There's another one," Longtree said wearily.

"We'll swing out a little farther this time," Bannon replied.

They turned south again and after five hundred yards a new set of machine guns opened up, stopping them cold. They crawled away beneath the hail of sizzling bullets and then scouted the far side of the hill. It wasn't long before more machine guns started firing at them.

By noon Colonel Smith realized that ahead of him was a vast Japanese defensive position. He couldn't figure out its complete configuration, but he knew the approximate location of some of the machine-gun nests and decided to knock out at least a couple of them. He withdrew all his units and requested an artillery strike on two of the machine-gun nests on Hill Thirty-one.

A dozen of the regiment's seventy-five-millimeter pack howitzers were towed to the front, and shortly before 1500 hours began their barrage. The big, powerful shells blew apart the top of the hill, cracking trees and loosening boulders, causing minor landslides. Although the jungle suffered considerable damage, the Japanese pillboxes weren't harmed at all. The Japanese soldiers crouched low to the ground, jammed their fingers in their ears, and waited for the barrage to stop.

In the headquarters bunker Major Uchikoshi had followed the day's events closely, aware that the Americans were trying to determine what was in front of them by patrolling. Now that Hill Thirty-one was under bombardment, Major Uchikoshi knew that the Americans were going to assault the fortifications there. It was like a chess game, and Major Uchikoshi decided that he must check the American assault.

He ordered that the bunkers on Hill Thirty-one be fortified with machine guns and rifles from bunkers not under shelling and that other Japanese troops set up a defense in front of those bunkers as soon as the shelling stopped, to impede the American advance.

Major Uchikoshi believed the communiqué from General Hyakutake, stating that the Americans were cowardly and were losing their taste for fighting. He thought that if he could stop this first American attack on the Gifu Line, they wouldn't have the determination to make a second all-out effort.

He ordered his men on Hill Thirty-one to stand fast and defend their positions to the last man. Then he look at his watch and waited for the barrage to begin.

The recon platoon would participate in the attack on Hill Thirty-one with George Company, commanded by Captain Dennis Orr from Lubbock, Texas. Captain Orr had closely clipped salt-and-pepper hair and was old for an officer of his rank. He had been an enlisted man before the war, receiving a commission in 1940 when the Army began its buildup.

Lubbock was a long way from Pecos, the area where Bannon was from, but they were both Texans and heard the wide open spaces in each other's speech the first time they talked. Orr's family were ranchers and Bannon had worked on a ranch, so there was an affinity between them right off the bat. While the artillery barrage went on, they sat together at the bottom of the hill, talking about horses and cows, trying to figure out if they knew anybody in common, but they didn't. Captain Orr had a slow, easy manner, as if he were going to set out on a hike instead of trying assault one of the machine-gun nests on Hill Thirty-one.

"You a married man?" he asked Bannon.

"No, sir." He noticed the gold band on Captain Orr's finger. "You are though, huh?"

"Yup. Got me a good little gal. She's back in Hawaii, looking after my youngsters. Got a boy fourteen and a girl twelve. The boy's tried to enlist already, but he wasn't able to fool anybody. He's afraid the war'll be over before he gets a chance to fight."

"He doesn't know when he's well off."

"No, he doesn't. I guess he's seen too many of them war movies, and of course he's been on Army posts all his life. Boys that age love war. They think a chestful of medals will make the girls love them more, but they don't realize they'll more likely get a chestful of bullets. Course, you can't tell them that. You can't tell a boy that age nothing." Captain Orr looked at his watch. "The barrage is gonna stop in about ten minutes. I think maybe you'd better get back to your men."

"Yes, sir."

In a crouch Bannon moved through the jungle to the recon platoon. He found them sitting in squad groups, smoking cigarettes and looking exhausted from the morning's patrols.

"We're moving out soon," Bannon told them. "Let's get ready."

The men checked their rifles and bandoliers of ammunition. They put on their packs and made sure nothing was dangling loose. It was another hot sunny day on Guadalcanal, and the top of the hill was covered by smoke from the howitzer shells. The top of the hill was gradually being pulverized, which would make for tough going, because there'd be fallen trees everywhere.

Bannon sat on the ground and took out a cigarette. His right side hurt him where he'd been cut by that Japanese bayonet. The stitches had been removed nearly two weeks before, but the wound bothered him if he did too much physical exercise, as he had that morning. The barrage on top of the hill sounded like rolling peals of thunder. Bannon figured it would soften up those machine-gun nests pretty well and might even put them out of action for good. He had no idea that the machine-gun nests were well protected by bunkers with thick walls and thicker roofs.

Nutsy Gafooley was listening to a message on the walkie-talkie. "Sarge," he said, "Captain Orr says the artillery barrage is gonna stop any minute now, so get ready."

The men groaned and grumbled as they got to their feet. They didn't know what was waiting for them at the top of the hill and wondered if they'd get through the day alive. DelFranco had returned and Bannon assigned him to the First Squad, retaining Nutsy Gafooley as his runner. DelFranco was in a foul mood and determined to show everyone he could soldier as well as any of them.

They all formed their skirmish line, linking up with George Company's First Platoon on their left and Second Platoon on their right. Company G would assault one of the pillboxes, and Company F the other. E Company would be in reserve, and H Company, the heavy-weapons company, would provide fire support.

The Second Battalion was ready to move out. Colonel Smith was behind them with his staff, close to the radio, looking through his binoculars at the wreath of smoke on Hill Thirty-one.

The barrage ended and an unearthly silence filled the jungle.

"Move it out!" shouted Captain Orr.

The recon platoon and George Company advanced through the jungle in a solid wave, the men holding their rifles at port arms, their helmets low over their eyes. Some wore raggedy shirts; others wore no shirts at all. They were filthy, smelled bad, and their mouths tasted like shit. But up they went, mechanically putting one foot in front of the other, knowing they'd come under fire at any minute, each hoping the first machine-gun burst wouldn't contain the bullet with his name on it.

There was no breeze, and all the birds and monkeys had fled the jungle. Only the insects remained, dive-bombing the GIs and sucking their blood. The GIs slapped the bugs, leaving red smears on their skin. The suspense was terrible. Every step brought them closer to the Japanese machine guns, and they knew the slant-eyed bastards were waiting for them. The bombardment couldn't have killed them all. They didn't know that the bombardment hadn't killed even one Jap.

Two-thirds of the way up the hill they heard *rat-tat-tat-tat* as the machine guns opened fire. The advance was stopped cold. Men dived to the ground and tried to burrow into it. Hot lead whizzed over their heads and Bannon thought, *Here we go again.*

"Fire your weapons!" yelled Captain Orr. *"Let's go!"*

The GIs fired up the hill but couldn't see a damn thing through the tangled jungle and lingering smoke from the artillery bombardment. However, the Japs could see them, because the GIs weren't dug in. The GIs' fire did no good whatever, and the GIs knew it.

"Keep Moving!" Captain Orr yelled. *"Get your fucking asses in gear!"*

The GIs gritted their teeth and crawled into the hornet's nest of bullets. They still were nearly four hundred yards from the machine guns, so they were able to make only slow, excruciating progress. It took an hour to crawl a hundred yards, and George Company suffered ten casualties. Finally they could advance no more. The Japanese machine guns were too much for them. You can't fight what you can't see. Captain Orr got on the radio to Colonel Smith.

"We're pinned down," he said, discouragement in his voice. "We can't move."

"Get your mortars set up and advance behind them!" Colonel Smith replied.

"Yes, sir."

Captain Orr called for his heavy-weapons platoon, and the mortars were set up behind the main line. Captain Orr's machine-gun squads established positions on the company's flanks and raked the jungle ahead with bullets. The mortars fired, blasting holes in the ground and wreaking havoc among the trees. They were firing blindly, but their purpose was to obscure the vision of the Japanese machine gunners.

"Let's go!" Captain Orr screamed. *"Move it out!"*

The GIs crawled up the hill behind the supporting fire. The Japanese machine guns continued shooting, but with less intensity and accuracy. The GIs felt that they finally were getting somewhere, but after fifty yards Captain Orr ordered a halt to let his machine-gun crews catch up.

Bannon took the opportunity to light a cigarette. He smoked it with his cheek lying on the moist earth, the scar on his side bothering him. He was getting a headache. *This fucking war,* he thought, getting mad. *I hate this fucking war. I hate those fucking Japs. I hate everybody.*

The new machine-gun positions were set up and they commenced firing. The mortars resumed their walking barrage.

"Forward!" shouted Captain Orr.

Company G resumed their slow crawl up the hill. The sounds of battle were deafening, and Japanese bullets whistled over their heads. Somebody down the line screamed as a bullet bore through his shoulder. Another man went slack as a bullet smashed through his helmet and entered his brain.

"Medic!" somebody yelled.

"Keep moving!" called Captain Orr.

Company G and the rest of the Second Battalion slithered up the hill. They were within three hundred yards of the Japanese machine guns now, but they still couldn't see anything. The GIs continued their crawl, taking an occasional casualty, and then, when they were about 250 yards from the Japanese machine-gun bunkers, they suddenly came under fire from other bunkers that they hadn't even known about.

All the Japanese bunkers were mutually supporting, and the bunkers now opening fire were able to rake the Second Battalion from the sides. The GIs were caught in a murderous crossfire, in addition to the fire from ahead, and twenty men were hit in the first few seconds.

All hell broke loose, and the GIs didn't have to wait for an order; they turned tail and crawled down the hill as fast as they could.

"Pull back!" Captain Orr ordered. *"Keep your heads down!"*

Some of the GIs panicked and jumped to their feet, trying to run away. They were cut down before they could cover five yards, and they went spinning to the ground, blood spurting from holes in their bodies.

"Stay the fuck down!"

The mortars and machine-gun squads were pulling back, too, so the company didn't even have fire support anymore. The retreat was turning into a rout as Japanese machine gun bullets buzzed in all directions. Private Citrino in Bannon's Third

Squad was shot clear through the pelvis and fell to the ground, screaming, but nobody stopped to pick him up; there was no time for that.

Captain Orr lay close to the ground and called Colonel Smith. "The shit has hit the fan up here! Put some artillery up on that goddamn hill!"

"Will do."

Colonel Smith called artillery and in seconds the howitzers were firing. The big guns were still zeroed in on the top of the hill, and once again it was smashed by artillery shells. The Japanese machine gunners couldn't see, and the resounding explosions all around them made it hard for them to think, but they kept firing anyway. Their shots went wild and the GIs jumped up, running down the hill to safety. Their packs bounced up and down on their backs as they sucked wind and ran as fast as they could. Soon they had enough jungle behind them to feel secure and slowed down.

Captain Orr was the last one to pull back, and he hadn't taken more than ten steps when a big Japanese machine-gun bullet hit him in the leg and sent him flying to the ground. He writhed and squirmed, trying to stanch the flow of blood with the palm of his hand, while his runner and executive officer dragged him down the hill.

When he'd caught up with the others, his medics rushed to him and worked on his leg while he gasped and called Colonel Smith again.

"My company's safe," he reported.

Colonel Smith heard the weird urgency in his voice. "What the hell's the matter with you?"

"I got a bullet in my leg."

"You'd better get down to the aid station."

"I'm okay. I can stay here."

"Are you sure?"

"I'm sure."

Colonel Smith received messages from his other companies, and it was all the same: Each battalion had had the shit kicked out of it on Hill Thirty-one. He realized the Japanese fortifications were even tougher than he'd thought.

He walked down the hill to his tent, chomping his cigar and wondering what to do next. His staff officers and aides followed him, feeling defeated. When they came to his tent, he told them to order all units to stay where they were, and then he went into his tent to be alone with his thoughts and his flask of jungle juice.

He sat at his desk and took the flask out of his footlocker, taking a swig, letting it burn all the way down. He thought the only solution to the problem of Hill Thirty-one was massive firepower and more troops. They'd pound the Jap positions on Hill Thirty-one and the hills nearby until they were softened up and then try again.

His tent was divided in two parts; the other part was the office of his sergeant major, radio operator, and executive officer. He tucked his flask into his footlocker and waddled out to the other office to call Colonel Stockton at Regiment.

"Sir," he said, after the call went through, "we've just been thrown back on our heels. There's more up there than we thought. I think it'll take the whole regiment to break through, and only then after we've softened up those hills."

"Do you have any better idea of where those nests are?"

"Yes, sir, but we still can't spot them exactly. The situation is all fucked up as usual. At least we've learned two things. The first is the Japs don't have any artillery up there, otherwise they would have shelled the shit out of us. The second is that they're pretty well dug in, because my own artillery barrage didn't make a dent in them."

"We'll bring up the heavy stuff, then. And we'll hit them from the air. They might be tough but they're not that tough. Anything else?"

"Not at present, sir."

"Call me when you get more information. Over and out."

As dusk fell on Guadalcanal, Colonel Stockton had a fairly clear picture of what was in front of him, although many pieces to the puzzle were still missing. He agreed with Colonel Smith that it would take more than the Second Battalion to bust through the Jap fortifications. It was time to call General Patch, who'd relieved General Vandegrift as top commander on Guadalcanal. Colonel Stockton stood next to his radio operator in his command-post tent as the call went through.

"This is General Patch," said the voice on the other end.

Colonel Stockton told him the bad news and didn't try to hide anything about the Second Battalions's defeat. "I think it'll take my whole regiment to wipe out the enemy in front of me, but first we'll need heavy artillery and air strikes."

"I'll give you whatever you need," General Patch said.

After the conversation Colonel Stockton felt optimistic about taking the Jap stronghold. If the Japs could be hammered by artillery and air power sufficiently, the Twenty-third Infantry Regiment could do the job. He retired to his office, sat behind his desk, lit up his pipe, and started working his with maps, laying out the tactics that would destroy the Gifu Line.

Chow trucks couldn't get through to the front, so the Second Battalion had to eat C rations for supper. The men were exhausted and chewed their food lazily. It was the end of Christmas day and they'd had no presents, no letters from home. Homer Gladley was still hungry after he finished eating—he was always hungry—and to distract himself he took his harmonica out of his shirt pocket and played "Silent Night."

The men listened, thinking of home. Bannon remembered his previous Christmas, which he'd celebrated with his girl friend, Ginger Gregg, and some of the people from the saloon where she worked as a waitress. They'd danced, gotten drunk, and had a grand old time, but now Bannon hadn't received a letter from her for nearly a month, and he wondered who she was dancing with this Christmas. *She's probably forgotten all about me,* Bannon thought.

Bannon tossed his empty C ration can over his shoulder and lit a cigarette. Gladley ended "Silent Night" and began "God Rest Ye Merry Gentlemen." Bannon wondered where Gladley got his energy from. Bannon was so exhausted, he wasn't sure if he wanted to finish his cigarette.

"Can I talk with you, Sarge?"

Bannon looked up and saw Private DelFranco. "Whataya want?"

"I want a transfer."

"To where."

"Anywhere but the recon platoon."

"How come?"

"I don't like it here."

"Why not?"

DelFranco kneeled in front of Bannon and looked him in the eye. "Because you don't like me."

Bannon spat at the ground. "Listen, DelFranco. I don't have time for this horseshit. I don't like you and I don't dislike you. I don't give a shit about you at all. Just do what you're told and you'll be all right."

DelFranco didn't budge. "You don't think I'm good enough for the recon platoon, do you?"

"I just told you to get the fuck away from me."

"Do you think I'm good enough for the recon platoon?"

"I ain't never thought about it. I told you I don't give a shit. When things settle down, you can put in for a transfer through normal channels. Now get the fuck out of here."

DelFranco stood and walked away. *He's acting like an asshole,* Bannon thought, and wondered how Butsko would have handled DelFranco. He decided that Butsko would have told him to fuck off too.

It was night in the hospital and the lights were out. Nurse Grimsby, tall, gawky, freckled, and not very pretty, was making her rounds. She was a nervous young woman, always worrying about something, and she was knock-kneed on top of everything else. Never married, she was revolted by all the screwing around done by most of the other nurses on the base, and she was trying to keep herself pure for the man of her dreams, whenever he came along.

Frankie La Barbara stood in the shadows and watched her approach down the corridor. He wore only his pajama bottoms and had a mad gleam in his eyes, because for some strange reason Nurse Grimsby turned him on. There was something about icy, tense, hysterical women that he liked, and moreover he knew he'd be sent back to the front soon, and he wanted to screw as many nurses as he could. He'd already made it with five of them and wanted to raise his total to an even half-dozen.

"Hi, Nurse Grimsby," he said as she came abreast of him.

She nearly jumped out of her shoes. "Who's there?"

"Frankie La Barbara."

"What are you doing hiding in the corner there?" She

smoothed her hair with her hands and then adjusted the wire-rimmed glasses on her long, thin nose. "You'd better get to bed this instant!"

"I got a pain, Nurse Grimsby."

"Where?"

Frankie pointed to his stomach. "Down here."

"You probably drank too much."

"I ain't had a drink all day. I think it's my appendix."

Nurse Grimsby wrinkled her nose, because she knew all about Frankie La Barbara. He was a wise guy and a goldbrick, and once she'd heard some nurses talking about what a good lover he was. She thought him a perfectly disgusting human being, but maybe he did have appendicitis. She'd better have a look.

"Come with me, please."

"Yes, ma'am."

He followed her down the corridor, looking at her skinny ass underneath her white dress. But he knew it wasn't that skinny. He'd seen her bend over once, and it had a nice shape. It wasn't a magnificent ass, like Nurse Gleason's or even Nurse Kilbane's, but it was a nice ass just the same and he wanted to reach under her dress and give it a pinch.

"In here," she said, opening the door to an examining room.

She turned on the light and entered the office. He followed her in, his straight black hair neatly combed. He'd shaved only an hour ago. He'd also taken a shower. Frankie La Barbara was ready to roll.

"Lie down here," she said.

"Yes, ma'am."

Frankie lay on the examining table, spread his legs, and looked up into her eyes.

He's flirting, she thought. *I'll bet there's nothing wrong with him.* "Where does it hurt."

He pointed to the pit of his stomach. "Right here."

She pressed down on the spot with the fingers of his right hand. "How does that feel?"

"That feels real nice, Nurse Grimsby."

She gave him a dirty look and pressed to the left. "How about this?"

"That feels even better, Nurse Grimsby."

She pressed to the right. "What about here."

"Oh, that felt wonderful, Nurse Grimsby. You have the nicest hands."

She looked sternly at him. "I don't think there's a damn thing wrong with you, La Barbara. What are you trying to pull?"

"This," he said, pushing down his pajamas and revealing a big nasty hard-on.

She made a little cry of surprise and took a step back, staring at the long, thick, throbbing monster in front of her.

"This is an outrage!" she said. "I'm calling the MPs right now!"

Frankie leaped up from the table and grabbed her wrist. "What are you gonna tell them, that I took my dick out?"

She tried to shake her hand loose. "Let me go!"

"Ssshhhhhh."

"I said let me go!"

He pulled her hand down and rubbed it against his joint. His pajamas were down around his ankles and he was stark naked.

"Isn't it nice?" he cooed into her ear. "Why don't you make it feel good."

Frankie was a good-looking Italian stallion with a golden tan, and Nurse Grimsby was a very sexually frustrated young woman. She'd only been laid a few times in her life and she hadn't liked it much, thinking there was something wrong with her, and she was tormented by torrid erotic dreams nearly every night. Frankie's pecker was hot and smooth, muscular, and thrilling against the back of her hand. Nurse Grimsby was starting to feel strange.

"Please let me go," she whispered, trembling all over as Frankie rubbed her hand over the head of his cock.

"I love you, Nurse Grimsby," he said, pulling up her dress. Frankie knew what her problem was, even if she didn't.

"Don't do that," she said, trying to regain control of herself.

"Just let me touch it," he whispered. "All I want to do is touch it."

"No."

She hugged her thighs tightly together as Frankie ran his

fingers up her smooth white flesh. Nurse Grimsby touched her free hand to his shoulder.

"I'm going to call the MPs," she said softly.

"No, you're not."

He reached the top of her thighs and touched his fingers lightly against her precious love-starved little gazoo.

"Oh, Nurse Grimsby, that's so nice," he said, licking her ear.

She nearly fainted. "Stop it, La Barbara."

"You don't really want me to stop it, do you?" he asked, sticking his tongue into her ear, massaging her underwear, and pressing her hand against his hairy canary.

Nurse Grimsby thought she was losing her mind. She wanted to scream for the MPs and run out of the examining room, but somehow she couldn't. It felt too good. The attack had been sneaky and sudden and had taken her by surprise.

Frankie knew that if you went slow with a dame like Nurse Grimsby, you'd never get anywhere. He let her hand go, grabbed the back of her head, and licked her lips, sending tickles up and down her spine.

"No," she moaned.

"Yes," Frankie said, licking her clenched teeth.

"Please."

"Relax."

"Don't."

Frankie's tongue was insistent and delicious, because he'd been chewing spearmint gum. She felt herself weakening—deep down she was normal, after all—and Frankie knew there were no frigid women, there were only inept men.

"I love you," he mumbled, while still kissing her.

"No, you don't. You're a bastard and everybody knows it."

"But I'm your bastard."

"Get away from me."

"I won't."

"I'll scream."

"Oh, no, you won't."

She opened her mouth to scream, and Frankie thrust his tongue into her mouth. That did it. She melted like chocolate in summertime. Frankie withdrew his hand from underneath her skirt and pulled her against him, rolling his tongue around in her mouth, pressing his joint against her belly. She whimpered, because she knew he was defeating her, but it was a sweet surrender. She placed her hands on his broad shoulders and squirmed her tongue against his, making little animal noises. He pulled up her dress in back and cupped her buttocks in his hands, squeezing hard, but not too hard.

Oh, God, she thought, *what am I doing?* She tried to regain control of herself, but it was too late. She ought to lock the door, because somebody might walk in. She ought to do a lot of things, but she couldn't. Her nipples tingled and she was feeling creamy and dreamy between her legs.

Frankie urged her toward the examining table and withdrew his tongue from her mouth. "Take your clothes off," he murmured, brushing his lips across her eyes.

"You take them off for me," she replied, because if she was going to be bad, she might as well be real bad.

Frankie chuckled, because women like Nurse Grimsby always turned out to be the wildest. He let her go, spun around, latched the door, and flicked off the light switch, plunging the room into darkness.

But not complete darkness. Moonbeams flowed through the window and she stood beside the examining table, hands at her sides, a smile on her face, waiting for him.

He unbuttoned the front of her white dress, and she held out her arms as he pulled if off. Now she had on only her bra, her Army-issue cotton underpants, and her nurse's hat. Frankie reached behind her, unhooked the bra, and peeled it away, uncovering two pert breasts, not too big but very nice, each one a tempting mouthful. He pulled down her underpants and she stepped out of them; he tossed them over his shoulder, then stood and looked at her long, slim legs. Although they turned in a bit at the knees, he thought they'd look great in black net stockings. She wasn't bad at all.

He picked her up and set her down on the examining table, then crawled on top of her, feeling her soft body beneath him. Her nipples felt like little pebbles against his chest. He rested his heavy artillery on her stomach and covered her face with kisses while she closed her eyes and wondered if this was one of those crazy dreams she had were she fucked and sucked all night long and in the morning did her best to forget what she'd dreamed. He moved his heavy artillery into position and she looked up at him, glowing in the moonlight. His eyes glinted evilly, and it made her extremely passionate.

She grabbed his joint and squeezed it hard, pulling it into her steaming furnace.

"Hey, take is easy," he said, thrusting his hips forward.

His cannon banged against her door, but somehow it couldn't enter. Either it was too big or she was too small. They struggled against each other, groaning and sighing, and gradually the opening widened. He worked his hips around and she guided it through the door. He sank in deeper and her vagina held his joint like a fist, expanding and contracting, pulsating and going into little convulsions.

Frankie nearly came, but he squinched his eyes shut and tried to control himself. He considered himself a skilled sexual artisan, and it wouldn't do to come so soon. But the stimulation was too great. Her long, slim body was too thrilling. She rocked her hips back and forth and Frankie thought, *Oh, my God, I'm going to come!*

"What's wrong?" she asked as he tried to get away.

"I'm coming!"

He pulled out as his cannon fired, covering her belly with hot cream, and she rubbed it against her breasts and tummy and between her legs, making the petals of her flower tingle while Frankie caught his breath, aimed, and jammed it in again, this time to the hilt, and pumped her slowly. She raised her long legs and wrapped them around his waist, wagging her ass from side to side, their bodies sticky against each other, and he thought of how delicate and wonderful she was, how fluid her motions, so unlike the crabby nurse she usually was, snapping orders at GIs, her shoulders hunched because she was so tall and wanted to appear shorter.

Now she was stretched out to her full length, and Frankie kissed her ear as he drilled deep into her well. He knew he'd get her before long. All the nurses wanted to do it, and the nutty ones like Nurse Grimsby usually wanted it the most. They fought it the hardest. But once they gave in, they fucked like wild animals, scratching your back until it bled, kicking their legs in the air, and talking dirty.

"Fuck me," she moaned. "Fuck me."

"Whataya think I'm doing?" Frankie La Barbara asked.

"Roll me over and do it to me that way."

He disengaged from her and she turned over on her stomach, sticking her cute little caboose into the air. Frankie found her hot spot and stuck it in again, humping and pumping, and she wiggled her ass and bit her hand, afraid she would get so far out she'd never come back again. Frankie reached around with his long, educated fingers and massaged her little dewdrop. She felt like a blossom that was opening wider and wider, sending out tendrils and petals into the world in a wild profusion of colors and shapes. Frankie stoked the ecstasy building inside her and it became more intense and fiery, radiating out to her fingertips and toes, making her scalp tingle, and then it exploded, utterly consuming her in sweet pleasure, drowning her in crazy joy. Her movements became erratic; she went into convulsions, struggling to breathe, clawing the sheet on the examining table, and at that moment—the moment when she thought she could not possibly tolerate anything more—Frankie fired another volley, filling her deepest recesses with hot honey, and she blacked out for a few seconds, hearing bells and birds, but then came back and felt him screwing her erratically, gasping in her ear, cupping her breasts in his hands.

Finally, exhausted, they went limp against each other, their chests heaving as they tried to breathe, Frankie resting his face against her hair and she reaching underneath her, touching the barrel of his gun with her fingers. They closed their eyes and rested for a while, nearly falling asleep, and Frankie was again aware of how good her body felt and how nice was the fragrance that lived in her hair. Pretty soon his joint was stiffening again. He prodded her with it, rolling her over onto her back and sticking it in.

It wasn't long before they were going at it like wild animals once more as the moon rolled across the starry sky and birds of the night sang their plaintive songs.

EIGHT . . .

The next day American artillery pounded the Gifu Line while the Cactus Air Force from Henderson Field dropped bombs and strafed the jungle. Colonel Stockton worked amid the din, planning his attack. The Second Battalion would assault what he assumed to be the front of the Gifu Line, with the Third Battalion covering the left flank and the First Battalion in reserve to move in on the right if necessary. He knew those Japanese fortifications were impeding the American advance, and he would have to break through if he hoped to maintain his credibility as a combat commander.

His men spent the day digging in to forestall the possibility of a counterattack. Ammunition was brought to the front on roads bulldozed by the Corps of Engineers. The dead and wounded were carried back to aid stations; the worst of the wounded would be shipped to New Caledonia. Mail was delivered to the front, a bundle being delivered to the recon platoon.

Bannon ordered a break and handed out the mail. The men crowded around him, trying to read the names on the letters, and Bannon's voice faltered when he saw his own name on an envelope in Ginger Gregg's unmistakable handwriting. He put the envelope in his pocket and hurriedly called out the rest of the names. The last letter was for Butsko; he'd have to forward it to the hospital in New Caledonia.

Bannon returned to his foxhole, which was five feet deep, with a grenade sump at the bottom. Before his ass hit the dirt he tore the letter open and started reading. Ginger said she hadn't written for a while because she'd been sick with the flu. She hadn't been able to work and had been lying in a feverish delirium in her room in Pecos. She said she still loved him and thought of him all the time. She said she missed him desperately.

Bannon's morale improved five hundred percent. He lit a cigarette and thought of Ginger with her red hair and the freckles on her back. He should have known she was sick. Only crazy jealousy had made him think that she'd forgotten him.

But then the needles of doubt began to prickle his mind. Was she lying? Perhaps she had been shacked up with some other guy and only said she had been sick. Perhaps her little fling with the other guy hadn't worked out and now she wanted to come back to him because she had no one else at the moment. Bannon felt sick in the pit of his stomach. He wished he could trust Ginger, but he couldn't. She'd been no virgin when he met her and he knew she'd had a lot of boyfriends. She'd screwed him on the first night they'd met, and probably she'd done the same thing with other guys. For all he knew she was probably still doing it. She might be with some other guy right at that moment.

He ground out his cigarette butt with his heel and swore aloud.

"Whatsa matter, Sarge?" asked Nutsy Gafooley, lying next to him. Nutsy hadn't even gone to the mail call, because nobody ever wrote him. "Get a Dear John?"

"Mind your fucking business."

Nutsy Gafooley shrugged and returned to the contemplation of his future. He believed that somehow he'd survive the war, just as he'd survived the worst of the Depression, and one day he'd be riding the rails again, watching America pass by his eyes, free from military discipline and the danger of war.

Bannon was wondering whether to answer Ginger's letter or not. He ought to forget her, because she was no good. When he'd first met her she'd had a rich wildcatter for a boyfriend, and often Bannon had heard her tell him lies on the telephone so she could spend the night with Bannon. The wildcatter's name was Edwards, and sometimes she had even told him she was sick. Now she was probably telling Bannon she was sick so she could take a trip to Mexico or someplace else nice with Edwards. Women lie all the time. How can any man trust them?

He remembered the letter for Butsko and took it out of his back pocket. "This is for Butsko," he told Nutsy Gafooley. "Take it back to Captain Orr's mail clerk and tell him to forward it to New Caledonia."

"Hup, Sarge."

Nutsy took the letter and crawled out of the foxhole, heading for Captain Orr's command post. Bannon lit another cigarette and tried to think about the next day's attack. But Ginger Gregg stayed in his mind, with her mischievous smile, the way she teased him by crossing her legs so he could see up her dress.

Irritable, he climbed out of the foxhole to see what was going on. A group of men were nearby, reading their letters, and he thought it was time to break up the bullshit and put the men back to work. He slung his M 1 and strolled in their direction, a scowl on his face.

Homer Gladley was in the middle of the group, reading a letter from his girlfriend, Annie Mae, back in Nebraska. In his left hand he held a picture of her, blond and innocent-looking. "Boy," he said, "I'm sure glad I got this li'l old gal waiting for me back home. I don't know what I'd do if she wasn't there."

Bannon heard him and thought of Ginger, all his nasty demons slithering into his mind. "They're all full of shit, Gladley," Bannon snarled. "Turn 'em upside down and they all look alike."

Gladley looked up at Bannon. "Huh?"

"They're all no fucking good."

Gladley wrinkled his brow, thought about that for a few moments, and then smiled. "Some of them are okay."

"Yeah? Which ones?"

"Annie Mae's a good ol' gal. I've known her since she was a little girl. Your problem, Bannon, is that you been hanging around with too many loose women."

"They're all the same." The little voice in Bannon's ear told him to stop it, but he was too angry and frustrated. "How do you know who she's with right now?"

"She's with her mom, fixing supper."
"How do you know that?"
"That's what she always does."
"How old is she?"
"Nineteen."
Bannon spat at the ground. "She's at that age."
"What age?"
"The age when women start fucking around."
Everything grew quiet, because all the men knew how Homer Gladley felt about Annie Mae and how dangerous he was when provoked. Gladley respected Bannon and decided not to take him seriously.
"Not Annie Mae," he said. "She's not that kind of girl."
"They're all that kind." The little voice screamed in Bannon's ear, but he ignored it. "She's probably fucking the mailman right now."
That did it. Homer Gladley flashed on a hallucination of Annie Mae having sex with old Bert Lucas, the mailman, and turned purple. The other men moved back out of the way.
"You take that back," Gladley said as he drew his 245 pounds to his full height.
"I ain't taking nothing back," Bannon replied.
Homer Gladley pinched his lips together and raised his two enormous fists. He lumbered toward Bannon, ready to fight, and Bannon looked at him through eyes narrowed to slits, realizing that Homer Gladley had more power than he but that he had the speed. Could his speed defeat Gladley's power? He thought of himself punching Gladley in the mouth and felt sick. He didn't want to hit Gladley. He liked Gladley.
"Aw, shit," Bannon said. "I didn't mean it, Homer."
Gladley stopped in his tracks. "You sure?"
"Yeah, I'm sure. Annie Mae's a good girl. She's not like the rest of them."
Homer didn't know what to do, because his mind worked slowly. Shaw stepped in between them and smiled. "I know where to get some jungle juice," he said. "The mess sergeant in Easy Company's got a good batch, I heard."
"Shit, let's get some," said Shilansky. "What do you say, Homer?"
"Hell, yes," Homer said.

Bannon turned around and walked back to his foxhole, cursing himself. A platoon sergeant was supposed to stop fights, not start them. *When Butsko gets back he'll really kick my ass when he finds out about some of the things I've done,* he thought.

Bannon jumped into his foxhole and pulled his helmet down over his eyes, detesting himself. In the distance he heard the men arguing about what to trade for the jungle juice.

At the Gifu Line, the Japanese soldiers lay on the floors of their bunkers, their fingers stuffed in their ears, as bombs and artillery shells fell all around them. A few shells had landed so close that shock waves caused some of the men to bleed from their ears. Many of the Japanese soldiers thought they were losing their minds, but all their lives they had been trained in the techniques of self-control, and not one of them cried out or even made a disparaging remark.

Major Uchikoshi sat cross-legged on the floor behind his low desk, trying to figure out the best way to meet the American attack he knew would come in the morning. He was wondering whether to move more men to the sector where the Americans had attacked the previous day, because he knew that that was where they'd come again. He didn't think they'd determined where his other bunkers were. He decided to add one more machine gun to each of the bunkers on the hill where the Americans would come.

As he was pondering these matters, his orderly brought him a bowl containing a few spoonfuls of boiled grass and leaves left over from yesterday. The men hadn't been able to go out that day to gather food, and all the coconuts were gone. He knew of a coconut grove a mile away, but it had nearly been picked clean, and the men couldn't leave their bunkers anyway. Major Uchikoshi was skin and bones, just like the rest of his men. His uniform hung loosely on his frame as if he were a scarecrow, and his eyes had sunk into his head.

I wonder how long we can hold out, he thought.

Colonel Tsuji, cleanly shaved, attired in a new Army uniform, walked through the long corridors of Imperial Headquarters in Tokyo, his sword hanging from his side. Everywhere he looked he saw well-fed staff officers carrying around briefcases, looking important, and smiling confidently while the Seventeenth Army was holding on by its fingernails in Guadalcanal.

Colonel Tsuji was in a furious state of mind. Everywhere he'd been since he'd left Guadalcanal he'd met officers who didn't understand the seriousness of the situation there. Everyone was confident that Japanese spirit would overcome the American material advantage, but he knew better. He'd been in the middle of the shooting war too long to have faith in slogans. He was resolved to tell General Owada the bitter truth when he met with him.

He entered General Owada's office and gave his name to the young orderly sitting at the desk. The orderly said General Owada was expecting him and that he should go right in. Colonel Tsuji opened the massive oak door and entered General Owada's spacious office. The general sat at his desk, the Imperial Palace visible in the distance through the window behind him. Colonel Tsuji marched stiffly to the desk and saluted.

"Please take a seat," General Owada said.

Colonel Tsuji sat down, adjusting his sword. General Owada had a tiny nose and a gray mustache. A staunch militarist, he was one of the fanatics who had helped bring down the civilian government of Prince Konoye, establishing General Tojo as prime minister of Japan.

"How good to see you again," General Owada said. "I believe you've lost weight, Colonel Tsuji."

"Rations are short on Guadalcanal, sir," Colonel Tsuji replied in his high-pitched voice.

"I have asked you here to give me, without any embellishments, the true picture of our situation on Guadalcanal, Colonel Tsuji." General Owada folded his hands on his desk and leaned forward. "You may begin now."

"We have about ten thousand troops left, and approximately one-third of them are fit for duty. One hundred men are dying each day as a result of starvation. We have little food and ammunition. The Americans outnumber us approximately three to one but have been unable to make use of their numerical superiority, because we have pulled back to new defensive positions and they haven't found us yet. Once they do, they will defeat us. Our men will fight valiantly, but they cannot win unless substantial reinforcements can be sent to Guadalcanal. I want you to understand, sir, that the situation is most grave, and I'm not embellishing anything. It must be seen to be believed."

"How is General Hyakutake?"

"Starving to death like all the rest of them."

"Has his ability to command been impaired?"

"No. He is an inspiration to all of us."

"Hmmm," said General Owada. "Have your many defeats on Guadalcanal influenced your bleak assessment, do you think, Colonel Tsuji?"

Colonel Tsuji raised his eyebrows. "You question my veracity, sir?"

General Owada didn't reply. He just waited patiently for his answer.

"I have told you the truth," Colonel Tsuji said. "In fact, perhaps I've made everything sound too positive, if anything. Within two or three weeks the Seventeenth Army will be destroyed unless something is done."

"So"—General Owada unfolded his hands and leaned back in his chair—"what do you propose?"

"We can defeat the Americans on Guadalcanal if we have the toops and equipment, sir." Colonel Tsuji felt his rage getting the best of him. "Why have we not been resupplied?"

"The Navy has been unable to furnish transportation."

"Why not?"

General Owada shrugged.

"But we have the most powerful navy in the world!" Colonel Tsuji shouted. "Why have they abandoned the Seventeenth Army on Guadalcanal!"

"Calm yourself."

Colonel Tsuji gritted his teeth. "Sorry, sir."

"We must always stay calm, no matter what."

"Yes, sir."

"The answer to your question is that we no longer have the most powerful Navy in the world. Our navy has suffered two enormous defeats: one near the island of Midway and the other in the Coral Sea."

Colonel Tsuji turned pale. "No."

"Yes. We do not even know the extent of the Navy's losses in those two battles because the Navy won't tell us."

"Won't tell us?" Colonel Tsuji blinked. "Why won't they tell us?"

"Pride. Stupidity. Who knows? But if they won't tell us, it must have been pretty bad."

"No wonder they can't resupply Guadalcanal. Can they evacuate the Seventeenth Army?"

"I don't know, but that decision hasn't been made yet. General Sumiyoshi would like to launch a major offensive against the Americans on Guadalcanal."

"With what?"

"Calm yourself."

Colonel Tsuji realized he'd raised his voice again. "Sorry, sir. But the Imperial General Staff must understand that it would be impossible to launch a major offensive against the Americans. We have nothing left. We don't even have rice."

"You may tell them yourself. A meeting has been scheduled for next Wednesday to deal with the problem of Guadalcanal. You, of course, are to attend."

Colonel Tsuji groaned. "Next Wednesday may be too late. Can't they hold the meeting sooner?"

"I'm afraid not."

"But the situation is desperate on Guadalcanal. No, it's worse than desperate; it's catastrophic. I told you that a hundred men are starving to death every day."

"I'm afraid the decision has already been made, Colonel Tsuji. The meeting will take place next Wednesday at nine o'clock in the morning. Be there."

"Yes, sir."

After the meeting Colonel Tsjui walked like a man in a trance through the long wood-paneled corridors of the headquarters building. It was incredible to him that the leaders of the Imperial Army were unable to respond to the plight of the Seventeenth Army on Guadalcanal. Colonel Tsjui wanted to draw his sword and attack the complacent, self-satisfied officers he passed in the corridor, but instead he headed for the door and his staff car so he could go home and have lunch with his wife, who would feed him raw fish and sake and make him relax.

NINE . . .

Before dawn the Twenty-third Infantry Regiment moved in a skirmish line toward the Japanese positions. The jungle smelled of gunpowder and burned trees, and the moon was obscured by a thick cloud layer. Holding their rifles at port arms and carrying full field packs, they made their way up the hill to get into position to attack as soon as it got light.

The recon platoon was still with Captain Orr's Company G, and Captain Orr limped behind the skirmish line, his thigh bulging with bandages, but he still had a lot of fight left in him and wouldn't let anybody else lead his company.

Bannon was in the middle of the recon platoon, and he swore that he was going to cut out all the bullshit and not let his personal feelings get the best of him anymore. His men were depending on him and he couldn't let them down. Butsko had never worried about anything except the next battle, and that's the way Bannon was going to be from then on.

When they were halfway up the hill, they came under observation by the lookouts posted by Major Uchikoshi. The lookouts returned to the forward bunkers and reported the presence of the GIs. Minutes later the machine guns opened fire on the Americans, who hit the dirt.

"Keep moving on your bellies!" Captain Orr shouted.

The GIs crawled up the hill, hearing the chatter of the machine guns. The veterans among them could sense that the

Japanese bullets weren't even coming close. The GIs crawled through shell craters and underneath trees knocked over by the previous day's barrage. The floor of the jungle was alive with rats and mice whose homes were destroyed, and they squeaked with fear as they ran away from the Americans.

Bannon looked ahead, trying to see the muzzle blasts of the machine guns, but the jungle was too thick and the machine guns too far away. In the darkness the skirmish lines became confused, as companies lost touch with each other and some companies moved more quickly than the others.

In his bunker Major Uchikoshi dressed in the darkness, his stomach cramped with hunger, as the machine guns fired in the distance. He hadn't expected the Americans to attack at night and knew they would be searching for the muzzle blasts of his machine guns, which would be easier to spot in the darkness. He made the quick decision to send riflemen out to stall the American advance so the machine guns could stop firing. He figured the machine guns probably weren't doing much good anyway.

He issued the order to Captain Yatsu, who transmitted it to the appropriate bunkers. Several minutes later the machine guns stopped firing, and the riflemen crept out of their bunkers and moved forward to engage the Americans. They were to take no risks and steadily give ground until daylight, when they would return to their bunkers for the real battle.

Bannon and the recon platoon were crawling up Hill Thirty-one when the Japanese machine guns stopped firing. The men in the recon platoon looked at each other and wondered why the Japs had stopped shooting at them. Bannon thought they should just keep moving and see what happened.

"Hey," said Private Ruslip from the recon platoon's Third Squad. "What the hell are we crawling for? The Japs aren't shooting anymore."

He stood and walked up the hill in a crouch.

"Get down!" Bannon shouted.

"What the fuck for?" Ruslip asked.

Beaaannngggg—one of the Japanese rifleman shot him, and Ruslip spun in the air, dropping his rifle, and crashed into a tree, sliding down its trunk.

"Medic!" somebody shouted.

"There's Japs straight ahead!" Longtree yelled.

"Keep going!" replied Captain Orr.

The men continued their upward crawl, and the Japanese riflemen leveled fire at them. The Japanese soldiers were so close that their muzzle blasts could be seen easily, and the GIs returned the fire. Those with Browning automatic rifles raked the jungle, and the Japanese riflemen began their fighting retreat, moving slowly toward their bunkers.

Bannon had keen, battle-tuned ears, and he realized there was only a screen of Japs in front of Company G. He believed that if the men charged, they'd overwhelm the Japs. He turned to Nutsy Gafooley. "Get me Captain Orr on the radio."

Nutsy called the captain, finally got through, and gave Bannon the walkie-talkie.

"Sir," said Bannon, "there's only a handful of Japs ahead. I think the company should rush them."

"We'll try it."

Bannon got set, and a few moments later he heard Captain Orr's roaring voice. *"Up and at 'em! Charge!"*

Company G and the recon platoon jumped up and ran as fast as they could at the Japs, who fired a few shots and then pulled back. The GIs tripped over branches and fell into shell craters, because it was too dark to see. Some got tangled up in hanging vines, and Homer Gladley ran directly into the trunk of a tree, nearly knocking himself out cold.

The attack stalled and the Japs found new positions, from which they fired at the GIs. Then it was the same thing all over again. Bannon realized his bright idea wasn't so bright, but Captain Orr didn't call to tell him so. On top of everything else, the G Company skirmish line had become disjointed. Captain Orr had to take time to straighten it out. Then the slow advance got under way again. The GIs inched their way up the hill and the Japs gradually retreated. The sun rose on the horizon behind the clouds, and the day became lighter. The Japs fired at the GIs, and the GIs fired back. Visibility improved and the jungle became a weird nightmare landscape of broken trees and uprooted bushes. The Japanese riflemen ran back to their bunkers and soon thereafter the machine guns opened fire. The advance stalled as it had two days ago, although many more GIs were involved. Despite their numbers, the GIs were still facing an impenetrable hail of fire.

Mortar squads set up their tubes, and soon they were lobbing rounds into the jungle ahead. They couldn't see the Japanese machine-gun nests, but their purpose was to obscure the vision of the Japanese machine gunners. The regiment moved forward again, the units on the flanks trying to work their way around the Japanese position, but they, too, came under machine-gun fire.

The air sizzled with bullets as the regiment moved slowly up the hill. Longtree crawled toward Bannon.

"I've found some tracks," he said. "If I follow them, they should lead us to bunkers."

Bannon realized that the tracks must have been left by the retreating Japanese soldiers and that the Japs might have made a serious mistake. He got on the radio to Captain Orr and told him that Longtree could follow the tracks and that the mortars should stop firing in that sector.

"Okay," said Captain Orr. "We'll give it a try. Send Longtree and one other man. I'll stop the company until he gets back."

Bannon looked at Longtree. "He said you can do it. Who do you want to go with you."

"You," Longtree said.

Bannon opened his mouth to say that he was the platoon sergeant and he couldn't go, but then he thought, *Fuck it, I want to see what's going on up there myself.*

"Nutsy, I'm going with Longtree. Watch the store until I get back."

Longtree and Bannon crawled forward. The rest of the platoon watched them disappear into the twisted, devastated jungle. Longtree kept his nose close to the ground, following the tracks left by the Japanese riflemen, and Bannon stayed close beside him looking ahead for movement in the jungle. They heard firing and shell bursts farther down the line, interspersed with the shouts of officers and noncoms. Slowly, quietly, Bannon and Longtree crawled over fallen trees and through shell craters. Their part of the jungle was unusually quiet; all the birds and animals had fled. Only the bugs remained, flying around Bannon and Longtree, biting them, raising welts on their skin.

They crossed a brook and made their way around some huge boulders. Longtree lost the trail on a stretch of ridge but picked it up again on the other side. They stayed close to the ground and moved slowly so they would be hard to spot. They passed through fields of fire covered by Japanese bunkers, but the Japs didn't see them.

Finally, near the crest of the hill, Longtree raised his hand. "There it is," he said.

Bannon looked ahead but couldn't see anything except more jungle. "Where?"

Longtree pointed. Bannon raised his binoculars to his eyes and barely made it out: It was the opening of the bunker, about twenty-five yards away. He could see the ugly snouts of two machine guns.

Bannon wished he had the whole platoon with him. They could rush the bunker in waves and take it without much trouble. But two men couldn't take it. Or could they? Bannon thought he'd better mark the position on his map. He took it out and made an *X* on the approximate position of the machine-gun nest.

"Longtree," he said, "do you think we could sneak up on them and drop grenades into the opening?"

"It would take a lot of time."

"We got nothing but time. I'll ask Captain Orr." Bannon held his walkie-talkie to his ear and called Captain Orr. There was no answer, so he called again. The airwaves screeched and crackled, and finally Captain Orr's voice came through.

"Sir," said Bannon. "We've found one of their nests."

"You have! Where is it?"

Bannon told him the coordinates of the machine-gun nest. "Sir, Longtree and I think we can sneak up on it and drop a hand grenade in. Can we try it?"

"Sounds like suicide to me."

"No, I think we can do it. They don't even suspect that we're here."

"It's too risky. Pull back about a hundred yards and wait for the rest of us to catch up."

"Yes, sir."

"Over and out."

Bannon let the walkie-talkie hang from the strap on his shoulder. "He said no."

"Why not?" Longtree asked.

"He said it's too risky."

"It'll be much more risky to take it head-on. These officers don't know shit from Shinola. They'd rather lose a hundred men trying to rush the nest than take it like we're going to. If we take that nest, nobody'll complain. Stay here and cover me. I'll drop the grenade in myself."

Bannon peered through the bushes at the opening of the machine-gun nest. It wasn't that far away, and Longtree knew how to move silently in the woods. "Okay, what the hell," Bannon said. "Give it a try."

Longtree took off his field pack and laid it down on the ground, because he wanted to travel light. Then he slipped silently into the jungle, and all Bannon could hear was the rustle of wind in the leaves and the sounds of gunfire not too far away.

Bannon made himself comfortable, lying on the jungle floor. Insects buzzed around his head, and he held his rifle ready to fire in case Longtree got into trouble. He watched Longtree move far to the right so he could sneak up on the machine-gun nest from the side. Then Longtree darted behind a tree, and Bannon couldn't see him any longer.

Longtree crawled through the thickest part of the jungle, stopping every few seconds to look and listen. This was the kind of fighting he liked: He and his wits against the Japs, instead of a lot of GIs charging through the jungle like a herd of elephants. He moved slowly and deliberately as the sun rose in the sky behind the thick ominous cloud layer. He passed a dead monkey torn apart by an artillery shell, and the splinters of trees were everywhere.

Longtree drew closer to the bunker. He could hear the chatter of Japs, and one of them knocked over a can, drawing verbal abuse from his sergeant. Longtree stopped and pulled a hand grenade from his lapel. He was only ten yards from the opening in front of the bunker. Leaving the pin in the grenade, he continued to crawl closer. He was quiet, close to the ground, and so stealthy that Bannon couldn't see him, even though

Bannon pretty much knew where he was.

Longtree worked his way to within five yards of the bunker's front opening. He could see the two machine-gun barrels and hear Japanese conversations from within. He was beside the bunker, concealed in thick foliage, and the Japs would have to stick their heads out of the bunker to see him. Crouching low, he pulled the pin of the grenade and held it in his right hand, grasping his rifle with his left hand. Leaping up, he dashed through the jungle toward the bunker, leaves slapping him in the face, branches scratching his uniform.

"Nani sono!" shouted one of the Japs.

Longtree turned loose the arming lever of the grenade as he charged through the jungle. He dived to the ground beside the bunker, drew back his arm, and tossed the grenade inside, then rolled away quickly. Japs screamed in a mad panic as the grenade fell in their midst; then they crashed heads as they bent over to pick it up.

It exploded, sending smoke and lightning out the opening of the bunker. Bannon was on his feet, running toward the bunker, holding his rifle at port arms, ready to fire at anything that moved. Longtree dashed around to the bunker's rear and saw a trench and a low entrance to the bunker. He took another grenade, pulled the pin, let the lever snap away, counted to two, and rolled it into the opening. It exploded, sending dust and smoke shooting through the cracks between the logs. Longtree dived through the hole and entered the bunker. It was filled with smoke and his hand touched down on warm, mushy flesh, the intestines of a Japanese soldier. The smell of gunpowder and entrails was strong in the air. The machine guns had been knocked off their pedestals and lay on the floor. Mutilated bodies were sprawled everywhere, and splashes of blood were on the walls and ceiling of the bunker.

Bannon crawled inside and joined Longtree. "Good work," he said. "I'll tell Captain Orr we've got the bunker. You keep your eyes peeled, because the Japs might want to take this back."

Longtree checked the Japanese machine guns to see if they were still operable while Bannon called Captain Orr on the walkie-talkie.

"Sir," Bannon said, "we've blown up that bunker and I

think you should send the men forward quickly before the Japs reoccupy it."

There was silence on the other end for a few moments. "Who told you to take that bunker!"

"You'd better send the men up fast. Over and out."

"But . . . !"

The walkie-talkie went dead in Captain Orr's ear. He wanted to hurl the walkie-talkie to the ground and smash it to bits. Once peple start disobeying orders, the whole concept of the Army started to break down. He handed the walkie-talkie to his runner and decided he'd worry about the Army later. The main thing now would be to occupy that machine-gun nest before the Japs tried to take it back.

Meanwhile, Longtree was dragging one of the Japanese machine guns through the low opening at the rear of the bunker. It was a Type 96 light machine gun; it was chambered for the 6.5-millimeter cartridge and had a tendency to jam. Bannon carried out pouches filled with oiled cartridges. Longtree set up the machine gun in the opening and Bannon fed bullets into the clip.

A Japanese head appeared around the bend in the trench ahead, and Longtree fired a burst that made the Jap pull his head back.

A Japanese hand grenade came flying through the air and landed on the roof of the bunker, where it exploded harmlessly. A Japanese head appeared on the top of the trench, and Longtree fired a burst that made the head duck. Then a hand grenade came flying down the trench and landed a few feet in front of the Type 96 machine gun.

"Get back!" Bannon yelled.

Both GIs retreated into the bunker and pressed their bodies against a bloody inner wall. The grenade exploded, sending a blast of smoke and flame into the bunker and blowing the machine gun into the air. Bannon's ears rang as he picked up the torso of a Japanese soldier and threw it into the opening at the rear of the bunker. He picked up some wood that had been a table and stuffed it in the opening too. He wanted to make sure no Japanese hand grenades came flying into the bunker. He realized that he and Longtree should not have occupied the bunker, because they were like rats in a trap. They should have stayed outside and waited for Captain Orr's men to catch up.

Bannon and Longtree got behind the torso and debris at the rear of the bunker and fired at everything that moved in the trench. Their visibility was poor and if the Japs had anything like a bazooka, they could shoot a rocket through the opening and finish off Bannon and Longtree easily.

Bannon fired round after round from his M 1. "Where's that fucking Captain Orr?" he said between clenched teeth.

Longtree didn't answer. He was too busy shooting at Japs swarming around behind the bunker. "I think we'd better get out of here," he said.

"Through the front hole?"

"That's the only way there is. I'll go first."

Longtree moved toward the hole, tripped over a dead Japanese soldier, and fell on his ass. He got up, made his way to the hole, and looked out. The coast appeared clear. He stuck his head out the hole and pushed with his legs.

Beeaaannnggggg—a bullet ricocheted off a log a few inches from his face, and he pulled his head back in quickly. "We're surrounded!"

Bannon cursed himself for getting stuck inside the bunker. Butsko would never have fallen into such a trap. Bannon thought he'd better call Captain Orr and tell him to hurry up. Machine-gun bullets and rifle shots zipped through the opening at the rear of the bunker as he raised the walkie-talkie to his face and called Captain Orr. It took a few horrifying minutes to get through.

"Sir," he said, "the Japs have got us surrounded in this bunker and you'd better get your men up here pretty fast!"

"Hold on, Bannon! We're almost there!"

Bannon let the walkie-talkie drop.

"What he say?" Longtree asked.

"He said to hold on!"

"To what!"

Smack—something hit the barricade at the rear of the bunker, and Bannon and Longtree knew what it was. They dived to the floor of the bunker and pressed their bodies against the walls, squinching their eyes shut, hoping and praying. *Blam*—the grenade exploded, and Bannon felt the heat wave against his face; his ears ached from the concussion. Dizzy and disoriented, he looked toward the back entrance and saw that the torso and junk had been blown away. A grenade came flying through the opening. He pounced on it and threw it back. It exploded as another grenade floated through the front window. Longtree caught it in midair and tossed it out the window again. It rolled down the slope and detonated.

Bannon and Longtree heard Japs jabbering all around them. There was no place to run and no place to hide. If they showed their faces in either of the openings, they'd get them shot off. All they could do was throw back hand grenades. Bannon and Longtree looked at each other, their faces pale.

"Well," said Longtree, "it's a good day to die."

"Like fuck it is!"

Two grenades flew through the backdoor opening, and Bannon and Longtree dived on them, hurling them out the front window, where another Jap was getting set to lob in a hand grenade of his own. The two grenades went off in his face, tearing his head off and ripping up his torso, and then his own grenade went off, blowing off his legs.

When the last sounds of the explosions died away, Bannon and Longtree heard a volley of rifle shots farther down the hill. They looked at each other and their faces creased into smiles. Company G was coming.

"Hey, we're over here!" Bannon shouted. He took off his helmet and waved it in front of opening that faced east. *"Here we are!"*

Beeaannnngggg—a bullet hit his helmet and knocked it out of his hand.

"Stupid son of a bitch!" Bannon pulled his hand back into the bunker and shook it, because it stung.

Longtree heard footsteps in the trench and dropped to his stomach, looking out. He saw Japs charging the rear door. He raised his rifle and fired shots into the trench as quickly as he could pull the trigger. Japs dropped to the bottom of the trench, holes in their legs and abdomens, twisting and whining in pain. The other Japs turned and ran away. Gunfire sounded all around the bunker. Bannon and Longtree looked from window to door frantically, wondering what was going on.

"Watch your right flank!" somebody yelled, and Bannon realized G Company was there.

"Hey, we're in here!"

"Who's in there?"

"Bannon and Longtree from the recon platoon!"

"Stay put!"

Bannon and Longtree crouched down and listened to G Company overrun the bunker and trench. Volleys of shots were fired, orders were shouted, and grenades were thrown. Bannon took out a cigarette and offered one to Longtree. He lit them with his trusty old Zippo.

"I told you it wasn't such a good day to die," Bannon said.

The sound of fighting diminished. Bannon got on his hands and knees and looked out the rear door of the trench and saw GI combat boots.

"Come on out of there!" somebody shouted.

Bannon picked up his rifle and crawled out of the bunker, his cigarette dangling out the corner of his mouth. Longtree came behind him. They stood up and saw the men from George Company standing around, looking at them curiously. Then the recon platoon came crashing through.

"Hey, what the fuck happened!" said Private Morris Shilansky. "Where'd you guys go?"

"Anything to drink in there?" asked Shaw, whose canteen was nearly empty.

"Lookit all the dead Japs!" said Nutsy Gafooley, looking around.

Captain Orr pushed his way through the crowd of men. "Break it up! What the fuck you think this is? Dig in around here! Let's move!" Finally he came face to face with Bannon and pointed his bony finger at Bannon's nose. "You disobeyed an order!"

Bannon grinned and winked and clicked his teeth. "We knocked out the bunker, sir," he said, pointing at it.

"But you disobeyed a goddamn order!"

"But we got the goddamn bunker."

They heard a jeep engine and turned around. A jeep was climbing up the slope, bouncing over logs and dipping into holes. Colonel Smith sat in the passenger seat, holding his helmet down with one hand, gripping the handle on the dash with the other, and chewing an unlit cigar. The jeep came to a stop beside the trench and Colonel Smith jumped out.

"Well, I'll be a son of a bitch!" Colonel Smith roared. "We've finally cracked the Jap line. Good work, Orr!"

Colonel Smith jumped down into the trench, kicked a dead Jap out of his way, and shook Captain Orr's hand. "How'd you do it?"

"Well, sir, um, actually these two soldiers from the recon platoon took the bunker, and the rest of us followed them up the hill."

Colonel Smith blinked as he turned to Bannon and Longtree. "How the hell'd you do it?"

"Waal," Bannon drawled, "we just sort of snuck up on 'em, sir."

Longtree nodded. "Yeah, we followed their tracks back here and tossed a few hand grenades at them."

"Very good work." Colonel Smith shook both their hands. "You can be sure I'll tell Colonel Stockton. All right, everybody, dig in and stay put until I find out where we go from here!"

Colonel Smith climbed out of the trench with the help of one of his aides. Captain Orr looked at Bannon and Longtree. "You heard him—dig in. And don't disobey any more orders."

"Yes, sir."

"And, Bannon, get yourself a helmet from someplace."

"Yes, sir."

Bannon and Longtree walked away with the recon platoon, joining the other GIs deploying around the bunker. Captain Orr watched them and wondered what to do about the insubordination, but nothing sensible came to mind. *Fuck it,* he thought. *The main thing is that we've got that damned bunker.*

Major Uchikoshi flew into a rage when he learned that Bunker Twenty-eight had been taken by the Americans, but he calmed down sat on the floor, wondering what possibly could have gone wrong. The strange part of it was that the bunker hadn't reported itself in danger or under attack. Another bunker had reported seeing Bunker Twenty-eight get blown up, and then efforts to reoccupy it had ended when Americans swarmed over the position. Somehow the Americans had taken the bunker by surprise. That must not be permitted to happen again.

"Captain Yatsu!"

"Yes, sir!"

Captain Yatsu, a short officer with a thick black handlebar mustache, approached Major Uchikoshi.

"Captain Yatsu, I want lookouts posted around all our bunkers twenty-four hours a day, and they will withdraw to the bunkers only when forced to do so by American fire."

"Yes, sir."

Captain Yatsu saluted and marched to the radio to pass along the order. Major Uchikoshi looked down at his map and made an *X* over Bunker Twenty-eight. He tried to figure out what the Americans would do next. Probably they'd try to use Bunker Twenty-eight as a staging area for assaults on nearby bunkers. If Major Uchikoshi had more troops, he could counterattack and drive the Americans away, but he had no other troops, little ammunition, and little food. In the distance he could hear machine guns, rifles, and mortars. The Americans were probing for more bunkers. Major Uchikoshi wondered how long it would take for the Americans to locate all the bunkers on the Gifu Line.

TEN . . .

George Company and the recon platoon dug in around the captured bunker as fighting raged in the hills all around them. Despite the shelling and bombing, the regiment made no more progress than the Second Battalion had made the day before. American soldiers were pinned down by machine-gun fire whenever they tried to advance. The shelling and bombing had wrecked the jungle but had little effect on the Japanese soldiers in their bunkers. By late afternoon Colonel Stockton broke off the attack and reported to General Patch that only one bunker had been knocked out.

"Well," said General Patch, "I don't think you need any more air or artillery support at this point, and I don't even think more troops would do any good. What you've got to do is find out what the hell you've got in front of you there, and I suggest that's what you devote your main effort to tomorrow. It should be obvious that you're not going to take that Jap position by assault."

"Yes, sir. I'll find out what's there. It may take a few days, but I'll find out what I need to know."

Colonel Stockton was embarrassed when he hung up the phone. He hated to call superior officers to report he'd failed to take an objective. It made him look bad. Do that too many times and they started to see you as a loser. When it came time to award general's stars, they passed you over.

Colonel Stockton went to work with his maps, puffing his pipe, trying to figure out the most efficient method of reconnoitering the Japanese fortifications. He continued working through chowtime, and as night came to Guadalcanal, Lieutenant Harper brought him a cup of coffee and plate of fried Spam and dehydrated potatoes. By eight o'clock in the evening Colonel Stockton had his plan pretty well worked out. The next morning the Third Battalion would relieve the Second Battalion, which would be placed in reserve. The Third Battalion would make a frontal attack on the fortifications, just like the one that day, but only to attract the Japs' fire and attention, while the First Battalion sent out company-size patrols to probe for the flanks of the Japanese position. The companies would be sent out in wide arcs until they worked around the fortifications. Sooner or later they'd have to find the flanks. The Japs had something big up there, but it had to end someplace.

The recon platoon was dug in near the captured Japanese bunker. It was pitch black on that little hill. Guards had been posted and the recon platoon was sacked out for the night.

Bannon smoked a cigarette with his head covered by his poncho so the burning end of his cigarette couldn't be seen. He was running the day's events over in his mind, trying to pick out his mistakes and analyze them so they wouldn't happen again. He wanted to be as good as Butsko, and Butsko seldom made mistakes. Butsko usually knew what he was doing, and it wasn't because he was unusually intelligent but because Butsko had a lot of experience and learned from it. Some people never learn anything from their experience. They're as dumb today as they were ten years ago. Men like that who came to the recon platoon never lasted very long, but all the old-timers were pretty sharp. Even Homer Gladley knew what to do when the shit hit the fan. But Bannon had made a mistake that day, and it had almost been fatal for him and Longtree. He should never had tried to hold that bunker against all the Japs in the area. It was poor judgment. If Butsko were around, he'd kick Bannon right in the ass and Bannon would be limping around for a few days.

Bannon couldn't remember any more serious mistakes. He

finished his cigarette, put it out, and pulled the poncho off his head, taking a deep breath of fresh air. Nearby, Nutsy Gafooley was on his back, snoring, his mouth open so wide that Bannon could drop a baseball inside.

Bannon was exhausted. He rolled onto his side and drifted off to sleep.

A few foxholes away Private DelFranco sat with his legs crossed, looking up at the sky. He wasn't too tired because he hadn't done much that day. He'd wanted to prove he was a good soldier, but when they had attacked the bunker the Japs ran away without putting up much of a fight.

Tomorrow I'll show them, DelFranco thought. *I may not be as big as the others, but I can shoot as well as any of them. Bannon'll realize I'm not the fuck-up he thinks I am.*

DelFranco was mad at himself. Living with other men in the middle of a war had made him more aware of his shortcomings. He realized he'd been too wishy-washy all his life, never committing himself to anything, always fooling around on the fringes of things. No wonder nobody liked him. No wonder he didn't have the courage to become a priest. He had never even had the courage to ask girls to go out on dates with him. He was disgusting.

But now he was resolved to take a stand on something. He was in the Army on Guadalcanal and he was going to be a good soldier or die in the attempt. Better to be dead than be a Caspar Milquetoast for the rest of your life. Saint Thomas Aquinas had said there were such things as just wars, and this war surely was just. Cardinal Spellman and all the other Church bigwigs had sanctioned it. There was nothing to hold him back. He'd just go all out and win himself a medal, and if he died, well, he was a Catholic in good standing and he believed in eternal life.

I'll show them all, he thought. *When this war's over, I'll become a priest for sure. Maybe I'll come back in the Army and become a chaplain. Bannon and all the others can see me and get their tickets punched. What a laugh that'll be.*

He lay on his back and looked at the stars glittering in the heavens, thinking of how wonderful it would be to be an officer and a chaplain in the US Army, with a few medals on his jacket to show he was as tough and resolute as the next man.

Betty Crawford got off the ward a little late that night and went directly to the nurses' mess hall for chow. A lot of other nurses were there, having finished duty late also, and she got in line with them, picking up an aluminum tray and having it filled with food by the cooks on the line. She passed through the line and sat at a long table with several other nurses whom she knew. The other nurses chattered about patients, doctors, and their love lives, but Betty was silent, because she was tired and irritable. Every day brought more wounded soldiers from Guadalcanal and New Guinea. There was so much work to do.

Nurse Dorothy Cochrane, wearing tan slacks and a tan shirt, with rouge on her cheeks and lipstick on her mouth, placed her tray of food opposite Betty Crawford's and sat down.

"Boy, look at you," said Nurse Gleason. "Got a date?"

Dorothy Cochrane nodded, chewing food quickly.

"Really? Who're you going out with?"

"None of your business," Dorothy said, her mouth half full of food.

"Aw, come on, tell us," said Nurse Gleason.

"Yeah, what's the big secret?" said another nurse.

"Is he so ugly you're ashamed to say who he is?" asked someone else.

Dorothy Cochrane was an extremely vain young lady, and that last remark ticked her off. "He's not ugly at all," she said, raising her nose in the air. "In fact he's quite good-looking."

"Then who is he?"

Dorothy Cochrane fluttered her long eyelashes. "Frankie La Barbara."

"Wow!" said one of the nurses. "He really is a dish."

"I suppose you could say that," Dorothy said nonchalantly, raising a forkful of beef stew to her heart-shaped mouth.

Nurse Gleason sighed. "I went out with him a few times. He's a lot of fun, but don't ever fall in love with him, because the only person he'll ever love is himself."

"People can change," Dorothy Cochrane said, because she was younger than the others and thought her femininity could conquer any man.

"They really don't change that much," said Nurse Gleason.

"We'll see about that," Dorothy Cochrane said.

"He sure is a handsome man," another nurse said. "I wish he'd ask me out sometime."

Betty Crawford was becoming increasingly irritated by the conversation going on around her, because she hated Frankie La Barbara. "I think he's loathsome," she said. "I don't understand what all you women see in him. He's an obvious liar and he's dumb."

"But he's got a body like Adonis," Nurse Gleason replied, a faraway tone in her voice.

"I still think he's loathsome."

"Well," said Dorothy Cochrane, snotty as hell, "if he'd never asked me out, I might say he was loathsome too."

Betty Crawford wanted to leap across the table and grab Dorothy by the throat, but instead she sat still and ate slowly, trying not to show that she was raging mad. *There's no way to win arguments like this,* she thought. *I'll just ignore that remark.*

But she couldn't ignore it. Inwardly she was furious. She thought of Frankie La Barbara with his cocky wise-guy smile. *He's screwing every nurse he can get his hands on,* she thought, *and evidently he's not having much trouble getting his hands on them. If he can do that, he mustn't be that sick. In fact, he doesn't look sick at all. He's probably paying off some personnel clerk someplace to keep him here, but why should he lounge around while other men are fighting for their lives at the front?*

I'm going to look into this, Betty Crawford promised herself. *I think it's time that bastard was returned to duty.*

ELEVEN . . .

On December 27 and 28, Colonel Stockton's wide-ranging network of patrols were unable to find the enemy's flanks or any gaps in his fortifications. Colonel Stockton was beginning to think he was facing a circular type of defense rather than a line. More patrolling would be required to determine its configuration, but patrolling was taking too much time. Yet, he didn't dare attack again, because the cost in men was too high. He'd have to keep patrolling.

The next morning the recon platoon moved out bright and early as part of the massive patrolling operation. Beginning at Hill Twenty-nine, they were to proceed south until they made contact with the enemy, but by noon they'd advanced 1,500 yards and hadn't encountered any Japs. They stopped for a break, and Longtree, restless as always, snooped around in the jungle ahead of them. In a small clearing he found the fresh tracks of a big wild boar and thought of pork chops and roast ham.

He walked back to Bannon and kneeled beside him. Bannon opened an eye. "You find anything?"

"No traces of Japs, but I found the fresh tracks of a big wild pig."

"How fresh?"

"Very fresh. He was here just before we got here."

"Then he's probably not too far away."

"He's probably looking at us right now. We could roast the son of a bitch over an open fire and have a feast."

Bannon salivated at the thought of fresh meat cooked over an open fire. "Take a few men with you and go after the pig. The rest of us will keep going south. We'll meet here at fifteen hundred hours."

"It'd be easier for me if I went alone."

"You'll need somebody with you in case you get in trouble."

"I never get in trouble when I'm alone."

"Do what you wanna do, but be here at fifteen hundred hours."

Longtree walked into the jungle and disappeared. He hadn't hunted since he was a civilian, and now he was alone, tracking down a wild animal like an Apache brave again. The tracks were so fresh that Longtree could smell the boar. A couple of times he spotted him through the thick foliage, but the boar ran away. Longtree stayed on his tracks.

A half hour later Longtree continued to track the wild boar. Sooner or later the boar would have to stop, and then Longtree would creep up and kill him with his bayonet, because a shot might attract Japs. The tracks led up a hill, and Longtree followed them. The sun was hot and the jungle sweltered in the heat, but Longtree crept along like a wild animal himself, glancing around, sniffing the air, having a wonderful time.

He heard a grunt and stopped. Pricking up his ears, he perceived a chomping, slurping sound ahead of him. Silently, Longtree got down on his belly and crawled forward. He peered through the bushes and spotted the brownish-red hide of the wild boar. It was eating grass. Longtree laid his rifle down and drew his bayonet. He slithered forward, his mouth dry, his eyes fixed on the hairy snorting beast. Longtree's boredom was gone; he felt keen and alive, only a few feet from his quarry.

The boar finished eating and raised its head. Longtree sprang at it, wrapping his powerful arm around the boar's thick neck, plunging his bayonet into the boar's belly. The boar squealed and struggled as Longtree ripped his bayonet across the leather flesh and the boar's guts spilled out. Longtree pulled out his bayonet, aimed for the boar's heart, and struck it with all his strength. The boar stopped struggling and blood gushed out when Longtree withdrew the bayonet.

The animal lay still on the ground, and Longtree felt triumphant. He wanted to do an Apache dance to celebrate the successful hunt, but this wasn't Arizona and there might be Japs around. He bent over the boar to gut and dress it so it wouldn't weigh so much on the trip back, and to keep the meat tasting sweet.

He pulled out the boar's ropy guts and cut them away with his bayonet. Then he sliced deeper into the boar's body cavity and tore out its heart, lungs, liver, and kidneys. He sliced the boar's throat so its blood would drain; when he was finished, the beast would be ready to be skinned and put over the fire.

Leaning against a tree, Longtree decided to have a smoke before returning to the rendezvous spot. He took out a cigarette and lit it up, feeling happy and satisfied with himself. It was almost as if he'd stepped out of the war for a little while. The military bullshit got on his nerves sometimes, but he put up with it as best he could. Someday, if he was lucky, he'd be back in Arizona with his people, and if he wasn't lucky, then he'd die like an Apache warrior: with his rifle in his hands, facing the enemy, and fighting hard.

He heard voices and his ears twitched. He heard them again; they were Japanese voices. Dropping low, he dragged the boar underneath a bush, then covered the guts and blood with leaves. He joined the boar in the bush and lay still as flies buzzed around the dead animal.

He couldn't see the Japs, but they were coming closer and sounded like a patrol. They passed by him, heading up the hill, and he wondered where they were going. Did they have a machine-gun nest up there? If they did, it was something Colonel Stockton ought to know.

Longtree looked at his watch. He still had over an hour until 1500 hours. He could see where the Japs were going, and then, if he hurried, he'd be able to meet Bannon and pass on the information. Taking an old shirt and some rope from his pack, he wrapped the boar in the shirt, trussed it with the rope, and strung it up so that other wild animals couldn't get to him.

Longtree picked up his rifle and slipped through the jungle in the direction of the voices he'd heard. He picked up their tracks and followed them up the hill. Moving as quickly as a cat, he made better time than they did and soon heard their voices again. He realized they were moving slowly, and when they spoke their voices didn't sound too loud. He angled to the side and came abreast of them.

Crouching in the leaves, he watched them pass. There were eight of them, all carrying burlap bags filled with something that didn't appear too heavy. They were skinny as scarecrows, their cheeks hollow and eyes burning. If Longtree had had the First Squad with him he could have wiped out all those Japs in about a minute.

He followed them, glancing around, trying to make certain no one was observing him. He neared the crest of the hill and heard shouts above him. It sounded like many Japs were up there. He slowed down and crawled froward on his belly, passing through the thickest part of the jungle, because it provided the best concealment.

Finally he saw figures moving in the foliage near the top of the hill. He spotted the small rectangular hole of a machine-gun bunker. Japs upended the burlap bags and grass fell out. *What the hell are they doing with the grass?* Longtree wondered. *Maybe they're stuffing mattresses with it.*

He thought he should see if there were any more machine-gun bunkers on top of the hill, so he roved through the jungle, searching around. He found another machine-gun bunker about a third of the way around the crest of the hill, but that was all. Now he could pick up his pig and go back.

Bannon looked at his watch. It was 1500 hours and Longtree still hadn't come back yet. The recon platoon lay around, smoking cigarettes, sipping water from their canteens, shooting the shit. They'd gone as far south as they could and hadn't encountered any Japanese positions. Bannon wondered if anything had happened to Longtree. He hoped Longtree had caught the pig, because a pork chop would be awfully nice after all the beans and crackers they'd been eating.

At 1515 Longtree emerged from the jungle, carrying the pig on his back. The GIs crowded around him, examining the dead animal. Longtree threw the pig down at Bannon's feet.

"Here it is."

"Took you long enough."

"I got sidetracked by a Jap patrol, but they led me to two Jap machine-gun nests."

Bannon sat up. "Where?"

Longtree pointed. "Over that way."

"Show me on the map."

Bannon took out the map and unfolded it. Longtree knelt beside him and tried to figure out where he'd been. Finally he placed his forefinger on the map. "Here."

"That's Hill Twenty-seven. I don't think any patrols have been out there yet. Let's go back and tell the colonel."

Bannon rounded up the recon platoon and told them they were heading back to Company G. The men moved out eagerly, their stomachs growling, their heads filled with visions of delicious roasted meat.

The recon platoon arrived back at their camp in an hour and a half, and the first thing Bannon did was report to Captain Orr. Captain Orr wrote down the information and delivered it in person to Colonel Smith, who carried it to Colonel Stockton at Regimental Headquarters.

Colonel Stockton sat at his desk, studied his map, and realized that an important discovery had been made. He hadn't known there were Japanese bunkers on Hill Twenty-seven, and the Japs on Hill Twenty-seven didn't know they'd been spotted. That meant they wouldn't expect an attack, especially a surprise attack at the crack of dawn. With Hill Twenty-seven in his possession, he'd have a good observation post from which to view adjacent hills, and if he could get some artillery up there, he'd be able to shell other bunkers as they were located.

Colonel Smith sat in front of the desk and studied Colonel Stockton, who was bent over the map, drawing lines with his pencil, figuring out the most economical way to assault Hill Twenty-seven. Colonel Stockton realized he wouldn't be able to attack the next morning, because the preparations would take too much time, but the next day, which was New Year's Day, should be right.

Colonel Stockton looked up from his desk. "This is good information," he told Colonel Smith. "Your men have done a fine job."

"They're your men, sir. The recon platoon had the patrol that scouted Hill Twenty-seven. They were someplace where they shouldn't have been, but I guess it doesn't matter."

"They weren't lost, were they?"

"I asked Bannon about it, but his answer was kind of hazy. I guess he was curious about the hill and sent somebody up to check it out."

"Yes, well, I've learned that it's not a good idea to keep the recon platoon on too short a leash. Give them room to maneuver and they'll be all right. They know what to do."

"They came back with a pig, sir."

"A pig?"

"Yes, sir. A wild boar. They hunted it down. I guess they're gonna eat it."

Colonel Stockton grinned. "What a crazy bunch they are. I'd better get a pork chop out of this somehow."

"Yes, sir. I'll have it sent you you by special messenger—after I get mine."

Colonel Smith departed for the Second Battalion, leaving Colonel Stockton alone with his map. Colonel Stockton puffed his pipe and felt fine, because at least he'd be able to tell General Patch that he'd found two more machine-gun nests. Although he didn't have a clear picture of the Jap fortifications in front of him, at least he could show General Patch that he was making progress.

Colonel Stockton bent over the map, planning his assault on Hill Twenty-seven. The best way would be to take it by surprise first thing in the morning, after climbing the hill during the night. The recon platoon would lead the way, since they had found the hill and knew what was up there. The Second Battalion would follow the recon platoon up the south face of the hill, and at the same time the First Battalion would conduct a wide envelopment, hitting the Japs from the west. He set H-Hour for 0630 hours on January first. The capture of Hill Twenty-seven would be a good way to start the New Year.

Longtree supervised the cooking of the wild boar. He was assisted by Nutsy Gafooley, who had considerable experience in open-air cuisine. They'd set up a spit over a fire pit, and the pig roasted over the flames, its skin crackling, filling the air with a marvelous odor.

All the men of the recon platoon were gathered around the pig, but none stared at it as ardently as Homer Gladley, the recon platoon's chowhound. His eyes bugged out of his head and his tongue hung out his mouth as his stomach rumbled.

"Ain't it done yet, Chief?" he asked Longtree. "Looks done to me."

"Just a few more minutes. Keep your shirt on."

Homer didn't think he could wait. He felt like diving onto the sizzling animal and biting its ass off. He licked his chops and shifted from foot to foot, nearly fainting from the fragrance wafting toward his mostrils. He held his mess kit in his right hand and his knife in his left hand. He thought he'd die if he didn't get some of that pig soon.

Finally, Longtree and Nutsy Gafooley decided the pig was ready. They lifted the spit off its posts and dropped the animal onto a bed of wide coconut palm leaves. When the animal landed, it broke apart and marvelous new fragrances filled the air.

"All right, boys," Longtree said, "dig in."

The men attacked the pig with their bayonets, and the first one to slice off a slab of meat was Homer Gladley, who stuffed it into his mouth, burned his tongue, and nearly choked to death, but he chewed like a wild man as he cut off another piece for himself.

"Don't make a hog out of yourself, Homer," Bannon said. "Leave something for the rest of us."

Homer cut off a few more slices and then retreated to a quiet spot to eat. He filled his mouth with roast pork and had orgasms of the tongue and throat, feeling the meat strengthen him and make him happy. It was almost as good as the pork his mama used to make back in Nebraska. It was the kind of meal that made life worthwhile.

Morris Shilansky sat down nearby with his plateful, picked up a slice with his fingers, and bit off half of it.

"Hey, Shilansky," Homer Gladley said, his mouth full, "I thought Jews weren't supposed to eat pork."

"I eat what I wanna eat," Shilansky said, chomping away.

Bannon reserved some choice slices for Colonel Stockton, Colonel Smith, and Sergeant Major Ramsay. Nutsy Gafooley delivered the food for Colonel Smith, and Bannon carried the rest through the jungle to Regimental Headquarters.

Sergeant Major Ramsay looked up from correspondence and requisitions as Bannon entered the orderly room, carrying platters of roast pig.

Bannon placed one of the platters on Ramsay's desk. "This is for you. The rest's for Colonel Stockton. Can I bring it in to him?"

"Lemme check." Ramsay picked up the phone, mumbled a few words into it, listened, and hung up. "Go ahead."

Bannon entered the colonel's office, the odor of the meat filling the tiny enclosure.

"Well," said Colonel Stockton, looking up from his map, "what have we here?"

"A little roast pork, sir."

"Set it down over here, boy."

Bannon placed it on the desk.

"Have a seat."

"Yes, sir."

Bannon sat on one of the chairs, and Colonel Stockton took his knife and fork out of a drawer, along with his canteen.

"Sure smells good," the colonel said, slicing into the meat. "How'd you get it?"

"One of my men snuck up on it and killed it with his bayonet."

"Sounds like quite a feat."

"He's an Indian, sir. He's real good at that kind of thing."

"Oh, yes, the Apache Indian. What's his name?"

"Longtree, sir."

Colonel Stockton placed a chunk of the meat into his mouth and chewed, rolling his eyes. "This is marvelous—simply marvelous." He continued eating, making sounds of satisfaction. When he finished he drank some water, then stuffed and filled his pipe.

"That's real nice work you did today," he said, puffing the pipe. "I'm not talking about the roast pork; I'm talking about Hill Twenty-seven. Butsko couldn't have done better."

"Oh, I think Butsko could've done a lot better, sir."

"Well, you're doing all right yourself. How's my recon platoon?"

"Okay, sir."

"What do you think of Colonel Smith?"

"He's a good officer."

"What about Captain Orr."

"A tough son of a gun."

"Good. I'm glad you're getting along well. Day after tomorrow you're gonna lead the attack on Hill Twenty-seven. Well, not you personally, but the whole recon platoon. We'll crack that Jap stronghold up there wide open. You'll go up the hill at night and take them by surprise at daybreak. Shouldn't be too much trouble. What do you think?"

"I don't know, sir. We'll find out when we get there, I guess."

"Yes, of course." Colonel Stockton grunted. He scratched his nose, feeling ill at ease with Bannon, because Bannon was so obviously ill at ease with him. Bannon was afraid of officers. Butsko wasn't afraid of officers. Butsko could even help plan operations.

"Well," Colonel Stockton said, "thanks for the chow. Good luck on the assault. Just do what you've been doing and you'll be all right."

Bannon knew he was being told to hit the road. He stood and saluted. "Yes, sir." Then he did an about-face and marched out of the office.

TWELVE . . .

The next day the regiment got organized for the assault on Hill Twenty-seven. Ammunition was brought to the front, and the line of march was established. Colonel Stockton's plans were discussed down through the echelons, and by mid-afternoon everybody knew what he was supposed to do. Then everyone had to wait, because they wouldn't move out until after dark.

The men cleaned their weapns and sharpened their bayonets. Some tried to sleep, but few could doze off; the tension and expectation were too much. There was always another hill to take, and then another valley, and then a river, and then another hill. The war just went on and on. There was no escape except in a pine box, and nobody wanted that kind of escape. They didn't even want to think about it.

Bannon sat against a tree and blew a plume of smoke into the air. The attack in the morning seemed like it wouldn't be too difficult, but anything could go wrong. Maybe there were machine-gun nests on that hill that Longtree hadn't seen. What if the Japs spotted them moving into position during the night?

If I'm lucky, I'll get my million-dollar wound, Bannon thought. *Just enough to send me back to the States, but not enough to fuck me up too much. But with my luck I'll probably get shot right in the head, and that'll be the end of me.*

Mail was delivered to Betty Crawford's station in the early afternoon, and she thought she'd pass it out right away, because she knew how important mail was to the wounded GIs. She glanced through the stack as she carried it out into the corridor, and on the bottom she was surprised to see a letter for Master Sergeant John Butsko. As far as she knew, this was the first letter Butsko had received since he'd been in the hospital.

The letter was mangled and dirty. According to the scribbling, it had been sent to Guadalcanal and then forwarded to New Caledonia. She figured it had been up on the front lines.

It was mailed from somebody named Dorothy Butsko, who lived in Hawaii. *Who is that?* Betty wondered. *His mother? His sister? His wife?* She passed the letters out to the men lying in bed, then went outside and gave letters to the men playing checkers, cards, and other games. Butsko was sitting alone under a tree, smoking a cigarette and reading a military manual.

"Sergeant Butsko!" she said as she approached. "I have a letter for you."

She handed him the letter. He looked at the return address in the upper left hand corner and groaned.

"Bad news?" she asked.

"Yup."

"How do you know if you haven't even opened it up yet?"

"Because it's from my wife, and she's always bad news."

Butsko grunted and tore open the letter. Betty walked away, wondering what Butsko's problem was with his wife. Somehow she couldn't imagine him as a married man living in a house with a wife and kids. She could only see him living in a barrack or a tent, cursing and giving orders, smoking his unhealthy cigarettes.

When she was close to the building she paused and casually looked around as if she were enjoying the view. Actually she wanted to get another look at Butsko. She saw him reading the letter, and he didn't appear happy.

After nightfall the Twenty-third Infantry Regiment moved out toward Hill Twenty-seven. There were sixteen companies in the regiment, with over a hundred men and officers in each company, so that added up to a lot of men traveling through the darkness with equipment and ammunition.

Some companies got lost, and other companies fell out of

radio contact. A few companies dropped behind and other companies moved too quickly. It was a big mess, but no different from any other major troop movement at night in difficult terrain.

Finally around midnight all the units were in position at the base of the hill. It was too early to advance, so everybody had to stop. The men sat around the jungle and weren't permitted to smoke. Some slept but most were too keyed up. The hours passed slowly and everybody had too much time to think. Then, at two o'clock in the morning, the order came to ascend the hill. The men got up, formed columns, and moved out. Their officers and noncoms urged them to be quiet, so they wouldn't alert the Japs, but it was difficult to be quiet in the thick, dark jungle, and there were stretches of steep, rocky slopes where men lost their footing and dropped equipment.

The recon platoon climbed the side of the hill that Longtree had been on the day before yesterday. Longtree led the way, trying to pick out familiar terrain details in the darkness, and behind the recon platoon came Company G, with Captain Orr limping forward with his men. At any moment they expected the Japs to open fire on them, but gradually they neared the crest of the hill and no Japs spotted them.

Now it was time to wait again. Exhausted, the men collapsed onto the ground, and this time nearly every one fell asleep. They and George Company were among the first units to reach the attack line, and the other units had to get into position. The attack was set for 0630 hours, shortly after dawn. The soldiers looked up at the sky and saw clouds obscuring the moon and stars. They hoped it wouldn't rain. It was hell to fight in the rain.

The wind picked up, and by 0600 hours the clouds had been blown from the sky. They could see the moon and the heavens glittering with stars. A faint glow appeared on the horizon; the sun was coming up. Officers and NCOs woke their men up and told them to get ready. Skirmish lines were established and the men checked their weapons and equipment. The officers glanced at their watches, waiting for the hands to reach 0630 hours.

The recon platoon stood around glumly as the top of the sun appeared over the trees, casting a golden glow onto their faces. They were grim, filthy, unshaven. They hadn't had breakfast and some had to take a shit, but there was no time. Their mouths tasted terrible. Some had trenchfoot. A few had a touch of malaria. But you had to forget about all those things when you attacked.

All the synchronized watches finally reached 0630 hours. In low voices the officers told the men to advance. The GIs moved quickly through the jungle, because they wanted to hit the Japs before the Japs knew what was happening. Bannon held his rifle in front of him, to keep branches and leaves from striking out his eyes, while glancing at the ground to make sure he wouldn't trip over anything or fall into a hole. The time for silence was over. The regiment sounded like a stampeding herd of cattle as it drew the noose around the top of the hill.

"Move it out!" yelled Captain Orr. *"Dress right and cover down! Let's hit 'em!"*

The sun was a red copper ball above the trees as Bannon and the recon platoon exploded out of the jungle and into the clearing. The Japanese soldiers were sleeping in the open around their bunker, and they jumped up in alarm, still groggy from sleep, reaching for their rifles and trying to retreat quickly.

They didn't have a chance. The GIs overwhelmed them before the Japs knew what was happening. The GIs fired their rifles from the waist, cutting down the fleeing Japs, and their screams of pain and alarm filled the air. Then the GIs got in close and went to work with their bayonets.

The remaining Japs realized now that they couldn't get away, and all they could do was stand and fight for their Emperor. They turned around and raised their rifles and bayonets with bony, wizened arms.

"Banzai!" one of the shouted. *"Tenno heika banzai!"*

"Banzai!" the others replied.

Bannon butted one of them in the face, stabbed another in the stomach, and slashed at a third, but that Jap blocked the blow with the barrel of his rifle and tried to kick Bannon in the balls. Bannon twisted to the side, receiving the kick on his outer thigh, and then he shot his rifle butt at the Jap's face, but the Jap ducked. Bannon's forward motion sent him crashing and they both fell to the ground, clawing at each other's face, trying to grab each other's throat, punching and kicking and kneeing.

They rolled over on the ground, their faces only inches apart, and Bannon could see the Jap's sunken cheeks and hollow eyes. Bannon punched the Jap in the stomach and was rocked by a punch in the mouth from the Jap, then each of them grabbed the other's throat and squeezed.

Bannon felt himself being suffocated, but he pressed his thumbs on the Jap's throat with all his strength. Hatred blazed out of the Jap's eyes as he coughed and gagged, trying to strangle Bannon, who thought he would black out at any moment. Bannon saw the specter of death in front of him and made one last supreme effort, tightening his fingers around the Jap's throat. Suddenly the Jap's fingers loosed around Bannon's throat. Bannon squeezed harder and the Jap's eyes rolled up into his head. The Jap went limp, and Bannon continued to squeeze, to make sure the Jap wasn't playing possum. Then Bannon jumped up, picked up his rifle and bayonet, and ran the Jap through.

Private DelFranco ran into the clearing like a madman, eager to kill Japs and prove himself a man. He found himself facing a Japanese soldier about the same size as he. DelFranco had been anxious to fight and kill, but now that he was face-to-face with a Jap, his mind went blank. He didn't know what to do first, and when he was aware that he didn't know what to do, he became terrified.

The Jap knew what to do and he did it, thrusting his rifle and bayonet at DelFranco's heart. Instinctively, DelFranco ducked out of the way. The Jap looked down at him, readjusted his aim, and the Jap charged him, holding his rifle and bayonet parallel to the ground.

DelFranco was so scared he nearly fainted, then realized he'd left his rifle and bayonet lying on the ground. He saw the Jap's rifle and bayonet streaking toward his heart, and all he could do was dive on it, clutching the barrel and stock of the Jap's rifle in his hands, deflecting the blow.

The Jap tried to pull his rifle away from DelFranco's grasp, but DelFranco didn't dare let it go. He held on in a mad frenzy as the Jap tugged and yanked, and then the frustrated Jap tried to kick DelFranco in the balls, so DelFranco let go of the Jap's rifle and jumped backward to avoid the blow.

Now DelFranco was unarmed and vulnerable again as the Jap stalked him. All around them men stabbed each other with bayonets and bashed each other in the face. DelFranco wanted to run away, but the Jap would stab him in the back. He didn't know whether to shit or go blind. *My God, I'm gonna die,* he thought.

The Jap lunged, and DelFranco dodged out of the way. The Jap lunged again, and this time when DelFranco dodged he saw a Japanese Arisaka rifle lying on the ground. He picked it up and got ready, and when the Jap lunged again, he managed to parry the blow just the way they'd taught him in basic training at Fort Cambell, Kentucky. The Jap feinted with his rifle and bayonet, suckering DelFranco into a parry that left DelFranco wide open. The Jap lunged again and DelFranco hopped out of the way, then slashed down at the Jap with his own rifle and bayonet.

The blade of his bayonet caught the Jap on the neck and sliced down to his collarbone. Blood gushed out, and DelFranco looked at it, astonished. The flow of blood to the Jap's brain was diminished, and the Jap blacked out, falling at DelFranco's feet. DelFranco looked down and couldn't believe his eyes. *How did I do that?*

The Jap stirred. DelFranco figured he'd better finish him off. He raised his rifle and bayonet and harpooned him through the chest; then, when he tried to pull out, the bayonet wouldn't budge, because it was firmly lodged in the Jap's ribs. DelFranco remembered that you were supposed to shoot your way loose when that happened, so he pulled the trigger and the Jap's chest exploded, sending blood, bone, and gristle flying through the air, much of it landing on DelFranco's uniform. DelFranco took a step backward, surveying the mutilated body of the Japanese soldier lying in front of him, the first man he'd ever killed in his life.

The dazed DelFranco would have been a sitting duck for a Jap just then, but the Japs had been overwhelmed in the first onslaught by the GIs. A few of them ran to their bunker, and Longtree ran after them, accompanied by Shilansky, Shaw, and Homer Gladley from the First Squad. They shot the Japs in the back, jumped into the trench, and charged into the bunker.

A few Japs were inside, and a volley of shots were fired from both sides. The GIs were moving quickly as they entered the bunker, making difficult targets, while the Japs were lying or kneeling on the floor. When the smoke cleared the three Japs were dead. One was a young lieutenant. Shaw and Homer Gladley were unscathed, but Shilansky had been shot in his upper left thigh and rolled around on the ground, howling in pain.

"Medic!"

Pfc. Blum entered the bunker with his bag of medicines and knelt beside Shilansky, cutting his pants away from the wound. Bannon and the rest of the platoon squeezed into the bunker to see what was going on as George and Easy Company swarmed over that part of the hill.

Suddenly the chatter of machine guns were heard. The bunker was being fired upon. GIs dived into the trench or hit the dirt where they were. It took a while for them to figure out that the bullets were coming from Hill Twenty-nine, but they didn't know exactly where the machine gun was.

Captain Orr crawled through the trench and into the bunker. *"Take cover and get ready for a counterattack!"*

The GIs loaded their weapons and got ready. The most likely time to get hit with a counterattack was right after you took something, when you were tired and low on ammunition. Japanese machine guns raked the bunker the GIs had just taken, and the GIs held their heads low, expecting the worst.

Captain Yatsu's face drained of color as the message came in on the radio. He swallowed hard and walked toward Major Uchikoshi, who sat cross-legged on the floor in front of his low desk, sipping a cup of weak tea.

"Sir," said Captain Yatsu, "bunkers Thirty-eight and Thirty-nine have been taken by the Americans!"

"What!"

"Bunkers Thirty-eight and . . ."

"I heard what you said!" Major Uchikoshi replied, jumping to his feet. He looked around frantically, because this was most unwelcome news. *"How did this happen? What went wrong?"*

"I don't know, sir."

Major Uchikoshi stomped to the radio, pushed the radio operator off his chair, and sat down.

"This is Major Uchikoshi calling Bunker Thirty-eight. Come in Bunker Thirty-eight. Do you read me? Over?"

"Up your ass with a ten inch meathook," came the reply in English.

Major Uchikoshi didn't speak English, but the voice told him Americans had captured the bunker. It was early in the morning; the Americans must have launched a sneak attack and taken the defenders by surprise. How had they taken them by surprise? He knew the answer. Bunkers Thirty-eight and Thirty-nine had never been attacked before and he didn't think the Americans knew where they were.

"Captain Yatsu!"

"Yes, sir!"

Major Uchikoshi stood up and walked toward Captain Yatsu, who expected to get the firing squad, although he was in no way responsible for what had happened.

"Captain Yatsu, I am hereby making you personally responsible for the security of our bunkers. We must be prepared for the Americans at all times. Evidently discipline became lax in Bunkers Thirty-eight and Thirty-nine. They saw no point in posting guards at night, because they didn't think the Americans knew where they were. That was stupid. There can be no more losses like these. Is that clear?"

"Yes, sir."

"Go to work on it."

Captain Yatsu sat at his desk to draft the order, and Major Uchikoshi paced back and forth in the bunker, his hands clasped behind his back. Now he'd lost four bunkers, and American patrols were constantly reconnoitering the Gifu Line, gathering new information about it every hour. Soon they'd have the bunkers pinpointed and their big attack would begin. Major Uchikoshi wished they'd attack and get it over with. The waiting and constant attrition, coupled with inadequate diet and little sleep, was driving him nuts. *They'll pay heavily for the Gifu when they come,* he thought. *The hills and valleys around here will be awash with American blood.*

If he had more men, he would have launched an instant counterattack to recapture those two lost bunkers, but he didn't have any men to spare. He lit a cigarette and sat at his desk again, sipping tea. Captain Yatsu's pen could be heard as he wrote the new orders on a piece of paper. The soldiers in the bunker sat at their machine guns, feeling dread over the loss of the two bunkers, trying not to look at each other, trying not to show their apprehension.

Butsko sat in the mess hall at the hospital, eating powdered eggs and Spam for breakfast. Men sat all around him, talking loudly, but he was lost in thought. The letter from his wife, Dolly, still disturbed him. She said she was worried about him, because he hadn't answered her last letter, which he'd torn up immediately after reading.

He hadn't heard from Dolly in over a year, and now he'd gotten two letters in two months. She said she still loved him and missed him, although when he'd last seen her they'd had a big fight and he'd punched her out because she was screwing other guys. He never thought he'd hear from her again. *Should I write her?* he wondered. *Oh, fuck it. What's over is over. No sense trying to get back what can never be.*

"Hiya, big Sarge!"

Butsko looked up and saw Frankie La Barbara wearing new green fatigues. He was grinning and rolling his shoulders, jumpy and wild, just like the old Frankie, the craziest son of a bitch in his platoon.

"I know you don't wanna talk to me," Frankie said, "but I just thought I'd come by to say so long. I'm going back to the front."

"Have a seat, Frankie. I'm not mad at you."

Frankie sat down. "Can't stay long." He looked at his watch. "Gotta leave in an hour."

"Say hello to the guys for me."

Frankie's mind wasn't on the guys. "I told them I'm still sick, but they won't believe me. Don't I look sick, Sarge?"

"You look okay to me."

"I still get dizzy spells. They say you never recover completely from malaria. I can't understand why they don't believe me, and I was paying off a couple guys in personnel too."

"Somebody must've got wise to you, kid. You're too fucking conspicuous. You gotta keep your head down and be calm."

"I'm gonna miss all these nurses," Frankie said, taking out a cigarette. "There's more pussy on this island than you can shake a stick at. You getting any, big Sarge?"

"Knock it off, willya, Frankie?"

"That's right. You don't like to talk about pussy. How come you don't like to talk about pussy? Don't you like to fuck, big Sarge?"

"I said knock it off, Frankie."

"Maybe I could break my legs," Frankie said. "Maybe I could climb on top of one of these buildings and jump off."

"You'd probably break your neck."

"That'd be even better. You want me to tell the guys anything for you?"

"I can't think of anything offhand."

Frankie puffed his cigarette and looked at his watch. "I'd better get going. Maybe I can get a blowjob before I leave. Take it easy, big Sarge. You want me to give you some names?"

"What kind of names?"

"The easiest fucks on the island. There's this nurse called Gleason . . ."

"Knock it off, Frankie."

Frankie grinned nervously. "Sorry, Sarge." He stood up and held out his hand. "I'll see you around like a doughnut."

Butsko shook his hand. "Go slow, Frankie. Watch your ass."

"You bet, Sarge."

Frankie walked away, bouncing up and down, snapping his fingers, looking everywhere, twitching his nose. Butsko shook his head and went back to his powdered eggs. He wished he could be like Frankie when it came to women, because Frankie didn't give a shit about them at all. He just fucked them and forgot them. He never fell in love. *My problem is that I fall in love with the bitches,* Butsko thought, *and once women find out you love them, they murder you.*

Butsko chewed the powdered eggs and took a bite of toast. *Maybe I'll write Dolly,* he thought. *It can't hurt nothing.*

THIRTEEN . . .

The men of the Twenty-third Infantry Regiment dug in on Hill Twenty-seven and wired their defense perimeter. Four seventy-five-millimeter pack howitzers were hauled up and fired for registration on the hills nearby. Colonel Stockton was jubilant about cracking the Gifu Line and reported his success to General Patch, who told him to press his attack.

Since the Second Battalion had been so successful on Hill Twenty-seven, Colonel Stockton decided to use it to assault Hill Twenty-nine the next morning after an artillery barrage. The First Battalion relieved the Second on Hill Twenty-seven and the Second moved into the foothills of Hill Twenty-nine, where they dug in. Artillery ringed the southern and eastern slopes of the hill and zeroed in on the summit. That took all day. After dinner the troops sacked out and no one had trouble sleeping, because they all were exhausted.

It seemed like they'd slept only a few hours before they had to get up again. It was dark and they ate C rations for breakfast as the artillery barrage began. The top of the hill flashed with the explosions and looked like a fireworks display, and the ground rumbled beneath their feet.

The barrage continued until it was light, and the troops lined up to make their assault. They were tired, grim-faced, and demoralized. The steady strain of fighting was getting to them. Many grumbled and said the regiment should be pulled off the line, because the men had been fighting so much.

The barrage stopped and the men moved up the hill. They'd only advanced a short distance when they came under scattered small-arms fire, and they all hit the dirt.

"Snipers!" somebody yelled.

The jungle became quiet as the men scanned the trees ahead of them, looking for the snipers. No one wanted to stand up and take the chance of getting a bullet in the face.

Colonel Smith called Captain Orr on the radio. "What the hell's the holdup out there!"

"Snipers, sir. We can't advance."

"What the hell do you mean, you can't advance?"

"The men won't advance against the snipers, sir."

"Oh, no?"

Colonel Smith threw the walkie-talkie to his runner and stood up. He was pissed off that the attack had been stopped before it had even started just because of a few goddamned snipers. He knew the men were afraid of snipers, but believed their fear was exaggerated. Those snipers weren't as accurate as the soldiers thought, and there usually weren't too many of them.

Colonel Smith trudged toward the front lines, followed by aides. He had a few shots of jungle juice in him and was determined to get the attack rolling again before Colonel Stockton called and screamed at him. Upon reaching the front line of the advance, he saw all the soldiers hugging the ground, hiding behind trees, cowering behind rocks.

"What the hell is this?" Colonel Smith shouted. *"It looks like a goddamned circle jerk!"*

Standing tall, he drew his Colt .45 and fired a shot in the air. *"Move out, you sons of bitches! What the hell you think this is!"*

The GIs looked the other way and made believe they didn't hear him.

Colonel Smith strutted to the front of the line and wandered around, firing his .45. The Jap lookouts for the bunkers on top of Hill Twenty-nine shot at Colonel Smith, but the bullets whistled harmlessly around him.

"You'd better get down, sir!" one of the GIs called out.

"Get down my ass! There ain't no reason to get down! You men get up on your feet and follow me!"

Nobody moved. The men pretended that they hadn't heard. Bannon buried his face in his arms and thought, *Fuck him. If he wants that hill so bad, let him take it himself.*

Colonel Smith kicked Nutsy Gafooley in the ass. *"On your feet, soldier!"*

Nutsy Gafooley acted as though nothing had happened. He just lay on the ground and thought of freight cars roaring over the Rockies.

Colonel Smith fired his .45 next to Nutsy Gafooley's ear and Nutsy jumped three feet off the ground, but when he landed he lay still again.

"The next shot's going right through your head, soldier!"

Nutsy jumped to his feet. Colonel Smith kicked Homer Gladley, and he got up too. Nutsy and Homer Gladley expected to get shot at any moment, but the Japanese bullets didn't even come close. They began to think Colonel Smith might be right.

"Get up, you sons of bitches! There ain't nothing to be afraid of!"

One by one the men stood. Colonel Smith lined them up and told them to move forward. The ragged skirmish line advanced up the hill.

"Marching fire!"

The soldiers raised their rifles to their shoulders and fired every third step, and bullets zinged into the jungle ahead. The Japanese soldiers weren't in the trees, as the men believed, and the Japanese fire really wasn't that accurate. They were only the lookouts for the bunkers on Hill Twenty-nine, and they fell back immediately.

"Keep moving! Dress right and cover down!"

The skirmish line advanced up the hill, and the Japanese lookouts continued to retreat. Colonel Smith watched Company G and the recon platoon disappear into the jungle, followed by the rest of the battalion. He jammed his .45 into his holster and puffed his cigar as he strolled back to his headquarters.

Meanwhile his battalion made its way up the hill. The first hundred yards were easy, but then they came within range of the machine guns at the top, and the battle got hot. The men dived to the ground and crawled toward the bunkers. After another fifty yards the fire became so intense that they couldn't move anymore.

Captain Orr, crawling behind his skirmish line, saw that his men couldn't proceed and knew it was pointless to order them to continue the attack. He called Colonel Smith on his walkie-talkie and told him so. Colonel Smith called Colonel Stockton, and Colonel Stockton called General Patch.

"What if I send you more men?" General Patch asked.

"More men won't do it. The machine guns will rip them apart. If we could see where the bastards are, we might be able to get them, but we can't fight what we can't see."

"Maybe they can be spotted from the air. Keep them busy and we'll try."

General Patch called General Roy Stanley Geiger, the commander of the Marine Air Corps detachment on Guadalcanal, nicknamed the Cactus Air Force bacause *Cactus* was the code name for Guadalcanal.

Geiger was stocky, broad-shouldered, and fifty-seven years old. He'd been awarded his wings at Pensacola in 1917, the forty-ninth naval aviator and the fifth Marine in history to earn them.

"What can I do for you?" Geiger said.

"I have some men pinned down by Jap machine-gun nests on Hill Twenty-nine, but we can't see where the Japs are. Do you think you can send up some spotters?"

"We'll try."

Geiger passed the order down, and soon a squadron of planes was warming up on the runway at Henderson Field. The pilots took off and flew west toward the Gifu Line.

Meanwhile the men of the Twenty-third Infantry Regiment maintained their positions and fired up the hill, keeping the Japs busy. The planes swooped down from the sky and made a run over Hill Twenty-nine. They saw the clouds of smoke indicating machine-gun fire, but the wind was blowing, so the gunsmoke dissipated quickly. The pilots couldn't see the machine-gun bunkers exactly, but they could estimate where they were and dropped yellow smoke bombs.

The smoke billowed into the air and could be seen clearly by the GIs, who opened fire at the jungle beneath the rising clouds. The entire regiment poured everything they had up the hill, their bullets and mortar rounds landing around the bunkers. This made it difficult for the Japs to fire, and the effects were realized immediately by the GIs.

"Forward!" shouted the officers and NCOs.

The GIs crawled up the hill in waves, covering each other, making slow but steady progress. By noon they were three-quarters of the way to the summit, making themselves clearer targets for the Japanese gunners. The attack slowed down and ground to a halt. Although the GIs were able to put pressure on the Japs, the Japs were well concealed and camouflaged, whereas the GIs weren't. The battle became a stalemate, with the GIs taking casualties, but not the Japs. Finally, at seven o'clock in the evening, Colonel Stockton broke off the attack. He ordered the regiment to stay exactly where it was; they'd jump off from that point in the morning.

Colonel Stockton called General Patch again. "Sir, they've stopped us cold, but we're pretty close to the summit. If you give me a good solid artillery barrage in the morning on the coordinates provided by General Geiger's boys, I think I can take the hill and everything up there."

"You got it," General Patch said.

Major Uchikoshi was infuriated by the American advance against Bunkers Forty-three, Forty-four, and Forty-five that day. Although the Americans didn't know it, those bunkers constituted the left flank of the Gifu Line, and if the Americans took that hill, the Gifu would be open to envelopment from the rear.

Major Uchikoshi dictated the following orders to Captain Yatsu:

(1) All bunkers will improve their camouflage so that they cannot be spotted from the air.
(2) The Americans can be expected to shell Bunkers Forty-three, Forty-four, and Forty-five in the morning; therefore the three mortars reserved for emergencies will be deployed at those bunkers and used to confuse the American effort.
(3) Additional rifle soldiers and machine guns will

be dispatched to those bunkers to strengthen their defense.

(4) If everything goes wrong and the Americans succeed in overrunning the positions, they will be counterattacked immediately by a detachment of riflemen formed from the defenders of the other bunkers.

(5) Captain Yatsu will personally lead the defense of bunkers Forty-three, Forty-four, and Forty-five.

Major Uchikoshi waited impatiently as Captain Yatsu wrote down the final order. When Captain Yatsu was finished, he looked up.

"Do you understand those orders?" Major Uchikoshi asked.

"Yes, sir."

"Do you have any questions?"

"No, sir."

"Good. Carry them out."

"Yes, sir."

Major Uchikoshi watched with narrowed eyes as Captain Yatsu dropped his equipment into his pack and closed the flap. Captain Yatsu hoisted the bag and thrust his arms through the shoulder straps.

"I'm ready to leave, sir," Captain Yatsu said.

"If the Americans take those bunkers, don't come back here."

"Yes, sir."

"You may go."

Captain Yatsu saluted. "Long live the Emperor!"

"Long live the Emperor!" Major Uchikoshi replied.

The Twenty-third Infantry Regiment posted guards and dug in on the side of Hill Twenty-seven. As darkness fell, all firing stopped and silence descended on the area. The men slept in their foxholes and Colonel Smith got rip-roaring drunk. He screamed at his subordinates, nearly set fire to his maps with his cigar, and finally went to bed, snoring loudly and forcing his aides to sleep as far away from him as they could.

The artillery barrage began just before dawn, waking everybody up. Big 105- and 155-millimeter cannons roared, plastering the hill with destruction but doing no harm to the Japanese soldiers in their bunkers. Captain Yatsu sat on a crate of machine-gun ammunition and ate some boiled grass for breakfast. He'd been constipated for three days, and his stomach felt as if it were filled with concrete. He was a little jittery, because he figured that day would be his last on earth. If the Americans didn't kill him, he'd commit hara-kira. That would be the only proper thing to do.

While the bombardment was taking place, the top military leaders of Japan were sitting down for a meeting at Imperial Headquarters in Tokyo. General Sugiyama chaired the meeting, which was to determine the facts of Guadalcanal. He began by inviting Colonel Tsuji to apprise them of latest developments on the beleaguered island.

The officers sat around a long wooden table, papers and pens in front of them. They wore dress uniforms, were well-fed, and Colonel Tsuji hated them all for their smug complacency. He rose to his feet resolved to tell them how bad things were for the Seventeenth Army.

He told them of hunger and ammunitions shortages. He described the valiant effort of the soldiers and the ruthless, nonstop onslaught of the Americans. He declared that the Seventeenth Army could not hold out much longer and that the soldiers must be either reinforced or withdrawn from the island. He painted the picture in the grimmest possible terms. Then he sat and folded his hands, waiting for the response of the leading military commanders in Japan. There was silence in the room for a few moments as the officers considered what Tsuji had said.

Admiral Fukudome, the chief of naval operations, was the first to speak. "Perhaps we should try some joint tactical map games before we reach a decision. That way we shall have a clearer picture of what to do."

"Games!" screamed Tsuji, going out of control. "It is the duty of the Navy to perform map games *before* emergencies arise! You all know the situation on Guadalcanal and yet you refuse to take action! I think all of you should resign!"

"Calm yourself!" said General Tojo, the prime minister of Japan and chief architect of the war.

Tojo was nicknamed The Razor, and he was nobody to mess with. Tsuji calmed himself down.

But Admiral Tomioka was insulted and didn't feel so calm. "What are you trying to say?" he screamed at Tsuji. "Are you trying to imply that naval commanders are incompetent?"

"Have you ever been to the front?" Tsuji retorted. "Do you know what's going on there?"

"How dare you talk to me that way!"

"Silence!" shouted Tojo.

Everybody shut up, because Tojo was the most powerful man in Japan, after the Emperor.

"I agree with Admiral Fukudome," Tojo said. "We should perform tactical war games to get a clearer picture of what is possible and what is not."

The officers adjourned to the big map table in the next room. On it were pieces of wood representing ships, soldiers, and airplanes. The officers moved the pieces of wood around, trying to predict what would happen if an effort was made to resupply Guadalcanal. At noon the decision was reached that less than one-fourth of supplies and troops would get through the American naval blockade of Guadalcanal.

"It is clear that we must withdraw," General Sugiyama said. He turned angrily to Admiral Nagano, top commander of the Japanese Imperial Navy. "You landed the Army without sufficient arms and food and then cut off the supply! It's like sending someone on a roof and then removing the ladder!"

"Well," replied Nagano, "how long can you expect us to provide reinforcements? Do you think our resources are inexhaustible? Why haven't you retaken Guadalcanal long ago? Where is the Army's fighting spirit?"

"We have plenty of fighting spirit!" General Sugiyama replied. "We need more men and supplies! We could have won long ago if we had *half* of what the Americans have! Up till now we've only received one percent!"

Colonel Joichiro Sanada had arrived from Rabaul only three days ago, where he'd conferred with the leading military commanders in the southwestern Pacific. "Every responsible commander in the Solomon Islands believes all troops should be withdrawn from Guadalcanal as soon as possible," he said. "Future military operations must not be jeopardized by continuing a campaign in which none of the front-line commanders has any confidence."

"No confidence?" asked Admiral Nagano. "Has the Army lost heart?"

"It has nothing to fight with," Colonel Sanada replied.

Colonel Tsuji felt himself going over the edge. "How can we continue to discuss this?" he demanded. "The facts are quite clear! The Seventeenth Army must be withdrawn at once if it cannot be resupplied!"

Tojo looked at Admiral Nagano. "If we were to withdraw the Seventeenth Army from Guadalcanal, how much time would it take for the Navy to do it?"

"The end of January," Admiral Nagano replied.

"The end of January!" Colonel Tsuji said. "That's too late! Why waste so much time while good men are dying? What's wrong with the Navy? Why won't Admiral Nagano tell us what's wrong with the Navy?"

"What's wrong with the Army?" Admiral Nagano replied.

"Silence!" hollered Tojo.

The room fell silent. Tojo thought of how well the war had gone in the first months. Malaya, Singapore, Java, Formosa, Hong Kong—all had fallen before the might of Japanese arms. The American Navy had been demolished at Pearl Harbor. The Philippines had been taken and General MacArthur had been forced to flee like the dog he was. But now, at Guadalcanal, great difficulties were arising. And something terrible had happened to the Navy at Midway and in the Coral Sea, but even Tojo didn't know the full extent of the catastrophe.

"It is not wise," Tojo said, "to make critical decisions in the heat of anger. I'll have to think this over and present my recommendations to the Cabinet. That is all. Meeting dismissed."

After the meeting, in the corridor outside, Colonel Tsuji approached his friend General Owada. "Did you hear what went on there? Are they all crazy?"

"You and I can do nothing to save the Seventeenth Army," General Owada said solemnly. "I think it's best that you become more philosophical about the matter. It's all in the hands of the gods now."

"It's not in the hands of the gods. It's in the hands of those idiots who were in that room."

"Colonel Tsuji, I have a suggestion for you," General Owada said. "I think you ought to go home and soak in your tub for a while. You're losing control of yourself. Good day, Colonel Tsjui."

General Owada walked away. Colonel Tsuji stared at Owada's back and thought of the starving soldiers on Guadalcanal.

Two squadrons from the Cactus Air Force soared down from the sky and dropped bombs on Hill Twenty-nine while artillery pounded it unmercifully. The Japanese soldiers in the bunkers were shellshocked and numb, but no one thought of surrendering. They lay on the ground and stuffed their bony fingers in their ears. Colonel Yatsu knew his position couldn't take much more of the artillery and bombs. It was time for desperate measures. The mortars would have to be deployed and fired. It would be extremely hazardous to set up the mortars with all the shells falling, but it would have to be done.

"Sergeant Sagamaki, set up the mortars!"

"The mortars, sir? Now?"

"Yes, now!"

"But, sir, we won't stand a chance out there!"

"I have just given you an order!"

"Yes, sir!"

Sergeant Sagamaki rounded up his mortar squads. The men moved listlessly and reluctantly. Captain Yatsu realized that the men didn't want to do it and that he would have to lead them personally. He stood and picked up a crate of mortar ammunition.

"Let's go!" he said. "Follow me!"

He dragged the crate of mortar rounds out of the bunker and into the smoke and flames of the bombardment. Shells exploded all around him and trees crashed to the ground. Choking from the dust and smoke, he set the crate of ammunition on the ground, expecting to be blown apart at any moment.

No one followed him out. He crawled back into the bunker

and grabbed a mortar tube from the hands of the terrorized soldier.

"If you men want to be cowards, I'll do it myself," he said.

His insult stung the men. To be a coward was the worst fate that could befall a Japanese soldier. The men followed him outside into the hell and havoc. A piece of shrapnel hit a private in the chest and nearly tore him in half. Another soldier was hit in the face with a bomb fragment and his head disappeared.

"Hurry!" said Captain Yatsu. "We can stop them if we get these mortars set up."

The men dropped the mortar plates in the trench and screwed on the tubes. Crates of ammunitions were stacked next to the mortars. Shrapnel whizzed all around them, chopping down trees and ripping apart the jungle. The ground heaved underneath as if an earthquake were occurring.

"Banzai!" shouted Captain Yatsu, dropping a mortar round into the tube beside him.

The round blasted out of the tube and soared high into the air, then fell to earth on the advancing Americans. The other mortar squads followed Captain Yatsu's example, and soon mortar shells were raining down on the front line of the American advance.

"Banzai! Give it to them!" Captain Yatsu screamed above the thunder of the bombardment. *"Hurry! Don't stop now!"*

The Japanese soldiers loaded their mortars as fast as they could as the earth trembled in the whirlwind of flames and death.

The mortar rounds dropped down on the Second Battalion, surprising the men. Their first thought was that their own artillery shells were falling short and landing on them.

"We're being shelled by our own people!" somebody yelled. *"Stop the goddamn shelling!"*

Bannon knew mortar rounds from artillery shells and realized the Japs were up to their old tricks. When the Americans conducted a barrage, the Japs shot back mortar rounds to make the Americans think their own shells were falling short. Often the trick worked because the Americans stopped their artillery barrage until they found out what was wrong.

"They're not our shells!" Bannon screamed. *"Hold fast!"*

Unfortunately American artillery *had* fallen short several times in the past, and many of the GIs thought it was happening again.

"Stop the artillery!" somebody shouted. *"They're aiming short!"*

Captain Orr also knew mortar rounds from artillery shells. *"They're not aiming short! Stay where you are!"*

The troops were scared. Many had been under bombardment before, and they didn't like it. Many pulled back, and some officers ordered their men to retreat.

Most of the men of the Second Battalion retreated down the hill, first on their bellies and then, when they felt safe, on their feet. The sight of other men running away increased their panic, and soon a rout was on.

"Hold it there, goddamnit!" Captain Orr shouted. *"They're only a few Jap mortar rounds!"*

Half of George Company and all of the recon platoon stayed where they were, but most of the Second Battalion ran away. Bannon ground his teeth and banged his fist on the ground angrily. After coming so far, the Second Battalion was giving up all the ground they'd won, and now they'd have to fight to take it back.

"Son of a bitch!" he muttered. "Goddamn stupid bastards!"

Several officers in the Second Battalion panicked and called the artillery units, screaming into their walkie-talkies that the bombardment should be halted immediately. The artillery commanders ordered a ceasefire to find out what was going on, and the battlefield became quiet except for the sound of the mortar rounds falling on abandoned positions.

Colonel Smith heard the artillery stop firing and saw his men streaming through the jungle in full retreat. A GI ran past him and Colonel Smith grabbed him by the shirt.

"You're going the wrong way, soldier!"

The soldier was pale and his eyes wild. "We're being hit by our own artillery, sir!"

"What the hell are you talking about?"

"We're being hit by our own artillery, sir!" the soldier repeated, scared to death.

Colonel Smith let him go and grabbed his radio, calling

front-line commanders and trying to figure out what was going on. After several heated conversations he found out most of his battalion was running away. Finally he reached Captain Orr.

"Sir," said Captain Orr, "the Japs have lobbed a few mortar rounds at us and the men think our artillery is falling short!"

"What about your company?"

"Half my company and all of the recon platoon is still here."

"Stay there and hold your fire! Let the Japs think everybody's gone! I'll get back to you once I turn this mess around!"

"Yes, sir!"

Captain Yatsu stood behind the mouth of his bunker and peered through his binoculars at the retreating Americans. The artillery bombardment had stopped and the Americans were running away. The ruse had worked!

"We've done it!" he shouted. "We've pushed them back!"

The men jumped up and down, cheering. They slapped each other on the back and grinned happily. They knew the Americans would come back, but at least they'd won the first round.

"I can hear them," Bannon said.

"So can I," replied Longtree.

Bannon pointed. "They're just up there, I think."

"I'll go look. Cover me."

Longtree crawled forward into the jungle. Captain Orr, checking on his men, noticed him. He moved toward Bannon.

"Where's that man going?"

"Can you hear the Japs?" Bannon asked.

Captain Orr closed his eyes and concentrated on his ears. He picked up the sounds of the Japs celebrating their successful trick.

"I hear them," he said.

"Longtree's gone to find out where they are."

Captain Orr thought for a moment. "Good idea."

"Did our mortar squads run away?"

"Two didn't."

"I think you'd better get them organized, sir, because we'll need them if Longtree spots those Japs."

Longtree crawled on his belly, keeping his face close to the ground. Branches scratched over his back and down his legs as he moved along. He slithered through shellholes and around boulders. He paused beneath bushes and listened to the chatter of the Japs, then moved forward again, heading toward their voices, which steadily became closer. The air was filled with the smell of gunpowder and burning vegetation. The higher he climbed, the clearer he could hear the Japanese voices, the sound of rifles bolts being closed, the bustle of men.

He saw bushes move in front of him, and a skinny Japanese soldier appeared, carrying an Arisaka rifle. It was one of Captain Yatsu's lookouts moving into position. He was headed straight for Longtree, and Longtree thought the Jap would spot him. He raised his M 1 so he could shoot the Jap first.

The Jap moved cautiously, and Longtree lined him up in his sights. It would be easy to kill him, but a shot would give away Longtree's position. Longtree lay still, and the Jap walked by him only a few yards away.

Longtree waited a few minutes, then crawled forward again. He correctly guessed that the Jap probably wasn't the only lookout in the vicinity. Longtree would have to be more careful than ever. He moved slowly, pausing every few minutes to listen, and then moved again. Sweat poured down his face, and he felt a tension headache coming on. He wished he could smoke a cigarette. He wondered why he'd volunteered to do this.

Then he saw it. In the jungle straight ahead, camouflaged by bushes, were the log walls of a bunker only twenty yards away. Longtree stopped, his heart beating wildly. A mad idea entered his mind: He could dash up there and drop a grenade into that slot before the Japs knew what hit them.

He took a deep breath and wondered if the idea was too wild. He might succeed, but then what? Could he get away? Was it worth a chance?

He looked at the bunker; it was a temptation. It would be a great accomplishment to knock it out when the whole battalion couldn't do it, even supported with artillery. It was the kind of challenge no warrior could walk away from, and underneath his US Army uniform Longtree still considered himself an

Apache warrior. A warrior's function was to perform heroic acts. He could not turn tail and run away from the bunker. It was too good an opportunity. What was death compared to the glory of a great personal victory?

I'll use two grenades instead of one, he thought, *but first I should get in a better position so I can attack from its blind side.*

He crawled slowly to his right, choosing the thickest part of the jungle for his path. His skin tingled with excitement as he made his way underneath trees cut in half by the shelling. The jungle was unbelievably tangled, with bushes uprooted and lengths of trees lying everywhere in weird angles. His mouth was dry with anticipation. He wondered how many Japs were in the bunker. Finally he reached a place where he thought he could launch his one-man attack. Staying low, he slung his rifle across his back so that his hands were free. He thought of the recon platoon farther down the hill and wondered what Bannon would do when he heard the explosions. *I don't care what he does. This is for me to do.*

He pulled two grenades from his lapels and yanked the pins, holding one grenade in each hand, pressing the levers tight. He looked at the bunker and took deep breath, thinking of great Apache warriors and especially the famous Mangus, who had been Longtree's grandfather. He sprang up and started running.

He let out no war cry, because he didn't want to alert the Japs, but he was moving quickly through the jungle and they heard him coming anyway.

"What's that?" Captain Yatsu said.

He looked through the hole in the bunker and couldn't see anything, but he could hear the sound of somebody coming at the bunker from the side. "Sergeant Sagamaki, come with me!"

Captain Yatsu and Sergeant Sagamaki dashed toward the rear of the bunker while the other Japanese soldiers looked at each other in alarm. Outside, Longtree ran swiftly toward the mouth of the bunker, kicking out his legs and gulping air. He leaped over a log, vaulted a shell crater, and kept charging. As he closed with the bunker he let the levers go, and they popped into the air, arming the hand grenades. In five seconds they'd go off.

He held both of the grenades in one of his big hands, dived toward the mouth of the bunker, tossed both grenades between the barrels of the machine guns and rolled away. His helmet fell off as he kept rolling, trying to get away from the mouth of the bunker.

Baaarrooooooommmmm!

The grenades exploded simultaneously, and a bolt of lightning shot out the mouth of the bunker. Outside, in the rear trench, the concussion knocked Captain Yatsu and Sergeant Sagamaki to the ground. Captain Yatsu scrambled to his feet and saw an American soldier running away. He snatched the Arisaka rifle out of Sergeant Sagamaki's hands and took aim.

Longtree was running as quickly as his feet would carry him. He was thrilled by the success of his deed and his heart beat like a tom-tom.

Crack!

Longtree felt as if he'd been hit in the back by a Mack truck. He lost his footing and everything went black. He crashed against a tree and fell to the ground.

Captain Yatsu rushed into the bunker and saw blood and guts. Wounded men groaned in pain, but most were dead, mutilated beyond recognition. "*No!*" he shouted.

Sergeant Sagamaki entered the bunker and blinked. He couldn't believe his eyes. The bunker had been designed to withstand the most ferocious attacks, but it had been wiped out by one American soldier.

Captain Yatsu knew the entire hill was threatened and that he'd have to do something fast. He looked at the radio; it had been demolished along with his men.

"Sergeant Sagamaki," he said, his throat constricted by horror, "go to the other bunkers! Get one-third of the men from each one and one-third of the machine guns and bring them here immediately!"

"Yes, sir!"

Sergeant Sagamaki ran out of the bunker. Captain Yatsu rushed to the opening of the bunker and laid Sergeant Sagamaki's rifle on the parapet, determined to hold off any Americans who attacked, even if it cost him his life. The stench of guts was almost unbearable, and Captain Yatsu tried not to look at the gore around him. He peered down the hill and saw the American soldier lying still against the tree. *At least I got him. At least I did that,* Captain Yatsu thought.

Bannon flinched when he heard the explosion. "What the fuck was that?"

"Sounds like hand grenades," said Nutsy Gafooley.

Bannon tried to figure what was going on. Longtree was the only GI up the hill and he must have got into trouble. But would the Japs throw hand grenades at him. No, they'd more likely try to shoot him. Then Bannon heard Captain Yatsu's rifle shot, and the picture became clear: *That crazy fucking Indian must have tried to toss a grenade at the bunker and then the Japs shot at him.*

He jumped to his feet. *"Let's go!"* he yelled. *"The Chief's in trouble!"*

Bannon ran through the jungle and up the hill, the rest of the platoon following him.

Captain Orr looked up and saw them advancing through the jungle. *"Where the hell are you men going?"*

"Follow me!" screamed Bannon.

Captain Orr had heard the grenade blast and the rifle shot too. The recon platoon was charging through the woods, and no machine guns were firing at them.

"On your feet!" he shouted. *"Follow the recon platoon!"*

The men who were left in George Company came up out of their holes and advanced up the hill. Ahead of them the recon platoon sped through the jungle, leaping over obstacles, a few of them tripping and falling, but they jumped up quickly and continued their rapid advance.

Bannon was in front, holding his M 1 high, and beside him was Nutsy Gafooley, carrying his rifle, walkie-talkie, bazooka, and bazooka ammunition. The ground that Longtree had crawled over slowly was covered by the recon platoon in a gallop, and the remnant of George Company followed them. Bannon batted branches out of his way with his M 1 and raced across the jungle on his long legs. Shots rang out in front of them as they were spotted by the lookouts, but the shots were few and Bannon realized there was little resistance up ahead.

"Keep going!" he shouted. *"Don't stop!"*

A Japanese lookout in front of him fired, and the bullet

whistled past Bannon's shoulder. He saw the Jap and fired a wild shot, which missed the Jap, but it upset the Jap sufficiently to ruin his aim. The Jap saw the jungle full of Americans running at him and held his ground, raising his rifle for another shot, but all the Americans opened fire on him, and one bullet hit him in the leg. Bannon jumped on his stomach with both feet, ran him through with his bayonet, and kept going.

"Charge!" he screamed.

The recon platoon charged among the other Japanese lookouts, shooting them down or whacking them with their rifle butts. The GIs stampeded through the jungle and swept up the hill, looking for the bunker and its Jap defenders.

Pow—a shot from Captain Yatsu's rifle brought down Private Cheatham from the Fourth Squad. *Pow*—another of Captain Yatsu's bullets whizzed over the head of Homer Gladley. Sergeant Sagamaki arrived at that moment with the men from the other two bunkers, and the men from the recon platoon saw them through the jungle.

"Attack!" Bannon shouted. *"Don't stop now!"*

Bannon jumped over a shell crater, and when he landed he saw the front wall of the bunker. Captain Yatsu fired his rifle and hit Pfc. Holgate from the Second Squad in the head.

"There's the bunker dead ahead!" Bannon screamed. *"Over the top!"*

The recon platoon swarmed up and around the bunker, charging into the men Sergeant Sagamaki had brought. Captain Yatsu ran out of the bunker and raised his samurai sword in the air.

Bullets were fired on both sides and grenades were thrown. Everything became confused in the smoke and movement of soldiers as the two sides closed with each other. Bannon ran at a Japanese soldier in front of him, lunged with his bayonet, and buried it in the Japanese soldier's stomach. He pulled it out, spun around, parried the thrust of a Japanese bayonet, and smashed the Japanese soldier in the face with his rifle butt. No more Japs were close to him, and he looked around, seeing a Japanese officer climbing out of a trench, brandishing a samurai sword.

"Banzai!" screamed Captain Yatsu, charging Bannon.

Bannon raised his rifle to shoot Captain Yatsu, but Captain

Yatsu was coming too fast. The Japanese officer raised his sword in the air to cut Bannon in two, and Bannon raised his rifle, blocking the blow with its stock, but the force of the stroke made Bannon's hands sting and nearly knocked the rifle out of his hands. He pushed his rifle stock forward and whacked Captain Yatsu in the face. Captain Yatsu's nose was flattened and blood squirted out, but he raised his sword to make a sideswiping blow at Bannon. Before he could get set, Bannon hit him in the face again, knocking his jaw loose from its hinges. Captain Yatsu was stunned. He struggled to keep his footing, and Bannon slammed him again, cracking open his skull. Captain Yatsu fell to the ground, his brains spilling onto the leaves. Bannon jumped over his body and looked for somebody else to kill.

Farther down the hill, Captain Orr saw the recon platoon and his own company overrunning the Japanese position and knew he'd better get more soldiers up the hill right away. He took the headset from his runner's backpack radio and called Colonel Smith. He reached Lieutenant Newton, who was one of Colonel Smith's aides.

"The colonel's busy right now," Newton said.

"Tell him it's urgent."

"Yes, sir."

Captain Orr waited a few moments and then he heard the voice of Colonel Smith. "What the hell's your problem, Orr?"

"Sir, the recon platoon and part of my company has captured a Japanese bunker. You'd better send whatever you have up here so we can hold it."

It took a few moments for Colonel Smith to digest the fact that Company G and the recon platoon were on Hill Twenty-seven. He chewed the stump of his cigar and looked around at his soldiers reorganizing after the retreat from the hill. "Hang on, Orr! We're on our way!"

He handed the headset to his runner and bellowed like a wild bull, ordering his men to charge up the hill. When they hesitated, he drew his Colt .45 and led the way. The men followed, first apprehensively, then with growing confidence when they realized the Japs weren't firing at them. The Second Battalion surged up Hill Twenty-seven, but some units soon came under fire from the other two machine-gun bunkers on the hill. They were stopped, but the rest kept driving and soon joined the recon platoon and Company G at the site of the bunker that had been taken.

Captain Smith was one of the first to reach the summit and immediately set to work organizing a defense, because he expected a counterattack. All was chaos atop the hill, for there wasn't much room and men were bumping into each other, looking for spots to dig in. The trenches around the bunker were so full, the men could barely find elbow room.

Japanese observers in the other two bunkers on Hill Twenty-seven saw that the effort to retake the first bunker had failed and now were faced with the dilemma of where to direct their fire. Their strength had been reduced drastically, due to the men and machine guns they'd sent to reinforce the bunker that had been taken. They radioed Major Uchikoshi for further instructions.

Major Uchikoshi was thunderstruck by the loss of the bunker, because his left flank now faced a serious threat. Pacing the floor of his bunker and out of cigarettes, he tried to think of what to do. He would have to accept the fact that the three bunkers were lost and continue the fight as best he could. He'd known it would come to this eventually but not so soon.

He sat before his radio and transmitted his orders to the defenders of bunkers Forty-four and Forty-five. "There will be no surrender," he said. "You will fight to the last man for the glory of the Emperor. *Banzai!*"

Bannon was wondering what had happened to Longtree. He told the recon platoon to dig in on the line facing the bunkers to the north and then went looking for him, crawling around the battle area on his belly. Something told him Longtree had been hurt, otherwise he would have shown up by now.

He crawled around, looking at the faces of dead and wounded American soldiers who were tall like Longtree. Medics worked feverishly on the wounded, and the dead were scattered everywhere. He saw many Japanese soldiers and GIs locked together in the final embrace of death, arms entwined, faces close together, blood intermingling, but no Longtree.

The Americans on Hill Twenty-seven set up their machine guns and mortars and fired at the Japs in adjacent bunkers.

Visibility was clear atop the hill and they could see where the Japanese fire was coming from fairly clearly, while the Japs sent a light concentration of fire their way. Occasional bullets pinged around Bannon as he made his way across the top of the hill, and then at the edge of a clearing he saw a medic from Company G working on the prostrate body of a soldier. Bannon knew instantly that it was Longtree. Bannon ran the final distance, dropping down beside the medic. Longtree lay on his stomach, his eyes closed and a big bloody bandage on his back.

"How is he?" Bannon asked.

"Real bad, but we can save him if we can get him down the hill." The medic was injecting morphine into Longtree's arm.

"What are you waiting for?"

"Stretcher bearers."

"I'll take him down."

"No, he'll have to go down in a stretcher."

"I'll make a stretcher." Bannon cupped his hands around his mouth. "Gladley!"

"Yo!"

"Get the fuck over here!"

"Yo!"

The medic looked at Bannon. "You'll have to be careful with him. He's got internal injuries."

"I'll be careful with him."

The medic crouched and moved away to help another wounded GI. Bannon looked down at Longtree lying still on the ground. Bannon felt sick in the pit of his stomach. He'd always considered Longtree the best man in the recon platoon, even a better soldier than himself, and he'd admired Longtree for his courage and silent, reliable strength. He didn't think the recon platoon would be much without Longtree on the point, leading the way.

Galdley came rumbling across the hill. "What's up?" Then he saw Longtree. "Holy shit, is he dead?"

"He will be if we don't get him to the battalion aid station."

"Gee . . ." Gladley said, his voice weak. He too was an admirer of Longtree.

"Take your shirt off and we'll make a stretcher."

Gladley and Bannon peeled off their torn, sweaty shirts and

tied them together in a makeshift stretcher. They rolled Longtree onto it and then picked up the ends, carrying him into the jungle, crouching low to the ground. Gladley went first. Bannon looked down at Longtree's head rolling from side to side. "Hang on, Chief," Bannon whispered. "You'll be all right."

FOURTEEN . . .

Colonel Smith set up a temporary headquarters in the trench outside the captured bunker, and as soon as his position around the bunker was consolidated, he called Colonel Stockton.

"Sir," he said, "we've got one of the bunkers on Hill Twenty-seven. There are two more bunkers up here and we can see them pretty well. I think I can take them with some help from your end."

The news made Colonel Stockton feel as if he'd been drenched with cool water. "Good work, Smith. What do you need?"

"I need an artillery strike on those two bunkers, and I'll want you to put pressure on Hill Twenty-five, to draw the fire from the bunkers there."

"Give me the coordinates on the two bunkers on your hill."

Colonel Smith told him the coordinates. Colonel Stockton told him he'd get right back to him. Both commanders broke off their radio connection, and Colonel Smith ducked as the top of his trench was raked by Japanese machine-gun fire. He looked to his right and left and saw his men raise their heads after the machine-gun fire passed. They placed their rifles and BARs on top of the trench and shot back at the Japs. Machine-gun and mortar squads were also firing at the Japs. Colonel Smith expected a counterattack at any moment, because he had no idea of how many Japanese soldiers were in that sector of the front. He hoped he could hold out until help came, not realizing how strong his position was.

Finally Colonel Stockton called back. "The artillery barrage will commence in ten minutes and will last for about fifteen minutes. Then send all your men forward and take those two bunkers. Don't worry about Hill Twenty-five. We'll keep them busy."

"Only fifteen minutes?" Colonel Smith asked. "Is that the all you can give us?"

"We're running low on ammo. You'll have to do the best you can. How did you manage to get that bunker?"

"One man did it, sir. A corporal from the recon platoon. From what I understand, he snuck up here all by himself and lobbed grenades into the bunker."

"You know his name?"

"Longtree."

"Anybody see him do it?"

"No, he was out here all alone."

"We'll have to work something out so he can get a medal."

"You may have to give it to his mother, sir. He probably won't live very long."

The artillery barrage began a few minutes later, covering the rest of Hill Twenty-seven with smoke and flames. Meanwhile the First Battalion of the Twenty-third Infantry Regiment pressed their attack on Hill Twenty-five. Colonel Smith passed along the word that the rest of Hill Twenty-seven would be assaulted as soon as the barrage stopped. The GIs checked their weapons and ammunition, making sure their bayonets were secure on the ends of their rifles. The machine-gun crews moved their positions so that they could support the attack once it got under way. Colonel Smith called his companies on the other side of the hill and coordinated the attack with them. The Second Battalion waited anxiously for the barrage to end so they could finish off the job Longtree had begun.

When the barrage stopped, the GIs came up out of their holes and raced across the ridge line toward the Japanese bunkers. The few remaining Japs put up a valiant defense, but they didn't have enough firepower and were dazed by the bombardment. The Second Battalion hit the bunkers on the run from all sides, throwing hand grenades, firing bazookas, and peppering the Japs with machine-gun fire. The GIs knew they had victory within their grasp, and that gave them renewed vigor. Their bazooka rockets and hand grenades entered the front and rear openings of the bunker, and the Japs didn't have a chance. They died for their Emperor and the GIs took Hill Twenty-seven at last.

They cleaned out the bunkers and dug in. Colonel Smith called Colonel Stockton and told him the hill was taken, and Colonel Stockton was overjoyed.

"Your men did a great job!" he said. "I'm coming up there to tell them so personally!"

"I've noticed something very interesting, sir," Colonel Smith said. "We're taking fire from the south but not from the north. I think this is the flank of the Jap fortifications in this area."

Colonel Stockton was silenced by the good news, because if Hill Twenty-seven was indeed the flank, they could start hitting the Japs from the side and the rear. It was the kind of bonanza that occurs occasionally in battles and changes the whole picture.

"You just hang on up there," Colonel Smith said. "I'll see you in a little while."

The battalion aid station consisted of a network of large walled tents that were covered by camouflage netting and situated in a jungle clearing. Soldiers lay on the ground, bleeding and unconscious or smoking cigarettes, their hollow eyes staring at the tops of the trees.

Bannon and Homer Gladley entered the aid-station area, carrying the unconscious Longtree, who was turning green. "This man needs attention right away!" Bannon shouted.

A medic wearing glasses looked up from the side of a soldier whose wound he was treating. "Set him down over there and we'll get to him when we can."

Bannon wanted to unsling his rifle and force the medic to treat Longtree at gunpoint, but there were so many other wounded men around that it wouldn't have been fair. Bannon and Gladley knelt beside Longtree, and their first thought was that they'd carried a dead man down the hill. Bannon pressed his ear against Longtree's chest and heard a faint beat.

"He's alive," said Bannon.

Bannon saw a doctor wearing a bloody white apron enter the clearing; he was returning from the latrine. Bannon jumped up and collared him. "Sir, could you look at my buddy? I think he's gonna die."

The doctor was a surgeon and he had wounded men inside on the operating tables to work on, but he saw the passionate concern on Bannon's face. "Where is he?"

"Over there, sir."

The doctor was a short, dumpy man who wore blood-flecked glasses, and Bannon led him to Longtree. The doctor knelt beside Longtree and took his pulse, which was weak.

"I don't see any wound," the doctor said. "What's wrong with him?"

"He's been shot in the back, sir."

"Roll him over easy."

Bannon and Gladley rolled Longtree over and the doctor saw the bloody bandage on Longtree's back. The bandage was sopping wet, which meant the medic on the hill hadn't stopped the bleeding effectively. The doctor knew that Longtree needed plasma immediately and that whatever was in him would have to come out.

"Take him in that tent there."

Bannon and Gladley rolled Longtree back onto their makeshift stretcher and carried him into the operating tent. They saw two doctors bending over soldiers, slicing into wounds. In the corners medics were sewing up incisions.

"Give this man some plasma immediately!" the doctor said. "Prepare him for surgery on his back!"

Medics took Longtree from Bannon and Gladley and laid him down on the ground. They set up a stalk with a bottle on it beside him and peeled the bandage off his back. The doctor washed his hands and put on rubber gloves.

"You men wait outside," the doctor said.

The doctor called for his scalpels. Bannon and Gladley watched him prepare to operate, and medics herded them out of the tent. They sat outside among the wounded, smoking cigarettes. Under normal circumstances Gladley would have tried to find a chow truck or mess tent to raid, but Longtree's condition had caused Homer to lose his appetite.

Bannon looked around at the wounded everywhere, bleeding and moaning. Some were knocked out by morphine, others hallucinated, and still others called for their mothers. Bannon hadn't been wounded seriously yet and knew his number would have to come up someday. He hoped he'd be able to handle the pain. It was better to be killed cleanly and quickly than suffer like some of the poor bastards around him.

"I hope he pulls through okay," Gladley said.

"He's strong—he'll be okay."

Bannon wasn't sure he believed that. Nobody was stronger than a bullet, not even Longtree. Who would be the point man from now on? He sifted through the faces of the men in his platoon, but not one of them could touch Longtree for sniffing out danger. The recon platoon wouldn't be the same without Longtree. He narrowed the field down to Shaw, Shilansky, and Corporal Gomez, and finally decided on Gomez, who was the trickiest of the bunch. Gomez would replace Longtree.

"I wonder what's taking them so long," Gladley said a half hour later. "That bullet must be in a bad place."

Bannon puffed his cigarette. He didn't know what he'd do if Longtree died. They'd been together ever since training in Fort Ord, California. It would be like losing a brother. *It's best not to get too close to people,* Bannon thought. *That way you don't miss them so much when they get hit.*

Medics carried a soldier on a stretcher out of the operating tent, and Bannon recognized the soldier as Longtree. He jumped up and ran toward the medics as they lowered Longtree on the ground.

"How is he?" Bannon asked the medics.

"He'll live. He'll be shipped to New Caledonia."

Bannon and Gladley felt relieved. They knelt beside Longtree and looked at his ashen features. Bannon placed his hand on Longtree's shoulder. "Hang on there, Chief," he said. "You're not ready to go to the Happy Hunting Ground yet."

"You guys had better get back to your outfit," one of the medics said.

Bannon stood up. "I'd like to thank the doctor."

"He's busy. You can't go in there now."

The medics returned to the operating tent. Bannon and Gladley slung their rifles and headed back to Hill Twenty-seven.

The jeep screeched to a halt in front of General Patch's headquarters near Henderson Field. Colonel Stockton jumped out of the passenger seat, gripped his briefcase tightly, and bounded up the steps. He entered the orderly room, full of staff officers and aides in neat, clean uniforms, and was ushered into the office of General Patch.

General Alexander McCarrell Patch sat behind his desk, looking at maps and communiqués, trying to coordinate the drive west to Cape Esperance. He was fifty-four years old, with a strong healthy build and a high forehead. During the First World War he'd commanded a machine-gun battalion, and between wars he'd helped develop the triangular concept of tactical warfare still in use by the Army. He was commander of all troops on Guadalcanal and Tulagi, designated as XIV Corps.

Colonel Stockton marched to his desk and saluted.

"Have a seat, Bill," General Patch said. "What's on your mind?"

"Sir, I wanted to report to you personally that we've made a major breakthrough in the Jap line in front of us. We've just taken Hill Twenty-seven."

General Patch looked down at his map. "Good work. How'd you do it?"

"One man did it, believe it or not. He crept up there and knocked out one of the key bunkers all by himself."

General Patch looked incredulous. "Jesus."

"He was hurt pretty badly, but he opened up the whole situation there. The rest of my Second Battalion followed him and took the hill. Nobody saw what he did, because, like I said, he did it alone, but I want to give him a medal."

"We can work that out. That's not why you came here, is it?"

"No." Colonel Stockton arose and bent over the map on General Patch's desk. "I have a plan to knock out the rest of that line. If we can get some heavy artillery on top of Hill Twenty-seven, we can pound the hills adjacent to it and take them too. Then we can proceed from hill to hill in the same manner, knocking out the Japs piecemeal while maintaining pressure on them everywhere else, but we'll need tanks."

"Don't have many tanks, Bill."

"Without tanks the cost in men will be too high. The men will be cut down by the machine guns in those bunkers, but they can advance behind tanks, and the tanks can get close enough to blast those bunkers away. We won't need many tanks. Just six or seven."

General Patch looked down at his map. XIV Corps had run into several pockets of resistance such as the one in front of the Twenty-third Infantry Regiment, but that was the closest to Henderson Field.

"Okay, Bill," General Patch said. "I'll give you whatever tanks we can spare. When can you attack?"

"The day after tomorrow."

"You have a pretty good idea of what the Jap line looks like up there?"

"Yes, sir. I'm patrolling constantly and gathering more information all the time. We'll keep patrolling tomorrow."

"How long you think it'll take to knock those Japs out if I give you the tanks and artillery?"

"A week."

General Patch looked down at the map. His troops weren't making much progress against the tough pockets of resistance west of the Manatikau River, and if Colonel Stockton knocked out what was in front of him, that would make more men available for assaults on the other Japanese fortifications.

"Okay, Bill. I'll give you what you need. Just clear out that mess up there."

It was evening, and Private DelFranco was strutting around the recon platoon area with his shirt off, showing a bloody bandage on his left shoulder where he'd been nicked by a Japanese bullet. A cigarette dangled from the corner of his mouth and the straps hung down from his helmet; he felt like a real soldier at last. He'd killed a few Japs on the hill that day, had shed some blood himself, and now figured he was as good as anybody else in the recon platoon.

He sat down with Shaw, Shilansky, Homer Gladley, and

the Reverend Billie Jones, who were among the most respected men in the platoon because they'd been around since the regiment first landed on Guadalcanal.

"Hiya, guys," he said. "What's going on?"

They'd been talking about Longtree, and DelFranco was interrupting them. DelFranco was an outsider, because he'd been with the platoon only a short while, and they clammed up. Shaw muttered something to DelFranco in response to his question.

"Whadja say?" DelFranco replied.

"I didn't say nothing," Shaw told him.

"I thought you said something." DelFranco looked around and grinned. "Great day, huh?"

"What the fuck's so great about it?" Shilansky asked, wearing a dirty, bloody bandage on his leg.

"Well, we took the hill."

"Big deal. This island's fulla hills, and we got a lot more to go."

"Yeah," said Homer Gladley, "and there's a lot more islands."

"God made lots of islands," Billie Jones said solemnly.

"Too many," Shaw said.

"Well," said DelFranco, "the way I see it, you just have to keep moving along and hope for the best."

"Oh, is that the way you see it?" Shilansky asked.

"Yep."

Shilansky shrugged. Nutsy Gafooley walked by quickly, heading toward the Third Squad.

"Where ya going, Nutsy?" asked Homer.

"Bannon wants to see Gomez. He's gonna be the new point man."

"No shit?"

"I wouldn't shit you." Nutsy kept walking along.

"Fucking suckass," DelFranco said, because he still hated Nutsy for taking over his job as Bannon's runner.

Nutsy Gafooley stopped cold in his tracks and turned around, glaring at DelFranco. "You say something, punk?"

"Yeah, I just called you a suckass, because that's what you are."

Nutsy wrinkled his brow and moved toward DelFranco.

Shaw, Shilansky, Homer Gladley, and Billie Jones got to their feet and stepped back. DelFranco rose, too, a little scared, snapped back to reality by the enormity of what he'd done. He'd insulted Nutsy Gafooley, who was a vicious man. But it was too late to back off, and he rose to his feet, trying to tell himself that he was as fearsome and deadly as any other man in the platoon.

Nutsy Gafooley raised his fists and advanced, murder and malevolence in his eyes. DelFranco grinned bravely and got into a fighter's stance, weaving from side to side. Nutsy drew close and feinted with a left jab. DelFranco dodged to the side to get out of the way of the punch that never came. That was just what Nutsy expected, and Nutsy unloaded a right hook, catching DelFranco on the side of his face. DelFranco heard harps and bells and staggered, and then Nutsy blasted him in the stomach. DelFranco doubled over and Nutsy hit him with an uppercut, splitting his lip and sending him flying backward. DelFranco fell onto his back and Nutsy jumped on top of him, raising his fist to pound DelFranco into oblivion.

Shaw caught Nutsy's arm in midair. "That's enough, Nutsy."

"I'll kill the son of a bitch!"

"Cool your motor now."

"Jesus Christ," said a familiar voice behind them. "I guess things ain't changed much in this platoon."

Everyone spun around and saw Frankie La Barbara, healthy, rested, and well fed, a grin on his face, wearing new green fatigues and carrying a rifle that still had the smell of Cosmoline on it. The men couldn't believe their eyes. Nutsy Gafooley climbed off the unconscious DelFranco and gathered around Frankie with the others. Nutsy was new to the platoon, but he'd heard stories about Frankie La Barbara.

"Hey," said Shaw, slapping Frankie on the back, "when'd you get back?"

"I'm just getting back right now."

"You're looking great, man."

"I feel great." Frankie was chewing gum a mile a minute and shifting from foot to foot, excited about being back with the gang. "You guys shoulda been with me on New Caledonia. I could get you laid every night."

"Yeah?" asked Shilansky, his nose twitching. "No shit?"

"I ain't shitting you. They got horny nurses coming out of the woodwork. I had one with tits out to here." Frankie held his palms in front of his chest. "I used to call her Torpedo Tits. She gave a fantastic blowjob. I used to come in her mouth and she loved it."

"Shit," said Shilansky, "I'm gonna try to get shot tomorrow."

"With your luck," said Frankie, "you're liable to get your dick shot off."

Everybody laughed. It was good to have old Frankie back again. Things wouldn't get dull with Frankie around.

"Then I had this tall skinny one with great legs and a nice tight pussy. I used to fuck her brains out in a broom closet. And I had this other cute blonde number who loved to sit on it and bounce up and down. And there was a brunette who liked me to fuck her in the ass."

Shilansky stuck his tongue out and screamed, "I can't take it anymore! Make him stop it!" He covered his ears with his hands but left an opening so he could continue to hear.

"And lissen to this one," Frankie said. "There was this nurse who was a fucking *captain*, and she used to give me handjobs right on the ward while I was lying in bed and she was supposed to be taking my pulse. And she was a knockout too."

Bannon heard the commotion and pushed through the throng around Frankie La Barbara. "Holy shit," he said, "look who's back."

"Well, if it ain't *Sergeant* Bannon," Frankie replied. "Well, you might have the stripes, you big hillbilly, but I'm the guy that got all the pussy on New Caledonia." Frankie held out his hand. "I finger-fucked a real sweetie-pie just before I left, and I never washed my hands since. Have a smell, Sergeant."

Bannon took a step backward. "You probably finger-fucked your ear and didn't know the difference."

"Oh, yeah? Smell and find out for yourself."

"You see Butsko while you were there?"

"Yeah, I seen him a few times. He's as rotten as ever. He ain't getting no pussy. Who'd fuck that gorilla? He spends all his time reading military manuals."

"How is he?"

"He should be coming back pretty soon. He looked pretty

healthy to me when I saw him two days ago. You like redheads, don't you Bannon? There was this redhead who loved to fuck all night long. I mean, it was pathetic. One night I . . ."

Frankie regaled the men with true and not-so-true stories about his romantic escapades on New Caledonia, and Private DelFranco slunk away, holding a bloody handkerchief against his cut lip. He felt humiliated and estranged from the other men, who still didn't accept him and now would be more contemptuous of him than ever.

Wait till we go against the Japs again, he thought. *I'll show them that I'm as good a soldier as any one of them. Then they'll have to respect me, the bastards.*

FIFTEEN . . .

The next day engineers cut roads through the jungle so that trucks could haul heavy artillery to the top of Hill Twenty-seven. Tanks rumbled through the jungle to the sector in front of Hill Twenty-five, which Colonel Stockton hoped to attack the next day. Patrols were sent out throughout the day to reconnoiter Hill Twenty-five and probe for other machine-gun nests in the Gifu Line. As the afternoon progressed, Colonel Stockton realized everything wouldn't be ready for the attack the next day, so he postponed it for twenty-four hours.

The next day the artillery was dragged to the top of Hill Twenty-five, where the mammoth 105- and 155-millimeter howitzers were set up and fired for registration. Again the patrols went out, and this time the recon platoon was sent to work around the other side of Hill Twenty-five, to determine whether a supporting attack could be launched from that direction.

Corporal Gomez was on the point, feeling a new sense of power and importance. Short and stocky, with a wispy mustache above his lip and eyes that were almost Oriental, he led the recon platoon around Hill Twenty-five and up its western approach. Although he'd been raised in Los Angelos, he knew how to be silent in the woods, because it wasn't very different from rolling drunks or being a burglar, which is what he'd done for a living before he joined the Army. You had to watch where you put your feet, and you had to be careful of what you touched. The principles of silence and stealthy movement were the same.

By noon they were halfway up the hill. Frankie La Barbara was exhausted, because he was in terrible physical condition. For the past six weeks all he'd done was sleep and screw nurses. He huffed and puffed, drinking from his canteen, and felt the old fear coming back, making him anxious and apprehensive. He realized that he'd forgotten a lot about being a combat soldier, and worried that he might make a mistake that could get him killed.

"Hey, Bannon, can't we stop for a break?" he asked.

"Not yet."

"What a hump you turned out to be."

The recon platoon slogged up the south side of Hill Twenty-five, expecting to make contact with Japs at any moment, when suddenly it happened: A shot from a rifle cracked over their heads.

They all dropped to their stomachs and looked at Bannon, who knew from experience at the Gifu Line that at least one machine-gun bunker was behind the Jap rifleman.

"Keep moving," he said. "Let's find out where their machine gun is."

The GIs crawled up the hill as more Japanese riflemen fired at them. The GIs stopped and fired a few volleys, then kept moving, steadily pushing the thin screen of Japanese riflemen back. After fifty yards they came within range of the machine guns, which began to chatter. Bannon raised his binoculars and tried to spot it, but couldn't see anything except a thick wall of jungle. He figured the Japs couldn't see them too well, either, so he decided to keep going.

The recon platoon advanced slowly up the hill beneath the hail of machine-gun fire. The closer they came to the summit, the closer the machine-gun fire came and the better Bannon could perceive the location of the machine-gun bunkers. He determined there were two of them on the crest of the hill and thought the recon platoon could get a little closer.

"Keep going!" he said. "Don't anybody fall back!"

"Hey, Bannon," Frankie La Barbara yelled from down the line, "you trying to be a hero or something!"

"Shaddup, Frankie!"

The recon platoon continued to crawl up the hill as the machine-gun fire became more intense. After another thirty yards, the Japanese bullets were getting too close for comfort, but Bannon now had a clearer idea of where the bunkers were. He took out his map, made little *X*'s on the spots where he thought they were, and put the map back into his pocket.

"Okay," Bannon said, "pull it back!"

Still facing the Jap bunkers, the recon platoon crawled backward down the hill, except for one man. Private DelFranco, who wanted to prove that he was a real soldier like the rest of them, didn't want to retreat. He was angry and frustrated and wanted to fight those Japs up there.

Bannon noticed him. "Hey, DelFranco, you all right?"

"Yeah, I'm all right!"

"Pull back!"

DelFranco couldn't make himself pull back. He craved action and the opportunity to prove himself. It would be unbearable to spend the rest of the day hanging around with his split lip, the laughingstock of the platoon because Nutsy Gafooley had beat him up easily the day before. He remembered Longtree's feat of heroism, assaulting a bunker all by himself. *Why can't I do that?* DelFranco asked himself. He'd heard that Longtree would get a medal, and DelFranco thought he might get one too. Then everybody would respect him. They'd call him the Fighting Chaplain someday.

"Hey, Bannon!" he shouted.

"I thought I told you to pull back, you little fuck!"

"I'm gonna try to take that bunker! Cover me!"

"I said get the fuck down here!"

"Cover me, Sarge! I think I can do it!"

"I said get back here!"

DelFranco set his jaw and crawled forward, dreaming of heroism and glory. The pressures of front-line combat had warped his already neurotic personality, and he actually thought he could do what Longtree had done. He headed for the thickest part of the jungle.

Bannon couldn't believe his eyes and turned purple with rage. *"I'll fucking court-martial you!"*

DelFranco didn't reply; he just kept going.

Nutsy Gafooley nudged Bannon. "Want me to shoot him, Sarge?"

"Shut up."

Bannon tried to think. He was tempted to continue his withdrawal and let DelFranco get killed, but you never knew, maybe he'd get through, doubtful though that was. Maybe the best thing to do would be to withdraw about fifty yards and make the Japs think they'd left. Maybe DelFranco would wake up and realize he was making a mistake. Bannon somehow couldn't bring himself to leave one of his men stranded, even if it was a twerp like DelFranco.

"Pull back!" Bannon shouted, hoping his order would be heard by DelFranco and bring him back to his senses.

But it didn't. DelFranco disappeared into the jungle, and the recon platoon continued its retreat down the hill. When the machine-gun fire died down, Bannon told his men to stop.

"What're we stopping for?" Frankie asked.

"We're gonna wait for DelFranco," Bannon said.

"What the fuck for?"

"Shaddup, Frankie."

"If he wants to get killed, let him get killed!"

"I said shaddup, Frankie!"

The machine guns stopped firing and DelFranco thought he had it made. He moved quickly through the jungle, so eager that he got up off his belly and walked on his hands and knees. He didn't know it, but the Japanese lookouts were coming out of their bunkers again to take their posts, fanning through the jungle in front of him. He heard faint rustling but thought it was only the natural sounds of the jungle, because he didn't have the ears of Longtree or Gomez. His heart beating wildly, flashing on himself standing at attention as General Patch pinned the Distinguished Service Cross to his shirt, he headed for the spot where he thought a Japanese bunker was.

One of the Japanese lookouts saw him coming and slowly sank to his belly behind a bush. He raised his rifle to his shoulder, drew a bead on DelFranco, saw the pack on his back, and smiled, because he knew it was full of American C rations. He waited until Del Franco came closer and wondered why the American soldier was making so much noise. Maybe it was a trap. The Japanese soldier was a seasoned jungle fighter and didn't care. He thought he could get away. He squeezed the trigger of his rifle.

Blam!

DelFranco twitched and stopped moving.

Blam!

DelFranco lay still on the ground. The Japanese soldier waited a few minutes to see if anything happened. Nothing did. He crawled forward and prodded DelFranco with his bayonet, but DelFranco didn't move. The Japanese soldier tore open DelFranco's pack, filled his arms with C and K rations, and carried them back to the bunker.

Farther down the hill, the men in the recon platoon heard the two shots and then the long period of silence. It didn't take much intelligence to know what had happened.

"Let's get out of here!" Bannon said. "Gomez, take the point!"

SIXTEEN . . .

The next morning the attack began with a massive artillery barrage from the top of Hill Twenty-seven and the lowlands. Bombers from Henderson field assisted in the roaring devastation, and fighter pilots strafed the jungle. At the bottom of Hill Twenty-five the tanks were lined up and the GIs deployed in three waves behind them. Tank engines belched smoke into the air, and tank commanders stood in the turrets of their vehicles, surveying their objective through binoculars. Farther back Colonel Stockton and the other commanders had their eyes glued to binoculars, anxiously awaiting the end of the bombardment.

The shelling and bombing continued for ninety minutes, and then the tanks and GIs advanced beneath its cover. Shells whistled overhead and every GI knew they were going to kick the shit out of the Japs. Simultaneous advances were made at other points on the Gifu Line to keep the Japs busy. In his bunker Major Uchikoshi knew something big was coming and ordered his men to get ready.

The shelling stopped and the tanks rumbled forward, smashing through the jungle. Behind them came the GIs, yipping and screaming. The Japanese machine guns in the bunkers opened fire, their bullets pinging harmlessly off the armor of the tanks, which now were buttoned down for action. The GIs huddled behind the tanks like baby geese following their mothers. The tanks knocked over trees and waddled across gullies, moving closer to the bunkers. The machine-gun fire became more intense and the Japanese soldiers heard the tanks coming, feeling cold fear inside them, because they had no defense against mobile steel fortresses with cannons and machine guns. They reported the presence of the tanks to Major Uchikoshi, who knew the Gifu Line was about to crack. But there was nothing he could do about it: He had no antitank weapons and he was under orders to stand and fight.

The tanks came into view of the bunkers, and the Japanese soldiers fired at them hopelessly. The tanks cannons were leveled on the bunkers and shells pumped out, blowing down the log walls, caving in the roofs. The Japanese soldiers still alive retreated from the bunkers and tried to make a last stand in the trench network surrounding them. The tanks fired their machine guns, cutting them down, then blew them up with their cannons. A few heroic Japanese soldiers charged the tanks with live hand grenades in their hands, but they were picked off by the machine guns and rifle fire from the GIs.

The order was given to charge, and the GIs poured around the tanks and charged the Japanese trenches while the tanks provided fire support. The GIs advanced with marching fire, tossing hand grenades, cheering wildly, going kill-crazy. When they got close to the trenches the tanks stopped firing and the GIs made their final rush, jumping into the trenches and taking on the Japs hand to hand.

The Japs were outnumbered and outgunned, but they fought bravely. Some pulled hand grenades and blew themselves up along with American GIs close by. The GIs swarmed over them and kept advancing, shooting and stabbing, stomping on Japanese faces, unleashing their frustration at being machine-gunned and stopped cold by the bunkers ever since the attack on the Gifu began.

It took two hours to overrun Hill Twenty-five, and the fight was over by noon. Colonel Stockton was so heartened by the success of the attack that he decided to keep going. He ordered an artillery strike on the adjacent Hill Twenty-three and told the tank commanders to move into position for another charge.

The tanks rolled down Hill Twenty-five and lined up at the

bottom of Hill Twenty-three, with the tired and victorious GIs taking positions behind them. The second artillery barrage began, this time without air support, but Colonel Stockton didn't think it was necessary. The tanks were all that was needed to do the job, he realized now, and he figured that if there had been two hundred tanks on Guadalcanal, they could have taken the whole island weeks before.

At two o'clock in the afternoon the second attack got under way, and it was the same story. When the artillery stopped, the tanks advanced with the GIs behind them. The machine gunners in the Japanese bunkers opened fire and the tanks homed in on them, firing shells, blowing them to bits. The infantry followed and mopped them up. Hill Twenty-three was in American hands at 1730 hours, and all resistance ended.

At the end of the day it was clear to Colonel Stockton that the Gifu Line was finished. All he'd have to do was keep attacking each hill with tanks until every Japanese bunker was destroyed. He figured three more days ought to do it. He ordered the tanks and troops to move into position at the foot of Hill Twenty-three in preparation for another attack in the morning. Then he left the field of battle to report to General Patch in person on the success of his day's work.

Major Uchikoshi knew what Colonel Stockton knew: that the Gifu was finished for all practical purposes. It was only a matter of days before each bunker, including his own, was systematically destroyed. The big question in his mind was whether he wanted to wait for that to happen and be killed like a cornered rat or take the initiative and go out in a blaze of glory?

The decision was not difficult for him to make, because all Japanese officers were programmed to think in wild, heroic terms. All Japanese officers believed in the theory of the One Sudden Decisive Victory ever since the Japanese fleet defeated the Russians at Port Arthur in one bold stroke in 1904. The theory of the One Sudden Decisive Victory had been behind the Pearl Harbor attack, which had succeeded tactically but not strategically, because it had not knocked America out of the war. Yet, the theory persisted, and Japanese military commanders were always looking for the opportunity to defeat their enemies in one spectacular stroke.

As the sun sank on Guadalcanal, Major Uchikoshi sat at his desk and worked out plans to attack the Americans. He reasoned that the Americans wouldn't expect a night attack and would be caught off guard. They would be confused and disorganized. A fierce determined onslaught might defeat them, especially if it was launched from their rear, and if it didn't succeed, at least he and his men could die like soldiers on the attack instead of huddling in their bunkers, being blown to bits by American tanks.

Major Uchikoshi had approximately 350 men left out of the 500 he'd had when the Americans had stumbled onto the Gifu Line. That would be a sizable force attacking suddenly at night from an unexpected sector of the front. He'd organize special detachments of men with grenades tied to their bodies, who'd propel themselves like human bombs at the tanks. The tanks would be his first concern. Knock them out and the rest shouldn't be too difficult.

He drew lines on his map, figuring out the plan of attack. His men would leave their bunkers and make their way down the hills, working around the Americans below and attacking from the rear. He knew the attack was audacious and many things could go wrong, but so had been the plan to bomb Pearl Harbor.

By eight o'clock in the evening he'd worked out all the details. Now the only thing to do would be to carry them out. There was no time to waste; he'd never have more men than he had then.

"Lieutenant Isogami!" he called out.

"Yes, sir."

"Summon all officers and noncoms to this bunker immediately!"

"Yes, sir."

Lieutenant Isogami got on the radio and made the calls. Major Uchikoshi studied his map in the light of the flickering kerosene lamp and realized that he and his men probably would not see the morning. The Americans were deployed across a broad front, and he knew there were a great many of them, perhaps a regiment or two, maybe even a division. It wouldn't be prudent to hit them in the center of their line, because he and his men would then have Americans on both sides. The best plan would be to hit them in flank and try to roll them back. It would be an almost impossible task, but perhaps, if the gods smiled on them, he could win a victory. Could Japanese spirit defeat American materialism?

That night Major Uchikoshi would find out for sure.

As the GIs slept beneath a full moon, the Japanese soldiers moved out of their bunkers and descended the rear slopes of the hills, where they wouldn't run into Americans. They assembled in the jungle and began their long march around the Gifu Line so that they could attack the Americans on their left flank.

The jungle was thick and the going was slow and arduous. Specially picked jungle fighters led the way, hacking their way through the thick vines and underbrush with their machetes. At one o'clock in the morning they came upon a coconut grove, and like madmen the Japanese soldiers fell on the coconuts, smashing them open, drinking the milk, and gulping down the meat. They all filled their bellies and Major Uchikoshi told them to move out again, for the Americans weren't far away.

Every Japanese soldier knew the odds against them, but they all agreed with Major Uchikoshi that it was better to die like a soldier than a cornered animal. They knew their attack had little chance of success, that it was in essence a suicide attack, but their spirits were high, for there was no more honorable a death than to give their lives for their Emperor.

At two-thirty in the morning Major Uchikoshi checked his maps and knew the American left flank was near. They could bump into it at any moment. He ordered a halt and his men had a last ceremonial drink of water, toasting the health of their Emperor and asking the gods to give them the strength to overwhelm their enemies.

They put away their canteens and threw off their packs so that they could travel light. The special detachments took their places at the head of the column, grenades strapped to their bodies. It was a solemn, almost religious moment as the Japanese soldiers thought of journeying to heaven together.

Major Uchikoshi moved his arm forward, and the soldiers with machetes ran forward to clear a path. The defenders of the Gifu Line followed, their rifles in their hands and bayonets fixed, ready to die.

Colonel Smith was sleeping soundly in his tent, when he felt his shoulder being rudely shaken.

"Wake up, sir!" said Captain Greewald.

Colonel Smith opened his eyes slowly, for he'd had a few belts of jungle juice before retiring. "What the hell's wrong now?"

"Fox Company reports enemy activity in the jungle to the south of its position!"

"What kind of enemy activity?"

"Captian Leach says it sounds like a sizable bunch of Japs!"

That's all Colonel Smith had to hear. He jumped out of bed and ran barefoot and in his shorts to the radio in the other section of the tent. The operator handed him the headset.

"Leach!" boomed Colonel Smith.

"Yes, sir!"

"What the fuck is going on out there!"

"Sounds like a couple companies of Japs at least! Maybe a battalion! Maybe more!"

Colonel Smith raised himself on his toes. "Now, listen carefully. I want you to hold on there as long as you can, but if it gets too tough, pull back slowly in a fighting retreat. Are you set up with your mortars and machine guns?"

"Yes, sir."

"Then start firing right now. Good luck. Over and out."

Excited, Colonel Smith called his other companies and told them to move to their left and be ready for a Jap suicide attack. Then he dashed to his sleeping area and put on his clothes, because he wanted to be where the action was. As he pulled on his pants, he heard the mortars and machine guns starting to fire.

The mortars rounds fell on the jungle through which the Gifu soldiers were advancing, and machine-gun bullets whistled through the leaves. The sound startled Major Uchikoshi, because he hadn't expected to be discovered so soon. He raised his samurai sword high in the air and ran forward, screaming at the top of his lungs.

"Banzai! Charge!"

His men followed him, and his machete bearers took positions at his side. The Japanese soldiers streaked toward the American left flank as the jungle exploded all around them.

"Everybody up!" shouted Captain Orr. *"Let's go!"*

The men put on their boots and scrambled out of their tents, grabbing their rifles and hanging bandoliers of ammunition around their necks. They plopped helmets on their heads and saw Captain Orr kicking tents and pointing south, where Fox Company was encamped.

"Hurry up! The Japs are coming!"

Bannon crawled out of his tent and jammed a clip of bullets into his M 1, hearing the sounds of battle coming from the direction of Fox Company, which was beside George Company and the recon platoon.

"Let's go, recon platoon!" he yelled. *"Move it out!"*

The recon platoon joined Bannon, their eyes sleepy and their helmets crooked on their heads. They heard Japs screaming and shouting *banzai* while machine guns stuttered into the night. The mortars had stopped firing, and everybody figured the Japs were already on top of Fox Company.

The GIs charged through the jungle. Everywhere they looked they saw other GIs, all heading toward Fox Company. Behind them they could hear the shouts of more GIs. The entire battalion was swinging to the right to meet the Japanese threat head-on.

Bannon galloped through the jungle and saw men in foxholes, firing machine guns and rifles. Before them were Japs pouring through the jungle, not more than twenty yards away. The Japs brandished rifles and bayonets and howled like wild animals as the soldiers from Fox Company cut down their front ranks, but still the Japs kept coming.

Bannon jumped into a foxhole in which two soldiers were firing rifles at the Japs. One was big and the other slight, and

Bannon blinked his eyes as he recognized the big soldier as Sergeant Page, the one he'd had the beef with a few weeks earlier.

"What you looking at!" Sergeant Page bellowed. "The Japs are over there!"

Bannon laid his rifle on the parapet and fired at a Jap ten yards in front of him. The Jap tripped and fell to the ground, a bullet through his neck. Bannon moved his rifle a few inches to the right and fired again. That Jap dropped to his knees and tumbled over, a bullet in his gut. Bannon fired at a third Jap and hit him in the leg, but the Jap kept running as if nothing had happened.

"Pull back!" shouted Captain Leach. *"Retreat!"*

The GIs backed out of their foxholes, and the Japs charged into their midst. The Jap with the bleeding leg ran at Bannon, and Bannon fired a shot from the waist, but the bullet whizzed harmlessly past the Jap, who lunged with his rifle and bayonet at Bannon.

Bannon raised his own rifle and bayonet, barely managing to parry the blow. The Jap crashed into Bannon, and both of them fell to the ground. Their rifles between them, they punched each other and tried to gouge out each other's eyes. Fighting frantically and desperately, they rolled over and over, clawing at each other. Bannon closed his eyes in the nick of time as the Jap's fingernail scratched over his eyelid. Bannon jabbed his thumb into the Jap's Adam's apple, and the Jap gagged. The Jap swung wildly at Bannon, who grabbed his wrist, pulled, and kneed the Jap in the balls.

"Ugh!" said the Jap.

Bannon kneed him again, and the Jap nearly fainted from the pain. Then Bannon jumped up, grabbed his rifle, and stabbed the Jap in the chest. As he was pulling his bayonet out, something hit him in the head. The next thing Bannon knew he was on the ground, looking up at a Japanese bayonet streaking toward him. He rolled over quickly, picked up an empty C ration can, jumped to his feet, and threw the can at the Jap, who ducked.

Bannon dived and grabbed the Jap's rifle, giving a mighty tug, pulling it away from the Jap, and then shooting the butt forward, smashing the Jap in the mouth. Eight teeth were knocked into the Jap's throat and he sagged toward the ground. Bannon got set to run him through when a bullet whizzed past his nose. He turned around and saw a Jap aiming a Nambu pistol toward him. Bannon didn't know whether to shit or go blind. He thought the party was over.

Something rose in the air behind the Jap and came down. It was the Reverend Billie Jones holding his rifle by the barrel and swinging it like a baseball bat. It hit the Jap in the head, cracking his skull apart. The Jap sagged to the ground and Bannon rushed forward, snatching the pistol out of his limp hand. He turned and saw a Jap running toward the back of Private Shaw, who was fighting with another Jap. Bannon raised the Nambu, took aim, and fired. The bullet whizzed past the Jap's nose, who stopped and looked at Bannon. Aiming more carefully this time, Bannon fired again, and the Jap went down to meet his ancestors. Bannon heard footsteps to his right and turned around. Three Japs were running toward him. He aimed, fired, aimed, and fired again. Two of the Japs dropped, but the last one kept running. Bannon aimed and fired when the Jap was only a few feet away. He plugged the Jap in the face, but the Jap's momentum carried him forward. He crashed into Bannon and they both fell down.

Bannon pushed the Jap off him and looked up. Another Jap was standing over him, raising his rifle and bayonet for a death blow. Bannon aimed up and pulled the trigger. *Click.* The Jap screamed for joy and pushed his rifle and bayonet down at Bannon, and Bannon rolled out of the way, saw a machete lying on the ground, and picked it up.

He bounded to his feet. The Jap charged and Bannon swung the machete from the side, crashing through the Jap's ribs. The Jap sank to the ground and Bannon tugged the machete loose, spinning around and whacking a Jap in the face, slicing through to his brain, blood spattering everywhere. The Jap dropped at Bannon's feet and Bannon charged forward, his adrenaline pumping madly, making him feel insane.

He saw a Jap standing over an American soldier, lying wounded on the ground. Evidently the Jap had wounded the soldier and was now going to finish the job. Bannon bellowed like a wild bull and swung at the Jap's back, severing his spinal column. The Jap fell over backward at an impossible angle and collapsed onto the ground. Bannon glanced at the wounded GI and saw that is was Sergeant Fowler, his old nemesis.

"You okay?" Bannon asked.

Fowler's eyes were at half-mast. "Thanks" was all he could say.

Two Japs charged toward Bannon and Fowler. Bannon stood over Fowler and swung the machete, batting one Jap bayonet out of the way. Bannon put all his strength into the backstroke and lopped off the Jap's head.

"Banzai!" screamed the other Jap.

He thrust his rifle and bayonet at Bannon's heart, and Bannon jumped backward, swinging his machete to the side, fracturing the Jap's left forearm. The Jap hollered and dropped his rifle, and Bannon raised his machete high, then brought the bloody blade down on the Jap's skull, splitting his head in two.

The Jap slumped to the ground. Bannon looked around and saw hordes of GIs wading into the few Japs who were still standing. He saw a Japanese officer with a Fu Manchu mustache and wielding a samurai sword get ripped apart by a burst from a Thompson submachine gun carried by a young blond GI who'd lost his helmet. He saw two GIs ganging up on another Jap and impaling him on both their bayonets. To his right Morris Shilansky bashed a Jap in the face with his rifle butt.

No more Japs were near Bannon. He lowered his machete and it dripped blood. Heaps of Japanese soldiers lay everywhere, and in the moonlight it looked like an open-air slaughterhouse. More soldiers from the Second Battalion kept arriving, but there were no more Japs to fight.

The GIs wandered around in a daze, looking at the carnage. Medics were tending the wounds of GIs who hadn't been as lucky as Bannon. Bannon leaned against a tree, took out a cigarette, and lit it. He didn't know it yet, but up in the hills only unmanned bunkers remained. He and the Second Battalion had just won the battle for the Gifu Line.

SEVENTEEN . . .

Emperor Hirohito, forty-two years old, sat stiffly behind his desk in his office in the Imperial Palace. He was small and spidery, with a wispy mustache and thick spectacles. The Japanese people believed he was a direct descendent of the Sun Goddess, and if they looked directly at him, they would be struck dead by his magnificence.

Before him sat Admiral Chuichi Nagumo, Chief of Staff of the Imperial Navy, and General Hajime Sugiyama, Chief of Staff of the Imperial Army. Both sat humbly and ill at ease, for they'd just delivered bad news to their Emperor.

The Emperor sat for a few minutes, the palms of his hands motionless on his desk as rain lashed the window behind him and made the branches of the trees in the garden outside wave hysterically.

"So," he said finally, "you wish to evacuate Guadalcanal."

"Yes, Your Majesty," they both said in unison.

"Didn't one of you say some time ago that 'the sun may fall, but never Guadalcanal'?"

"Not I, Your Majesty," said Nagumo.

"Nor I, Your Majesty," said Sugiyama.

"Somebody said it. Everybody had so much assurance then. The Americans were soldiers of poor quality, I was told. Why are soldiers of such poor quality forcing us to think of evacuating Guadalcanal?"

General Sugiyama cleared his throat. "A number of mistakes were made, Your Majesty."

"Why were they not corrected?"

"Events moved quickly. Perhaps the mistakes could have been corrected if the Army had been resupplied adequately."

General Sugiyama and Emperor Hirohito looked at Admiral Nagumo.

"Why," said Emperor Hirohito, "were you unable to resupply the Army?"

"Their navy was too strong for us," Admiral Nagumo said hoarsely.

"Before the war I was told we had the strongest navy in the world next to the British Navy. Then I was told that we destroyed the United States Navy at Pearl Harbor. Now I am told that the United States Navy is too strong for us. How can this be?"

"It is a very complex matter, Your Majesty, but to simplify it, let me say that the combined fleet is spread throughout the Pacific, guarding Your Majesty's many interests, and we could not divert ships from other places to Guadalcanal."

The Emperor's expression was like stone. "It is my impression that we have lost Guadalcanal because the Americans have greater air power. Why is it that Americans take only a few days to build an air base, while it takes us months? Isn't there room for improvement?"

"Yes, Your Majesty," Admiral Nagumo said, bowing his head. "I am very sorry indeed for what has happened, but you see, the Americans use machines whereas we must rely on manpower."

"Why cannot we use machines?"

Admiral Nagumo looked at General Sugiyama. They were both on the spot, and they had no good excuses. The military government had wanted the war; now they had it, and it wasn't turning out the way they'd thought it would.

"Your Majesty," said Admiral Nagumo, "one can only tremble in awe before your displeasure. We vow to do better in the future."

"Yes, Your Majesty," General Sugiyama added, "in the future there will be no more mistakes. The Americans might win Guadalcanal, but it is an insignificant island and it will be the last one they win. One day we shall take it back for Your Majesty."

Hirohito's face remained expressionless. "When can my men be evacuated from Guadalcanal?"

"The end of January, Your Majesty."

"That long?"

"It will take time to coordinate the effort, Your Majesty."

"I give my permission herewith to withdraw from Guadalcanal," Emperor Hirohito said. "And in the future the Army and Navy should do their best, as they have just promised."

EIGHTEEN . . .

Butsko sat in a gin mill near the docks of Nouméa on New Caledonia. He was wearing new green fatigues, because he was shipping out the next day, going back to the front. His sleeves were rolled up over his massive biceps and his yardbird hat stuck out of his back pocket as he raised his hand.

"Gimme another drink," he said.

Soldiers and sailors sat all around him in the bar, and from the jukebox a woman's voice sang "There'll Be Bluebirds over the White Cliffs of Dover." The gin mill was called the Lotus Lounge and was owned by a Chinaman, who worked in the kitchen with his wife. The Lotus Lounge was a hangout for servicemen who liked to drink and get rowdy and nurses who liked a wild time. There were also some hookers who'd made their way to New Caledonia, a few schoolteachers, and one defrocked nun. Men always outnumbered women by about twenty to one.

The bartender was a brutish-looking former merchant seaman named Otis who'd gotten beached on New Caledonia a few months before Pearl Harbor. He walked up to Butsko. "The same?"

"Yeah."

Otis drew a glass of beer and poured a shot of whisky, placing them before Butsko, who threw some money on the bar. Butsko raised the shot glass, knocked half of it back, then sipped the cold, foamy beer.

Around him guys laughed and a woman screamed as somebody goosed her. Many fights had taken place in the Lotus Lounge, and the scuttlebutt was that it would be placed off limits before long. Looking at himself in the bar mirror, Butsko saw the closely-cropped regulation haircut he'd gotten that day, and behind him red and yellow Chinese lanterns illuminated the bamboo walls. It was nine o'clock in the evening. Still looking at the mirror, he saw a slim blonde appear next to him. He turned to her; it was Betty Crawford, wearing tan slacks and a tan shirt with a couple of the front buttons undone and the sleeves rolled up.

"Hi," she said, smiling nervously.

"'Lo."

There were a few moments of awkward silence as they looked at each other and away from each other. She appeared as if she were going to jump out of her skin.

"Buy you a drink?" he said.

"Okay."

He got up from his stool. "Here, have a seat."

"No, it's okay. I'll stand."

"I said have a seat."

Butsko held her shoulders, moved her to the side, and pushed her onto the barstool. She reached into her shirt pocket and took out a cigarette. He pulled out his Zippo and lit it up.

"Thanks," she said, blowing smoke toward the ceiling.

"What're you drinking?"

"I'll have a beer, please."

Butsko reached across the bar and grabbed Otis's shoulder. "Bring the lady a beer."

"Gotcha."

Butsko took out a cigarette and lit it, looking down at Betty Crawford. The light from the lanterns gleamed in her golden hair and made a sheen on the side of her face.

"I thought you'd be here," she said.

"Everybody's gotta be someplace."

She looked around. "I've heard of this place. It's a real dive."

"You can't expect much in a town like this. Maybe you

shoulda stayed in the officers' club back at the post."

"Maybe I should've done lots of things."

"We all shoulda done lots of things."

Otis brought the glass of beer for Betty. Butsko ordered another double shot for himself, then downed the half-shot he still had in front of him.

"You really put that stuff away, don't you?" she asked.

"I'm shipping out tomorrow. They gave me partial pay today. What else am I gonna do with the money?"

"You could send it to your wife."

"Fuck my wife."

Butsko wiped his mouth with the back of his hand. He was a little high and feeling rambunctious. He puffed his cigarette and looked down at her.

"You know, you don't belong here."

She raised her eyebrows. "Why not?"

"Because you just don't belong here. I bet you never been here before."

"No, I haven't."

"What the hell are you doing here?"

She looked him in the eye. "I think you know what I'm doing here."

Butsko inhaled his cigarette and blew the smoke out the side of his mouth. On the jukebox somebody was singing "Sleepy Lagoon." He shrugged.

"I'm not sure I do."

"Oh, yes you do."

He thought about it for a few moments. "Maybe I do."

She stubbed out her cigarette and sipped her beer. Butsko looked at her gently curving nose and blue eyes. Her hair was parted on the side and kept out of her face by strategically placed bobby pins. She placed her beer glass on the bar and looked up at him, making an uncertain smile.

"Do you want me to leave?" she asked.

"No."

Otis brought Butsko's double shot. Butsko held it in the air, gazing at the amber fluid. "Down the hatch," he said, and brought the glass to his lips.

He tilted his head back and dumped the whiskey into his mouth. She looked at his gigantic bicep, the spread of his chest, the hair showing through the opening of his shirt. He slammed the bottom of the empty glass down on the bar and reached for his beer, gulping it down.

"Let's get out of here," he said. "Too many people."

Butsko left a few dollars on the bar and Betty stood. Butsko bulled his way to the door and she followed him through the throng of drunks and revelers. Butsko pushed open the door and held it for her. She stepped onto the sidewalk and smelled the salt air from the bay and the fragrance of tropical flowers. Butsko joined her on the wooden plank sidewalk and lit another cigarette. The moonlit masts of ships could be seen in the distance, and a jeep sped by in the street. Soldiers and sailors in work uniforms passed back and forth on the sidewalks.

Butsko held out his pack of cigarettes for her. She took one and he lit it with his Zippo.

"Are you drunk?" she asked.

"Hell, no."

"You were really putting it away in there."

"Where I come from, everybody drinks like that."

"Where are you from."

"A little steel town in Pennsylvania."

"You worked in a steel mill before the war?"

"No, I was in the Army before the war. I'm Regular Army. Where you from?"

"California. Town called Palo Alto."

"That where the guy you're gonna marry's from?"

"Yes."

They walked toward the waterfront and saw the fleet anchored in the bay. A faint breeze blew in from the ocean, and the moon made a squiggly path across the water. A ship was being unloaded on a wharf nearby and a truck zoomed by on the street. Butsko and Betty came to a railing above the water, and Butsko leaned against it, looking at the ships.

"I'll be on one of them tomorrow," he said.

"I guess you'll be glad to be getting back with your men."

"Yeah, I'd like to see them again."

She remembered how he'd looked when he'd first arrived at the hospital with a big hole in his chest. She knew something like that could happen again to him—or even something worse. He looked at his watch.

"It's after ten," he said. "What time you have to be back to the hospital?"

"Tomorrow morning."

"Don't you think that you ought to be getting back?"

"Do you want me to go back?"

"No."

"Then why'd you ask."

"I wanted to give you one last chance."

"What for?"

"Because you might be having second thoughts."

"About what?"

"About this, because you're supposed to be getting married, aren't you?"

"Forget about that," she said. "You won't be the first boyfriend I've had since I got engaged."

"Oh."

"Are you having second thoughts?"

"No."

Butsko flicked his cigarette into the sea. He turned to her and she turned to him. They looked at each other for a few moments. Then she raised her face and he made himself shorter so he could kiss her. Their lips met and his arms wrapped around her. It was not a mad, passionate kiss, but a hello kiss, a It's-nice-to-kiss-you kiss.

"You're so strong," she said, pressing her cheek against his chest.

"You're so pretty," he replied. "All the guys on the base are after you."

"But you weren't."

"Oh, yes I was."

"You didn't do anything about it."

"Oh, yes I did, because you're here with me now aren't you?"

"Well, I'll be damned," she said.

They laughed. He placed his arm around her shoulders and she hugged his waist as they walked away. The streets were lit by lampposts and crowded with soldiers, sailors, and natives. Some were on their way to or from work, and others were drunk. Butsko took her to a seedy little hotel on a sidestreet where servicemen took the nurses or whores or other women they picked up. Butsko didn't ask her if she'd been there before, because he didn't want to know.

They entered the small, cluttered lobby, and a ceiling fan spun round above their heads. A Chinaman was behind the desk and Butsko checked in, using a false name, while Betty crossed her arms and made no effort to hide her face from the Chinaman. Butsko paid some money and got a set of keys. He placed his arm around Betty's waist and led her to the stairs.

They climbed the stairs to the third floor and walked down the hall, the floorboards creaking beneath their feet. Butsko inserted the key in the lock of the door and pushed it open. They entered a small dark room, and Butsko closed the door and latched it while Betty flicked on a lamp.

The bed had a steel frame painted white, and its mattress had a big crater in the middle. The sounds of the street could be heard through the open window. A worn rug lay in front of the bed.

"What a dump," Betty said.

Butsko pulled back the bedspread. "The sheets are clean."

Betty clicked off the lamp, and moonlight streamed through the window. "Looks better with the light off."

She unbuttoned her Army shirt, and Butsko sat on the bed, unlacing his boots. They undressed, glancing at each other, curious and eager. Betty was a little apprehensive, while Butsko knew exactly what he had to do.

They embraced standing on the rug. Betty hugged him tightly, feeling his body like a mountain against her, rubbing her lips across the hair on his chest as he squeezed her against him, exulting in her youth and beauty and running his hands over the smooth skin on her back. Their lips touched and opened; their tongues entwined. She moaned softly and he felt her proud, firm breasts against him, driving him wild.

He lifted her in his powerful arms and laid her down on the bed, then lowered himself on top of her and kissed her hungrily. It had been so long since he'd had a woman, and she was so lovely, so soft, as fragrant as flowers, with a purity and innocence that was enchanting.

Betty felt overwhelmed by his rough, raw masculine strength, and it was just what she needed, just what she wanted. She'd lied to him before; she'd had no other boyfriends since becoming engaged, but she knew Butsko might feel guilty about being the first one and he'd think he was ruining her life. His conscience would bother him, and she didn't want it to bother him when he was back with his men on Guadalcanal. She just wanted him, and the thought that he was leaving had driven her to the waterfront and made her lie.

And now she had him. She arched her back as he entered her, and she felt overwhelmed by lust and passion. She spread her legs wantonly and raised her knees in the air, rocking back and forth, scratching her fingernails across his back as he held her buttocks in his big hands and worked her, chewing her ears, kissing her chin, licking her lips. The bed creaked noisily, and down in the street below a group of drunken soldiers argued as they passed by, but Butsko and Betty Crawford barely heard them as they kissed and loved and made the war go away.